CONTACT

Fighting the Machines - Book 2

by

David Geoffrey Adams

Copyright

First edition. October 31, 2020.

Contents

Prologue

Ten years ago, the starships Einstein, Anticipation and Europa fled the Solar System escaping an invading alien fleet of ships.

Einstein's own probe watched as the Earth, despite desperate defensive efforts, was destroyed. Europa, hidden in Earth's shadow, escaped only as massive missiles split the planet's surface but managed to cross the warp boundary and defeat the efforts of other ships to intercept it.

Einstein having retrieved its probe then sought a possible home to rebuild the human race. After almost seven years it has found a planet that might have been prepared for man.

But Eden, prepared by an ancient race, is protected by AIs left thousands of years before, who are now waking from their electronic sleep.

1. A Watcher Awakes

The skeleton crew still on the Einstein's bridge were on a low level of alert but it would have made no difference if they had been at a high state of awareness. Nothing happened to trigger the ship's sensors but, on the other side of the system, circling one of the gas giants, a computer, already ancient in Roman times, stirred from its electronic sleep as its array of sensors, spread across the system, reacted to the increase in radio traffic arising from the various craft involved in the repeated transfers from the starship to the planet.

For several orbits the powerful AI had been at full operational capacity but it was still unable to decide where the beings, whose activities had caused its array to trigger the alert process, could have come from.

There was no possibility of intelligent life having evolved into a space faring species on the second planet itself. While there had been good conditions for life to evolve, it was too soon for that life to have moved beyond basic non-sapient animals.

Its database contained all the languages of the known civilisations but the signals intercepted did not match any of those. The AI was forced to conclude that the beings must have originated from a star system outside of the volume covered by its designers.

Even though its internal systems could react rapidly the core was still limited by the speed with which its multiple units spread across the system could be contacted. Tight beam signals flashed from the central computer taking hours and even days to elicit a response.

Not all of its sensor units had survived the time that had elapsed since the last communication from its builders and even with its own capability for superfast analysis it took some time before it decided that a gap in the outer edge of the monitoring units must have allowed something, a ship perhaps, to move into the inner system unchallenged.

So, a single message was sent to one of the arrays, hidden on the moon of planet two, seeking video of the planet. A few hours later the AI was, if such an entity can be said to be, confused. Another of the sensors, in this case orbiting planet three, had sent data indicating that planet two had gained a second moon. Too big to be a ship, if the AI's database was correct, but for a small asteroid to have achieved a geostationary orbit seemed even less likely. Data from planet two confirmed the impossible. A ship almost fifteen times the size of any other known starship.

For an entity capable of high-speed thought, the several milliseconds it took to come to its next decision could be compared with a life time for biological beings. Nevertheless, the messages sent to the sensor array on two's moon and to a hidden base on planet three were simple. "ACTIVATE".

2. A Change of Command

"Captain on the Bridge." The ship's computer announced Ellen's arrival following her shuttle's trip up from the planet.

"Good morning, Captain." Her first officer greeted her, as the rest of the bridge team came to attention, contrary to her standing instructions that they should not formally acknowledge her arrival.

"Commander. Good morning everyone, as you were."

Crossing the bridge to her ready room, Ellen indicated that John should follow her.

"Lieutenant, you have the com." John said to Tung-Mei Cheung and entering the captain's room he came to attention, conscious of the formality of the occasion.

"At ease, John." said Ellen with a smile. Turning to her desk, she continued, "Computer, activate file Commandtransfer1. Authority code nine seven four one epsilon omega."

"Acknowledged. File activated. Full implementation requires Commander Lees' code."

Ellen moved to one side to allow John access to the desk. "John, once you enter your code the transfer of the Captaincy to you will complete. I should warn you that my own authority code and command status will be suspended indefinitely. However, in extremis, it will remain possible for me to take command. I don't anticipate any such situation arising but the computer security systems refuse a permanent block. I will retain access to the computer's memory banks and data for administrative type purposes. No command access other than in emergency. That will be yours from now on. OK?"

"Ellen, you are sure about this?"

"Yes, this isn't a sudden decision. I have been planning it almost from the first landing. Time for a different challenge, John."

"In that case, I accept. Computer complete file, Code six, eight, eight, psi, delta nine."

"Acknowledged, Captain John Lees. Command transfer is complete. Admiral Bayman, please repeat code for recording."

"Computer you stated "Admiral"?"

"Correct, Admiral. Command transfer core programming overrides such actions unless either the Captain is deceased or is being promoted. My systems therefore must authorise access only to the Captain or a senior officer such as stated."

"I see. Not what I intended but what must be must be. Code nine seven four one epsilon omega." Ellen responded.

"Admiral Bayman, please note that certain areas of the ship are no longer automatically open to you unless authorised by command crew."

"Computer, noted."

"John, have you considered who you would like as your first officer?"

John paused for a moment. "I have. I know you suggested Cheung but after a little thought I believe that Jaeger is a better choice at this time. He has a wider range of experience. Tung-Mei is good but I don't think she is quite ready yet. I would look to get her to take over the Communications section."

"Understood, I assume that Pawl has helm experience from before joining the Einstein?"

"He ran Lunar to Mars transfers for a couple of years, Cheung's helm experience is almost wholly with us and she has less command experience."

"I think we should get him in then, don't you think? Assuming he is on duty, that is."

"He is due on the bridge in the next few minutes. Computer, message to Lieutenant Jaeger. Request him to come to the ready room. Do not advise him of change of command."

"Acknowledged."

Ellen and John decided to sit down and wait. Then a few minutes later, John's communicator pinged - "Captain to the Bridge - urgent."

3.   Back on Eden

The argument had been raging for some time and Jing, who had, in Ellen's absence, agreed, to chair the meeting was struggling to maintain control. She had not been ready for those present to be divided into two opposing factions, each with such strongly held views.

"People have really thrown everything at the work and have had no chance to relax since the first landings." Helga Neilson repeated for the umpteenth time.

Anita Pavel interrupted, yet again. "We must have a communication system that will double as a source of entertainment and access to the town's central database. There are only two ways to do this either local radio with Bluetooth technology or better via some form of cabling. Yes, we can hold open air theatre and music events but we can't bring everyone into the same place other than on very special occasions." She continued not allowing anyone else the chance to comment. "It's rubbish that no-one can spare the time or provide the equipment to complete a network. If we don't find a way to do this, we will start to see problems."

Finally, Anita ran out of steam and Jing turned back to the other side but before she could speak Helga broke in. "We must remember that we have probably the best group of highly motivated, intelligent and willing people ever brought together but that doesn't mean they are immune from issues such as depression and other mental problems. Don't forget the loss of Earth must still hurt and disturb even the strongest."

7

At last, Jing thought. "Anton?"

Anton Tyler was quite a small man but made up for that with his stance and driving attitude. While strong-minded, Jing knew that he was, nevertheless, always open to a reasonable and sustainable argument.

"I'm sorry, Jing. As I have said several times," his irritation was clear, "I and my colleagues do not easily dismiss the proposals put forward by Helga and Anita. Our view is that there are other things that are more urgent and we do not have the people or, for that matter, the equipment."

"Haven't got the equipment! You have to be joking! First it was people - now equipment!" Anita shouted.

"Please let Anton finish, Anita." Jing interceded with a calmness she really did not feel.

Anton continued. "I know that we were given a flying start by the stores on Einstein but fibre optic cabling was clearly not seen as being of the highest priority and we only have a limited amount. As yet we cannot manufacture additional cable without diverting production from the work on the accelerator and associated kit and we need to get those in place to provide the town with heat and power for the winter."

"But what's the point, Anton? If we can't relax or have easy access to the central database?" Helga's frustration was clear. "Surely we can afford a delay of a few months?"

Finally, seeing that no progress was being made, Jing called a halt with a comment that drew a gasp from everyone else.

"Look everyone, I need to consider what I have heard and then discuss with the Administrator how we might go forward. I would say that I am disappointed with the content of both arguments. Neither side made any reference to those individuals whose needs, as a group, you do not seem to have thought of."

"Sorry?" Anton reacted slightly quicker than the others.

"We talk about the four thousand that came down from the Einstein to settle the planet. We don't forget the five hundred odd crew and support teams that will be staying with the ship. But we seem to miss the needs of those of our families who still need our support. Our children." As her audience caught its breath in recognition, she continued. "Almost six hundred ranging from nine to seventeen but, because we only ever see a few at a time, I accept it is easy not to think about their needs as a group. Education as well as, yes, entertainment. On the Einstein providing education was fairly straight forward, albeit via remote video conferencing and computer-generated lessons. We have been planetside for almost two years and everyone including the kids have been occupied in setting up our home. Now we need to review how we arrange their education going forward and I believe that it is inevitable that that will mean finding a way to provide remote teaching again as well as, perhaps, centralised schooling for the younger ones. Leave things with me and we will get back to you once Ellen has returned from orbit."

It was a subdued group of people who left the meeting, heading off to their various jobs around the town. Just after leaving the building Anton turned back to Anita.

"Anita, I think we need to chat further. This evening perhaps?"

"Really?" Anita growled.

"I need to talk with my colleagues and with the guys on Einstein. Tomorrow then?"

"Better make it early afternoon. You had better have something worth hearing."

They went their separate ways without further conversation while Jing returned to her office and sat down to ponder. She had little time to do so though.

"Commander, can you spare a moment?" It was Stefan Kovak, one of her researchers from the Titan station team, who disturbed her thoughts.

"Stefan, come on in and it's not Commander anymore." She smiled. "What do you need?"

"Jing, then. You know that I've been spending time with the team researching the use of lighter metals than normal."

"I was aware. We still haven't managed to find any deposits of metal heavier than aluminium, have we?"

"No, and we shouldn't be too surprised. This system is young in astronomical terms and there aren't enough older stars in the neighbourhood to produce heavier elements in any serious quantities. What I would like to do is to use some drones plus a shuttle to survey the other side of the mountain range across the water. No promises but while that area is younger in geological terms it is just possible, we might find useable deposits of other metals."

"Why do you need the OK from the administration team?" Jing was a little nonplussed.

"Not sure that we do, but we'll be using quite a lot of current mobile resource and it may be that there are other demands that are more important, that we aren't aware of." Stefan was unapologetic at asking and, smiling, he continued. "My colleagues doubt that but I wanted to be sure."

Jing thought about the request for a few moments before deciding that she could authorise the expedition. "You can take whatever is necessary subject to two conditions."

"Which are?" Stefan's confidence ebbed a little.

"No more than twenty days total time from start to return. And I want you to take two of the older youngsters, sixteen or seventeen years old with you. Think of them as apprentices on a learning curve. I am sure that your team will already have had interest from a few would be metallurgists or similar anyway. I have other educational issues to handle but this is the type of exercise which will become more important over time. OK?"

"I think that we could comply with that idea. You're right we have had one or two loitering around the labs and this would be a good test for them. Thank you, Jing."

"When do you intend to leave?"

"We should be able to start out tomorrow. I guess we will need to get sign off by the parents first?" Stefan knew that his question had to be rhetorical but was not looking forward to talking to the parents.

"You will." Jing smiled, guessing the reason why but deciding not to let Stefan off the hook. "Good luck."

After Stefan had left, Jing settled into preparing a summary of her views on the earlier meeting ready to provide her boss and partner with the recommendations she had already arrived at.

4. The Watcher is Discovered

John ran on to the bridge ahead of Ellen.

"Captain on the Bridge." The duty crew looked up in startlement before turning back to their stations with bemused expressions.

"Computer, all bridge and engine room crew to their stations." John ordered.

John raced to the command chair as Lieutenant Cheung moved to the First Officer's station. Despite the confusion, she anticipated |John's question.

"Commander, we have intercepted two radio signals. One from Eden's moon towards the sun, and a second one which appears to have been sent to planet three. The second signal appears to have come from the direction of the sun."

John and Ellen exchanged looks of amazement before Ellen calmly announced her decision to promote John to Captain. "I would have preferred to announce this in a more orderly situation but it is as it is. We can handle the detail later"

"I assume we do not understand what the signals mean. Do we have any comparison with the languages contained in the warning signal we received to warn us against the landing with the apparent biowarfare outcome?" John asked the question even as he started analysing the data at his own station.

"We don't think so. They were very short bursts, probably compressed data. It was complete chance that we intercepted them at all. It just happened that one of our comms satellites over the settlement was in line of fire, as it were, for the signal to planet three. The probe we had sent to survey planet four was, again, just in the right place."

"Do we have enough to be able to identify the exact locations on the two bodies?" John rubbed his chin thoughtfully while he tried to fathom a sensible response to a situation that he was struggling to understand. Just what had they run into?

"Nothing on the planet, Captain. We think we have limited the area on the moon to one of the craters just visible from the planetary surface." Cheung's response helped John to focus on an appropriate course.

"Right. Launch a probe towards planet one. You know, we must come up with some names for the planets. A second probe towards that part of the moon." He continued. "Lieutenant Piper, I want an IPS prepped for a trip to planet four."

"Planet four, Captain?" Judy's question was echoed by looks of surprise from the other bridge crew members.

"Yes, I propose a routing that would allow the craft to carry out a gravitational swing around that planet on to a course that would allow a close flyby of planet three. By cutting power it will limit the likelihood that it will be seen to be deliberately trying to find whatever is there. Possibly a single orbit to try and get a fix."

"Aye, Captain, I'm on it." Judy headed for the exit and the docking area while Tung-Mei took her place at the helm.

***   ***   ***

The sensor on Eden's moon responded to the instructions sent to it, switching from passive to active mode and started to probe the nearby object.

On planet three, long dormant machines began to wake.

***   ***   ***

As Judy left the bridge, she was passed by Pawl heading the other way to take up his position. "Pawl, watch out! Ellen's not captain anymore. She's resigned and promoted John!"

"What!" Pawl was as startled as any of his bridge colleagues.

"Can't stop, on a mission."

Meanwhile, John and Ellen agreed that she should return to Yablon and brief her team.

Pawl entered the bridge passing Ellen, only to be stopped by her at the door. "Congratulations, Pawl" Before he could respond she was gone, heading quickly to the docking bay. Her shuttle was ready and within a few minutes they were making a rapid descent from orbit back to the settlement. While her pilot concentrated on flying the craft, Ellen got on the radio to Jing asking her to get the Pipers and other lead researchers together in time for an immediate meeting once she was on the ground again.

Back on the Einstein, Pawl was in the Captain's ready room with John.

"Pawl, there is now a need to appoint a new First Officer. Ellen and I are agreed that you are ready for that position."

"Captain, sorry, I mean John. Are you certain? Surely there are others?"

"Pawl, your own spread of experience is wider than the other candidates, as it were. No one, of course, is yet aware of this process apart from yourself. Assuming you accept the position, I will have a conversation with the other bridge officers before announcing the changes to the ship's crew at large. You are, of course, free to refuse, if you really do not feel ready."

"I would be honoured. It is just a shock to hear of Ellen standing down from the Captaincy. John, I will not let you down. Thank you."

"Right, Commander. Let me bring you up to speed."

Shortly afterwards, after discussing John's plan for the Deimos to survey the third planet, the two men had their first operational argument in the Captain's ready room.

"Captain, you have to remain here. We don't know what is going on. At the same time, we need my experience on interplanetary craft. Yes, any of the bridge crew with flight experience could handle the ship but we might need something out of the ordinary. I suggest that I take the Deimos with Hidecki Yamata as my co-pilot."

"Hidecki Yamata?"

"He has loads of experience. If you remember he was on board the Phoebe when it was given the job of delivering Ellen to the Einstein back at Saturn. He ended up staying when we learnt about the alien fleet. We then need, I would suggest, an engineer and a comms expert with linguistic ability."

Finally, John sighed. "I don't like it but I guess that I must accept. There are times when I wish I were Jim Kirk; he wouldn't accept that you are correct. Get yourself down to the Deimos and launch as soon as you and your team are ready and good luck."

"Thanks, John." Pawl paused. "Sorry, who was Jim Kirk?"

"Oh dear, we will have to introduce you on your return. I'm sure that there are some of the original series in the entertainment database. Now get going. I need to brief the team properly."

***   ***   ***

Over the next hour, John held one-to-one sessions with the other bridge officers to appraise them of Pawl's promotion. Only Cheung showed real disappointment at not being selected and it took John longer to explain the logic behind his decision. In the end it was his plans to extend her role across those gaps in her experience that needed strengthening which helped her understand why she was not yet first choice. As she started to return to the bridge she turned back for a moment.

"John, you know I'm a little disappointed not to get that promotion but I am pleased for Pawl. One thing though, will he need to get our relationship cleared by the doctor's team. You know, under the rules set up when we first left Centauri? I mean," she hesitated, "it was OK when we were both lieutenants but, as he will now be senior to me?"

John laughed, "You kept that low profile didn't you. I can see no reason why it should need clearance. Don't worry, I will get the relevant people to tick the right boxes. Now get yourself down to the Deimos, you might want to say cheerio. Pawl is taking command of the probe to planet three."

The last of his one-to-ones was with Judy, who had returned from the docking area. It was less of a surprise to her due to hearing of Ellen's plans the previous evening. Although the formal meeting was shorter than most, her return to her post was delayed by her emotional reaction.

Following that John left his room moving back on to the bridge. The computer's usual "Captain on the Bridge" was received with surprise by the more junior members of the bridge team and John had to reinforce Ellen's previous rule.

"As you were everyone, there is no need to change from the previous ruling. We might be in standby mode for the moment but Ellen's view remains correct. We can't have everyone stopping what they are doing just for a piece of courtesy which is perfectly well known."

5. Searching for Answers

Ellen's shuttle landed close to the town and within a few minutes she and Jing had been reunited. They had little time alone though, as the rest of the team Ellen had called to join the meeting arrived, almost at a run.

Over the next hour Ellen explained all that had been going on and the actions being taken by the Einstein to respond. Throwing the discussion open to comments, she took the opportunity to grab a drink of water before settling down to listen to the various thoughts of the team.

A little to her surprise there were more questions being asked than were being answered. The overall concerns were summed up by Alan Piper.

"Ever since the early days of our journey we seem to have been haunted by past civilisations or dangerous locations that appear to have been affected or monitored by what seem to be automated systems. The anomaly at Jupiter, the bio warning. We didn't find anything at Centauri or in Hyades but I am beginning to wonder if that was just chance. Our real problem is that we don't know what the messages the Einstein has intercepted mean. Is this another automatic system? And, if so, what is its purpose? To record? To report? For whom and how?"

"Alan, you imply that these might be, how can I put it, live messages from the direction of One to Three and Eden's moon? Surely the initial survey of the system should have found evidence of an advanced civilisation?" one of the engineers, Waru Fujino, responded.

"I don't think that is necessarily the case, Waru. We may just have caused a dormant system to wake. Whatever, it doesn't change the problem we face. How do we respond? As it stands, I think that John has taken the right actions. For the moment all we can do is watch and wait."

"There is something else we could do." Ellen raised her gaze to the others. "Name the other planets. John did comment that having to constantly refer to planets by a number is irritating! He hasn't come up with any ideas himself but I wonder if this group could suggest some names?"

The opportunity to relax, for a little while, was welcomed with a lively discussion. In the end a consensus for the three other planets closest to the sun was reached.

"We are agreed then. Eden's moon to be Selene, planet one to be Heira, three Cain and four Abel. I suggest we invite the rest of the town to propose names for the other planets from five outwards." Ellen summed up the meeting. "Let's call it a day. You all know what you need to do. I suggest we get back together tomorrow afternoon."

*** *** ***

Back on the Einstein, its Captain decided to raise the ship's status to a higher degree of alert. With the bridge now fully manned, he authorised the launch of the probe to Selene. Shortly afterwards the Deimos slipped out of the dock and started its mission towards the fourth planet.

"Commander, no more than three quarters power on the way. Leave a little hidden, just in case." John's tone indicated his concern that this action was not without risk.

"Yes, Captain. Maximum seventy five percent power. We'll keep in touch."

John started a reply only to be interrupted by Tung-Mei. "Captain, live feed from the moon flyby coming in."

"Right, Lieutenant. On main screen. Pawl watch out for anything unusual."

The main screen fluctuated before showing the surface of Selene. Like most moons and startlingly like the early close ups of the lunar surface the moon was largely grey and cratered. The probe began circling in a tight orbit.

"Captain, best to focus on that side of the moon facing Eden. Like most single satellites it is tidally locked. If there is anything monitoring the planet it has to be located on that side."

"Alejandro, I thought you were planetside?" John was surprised but pleased to find his senior astronomer had joined the bridge crew."

"I was, Captain, but I grabbed a lift back with the shuttle that dropped Ellen. I thought I might be of help and, if I'm honest, I really didn't want to miss seeing the pictures live." Alejandro smiled.

"Good to see you. Now tell me what we are seeing."

Over the next hour, as the probe completed two orbits, there were only limited changes in the view, arising as the orbit was adjusted by the remotes switching the vehicle onto a different path, so that it would gradually cover the majority of the surface. Then, on the third orbit, a particularly deep crater came into view. It was apparent that its depth was such that it should have been in almost permanent shadow but, to the watcher's astonishment, the bottom was glowing with a steady synchronised beam of blue-white light.

"Alejandro, could that possibly be a natural phenomenon?" John turned to the astronomer, who himself looked stunned.

"Captain, I cannot see how. This must be what we are looking for, or at least an element of it. What I don't understand is why we haven't spotted the light from the ground. I will have the team try and see where the beam makes planetfall."

"As soon as you can, please." John turned back to the screen just in time to see another change on the surface. "There, what is that? It looks a little like an aerial."

"Captain, it seems to be the source of a signal similar to the earlier one." Judy Piper was at the helm monitoring the situation. Calmly checking the on-going reports from the Einstein's own sensor array, she suddenly gasped and jerked almost to attention. She was so startled that she lost the formality of the bridge.

"John, sorry, Captain. We are being scanned. The signal seems to be searching the hull."

"Comms, elevate the firewalls to maximum security." Then thinking rapidly John continued. "Leave the primary access levels unsecured."

"Captain?"

"We should allow the scanner to get a little information, assuming that that is what it is looking for. Basically, our first contact messaging and basic language data but no more than that. In fact, I don't think we should rely on the virtual firewalls. Shutdown the mainframe links other than those to life support and the bridge. Helm, move us into a higher orbit, one hundred klicks further out."

"Aye, Captain. One hundred klicks higher."

As the Einstein slowly manoeuvred into its new orbit it became apparent the scanner was managing to maintain contact and had latched onto one of the sensor pods on the ship's hull.

"Comms, I want to know what data is being extracted. Also has the scan tried to dig any deeper? If we can tell."

"That will take some time, Captain. We will need to carry out analysis using the computer once we know that the link has been cut and after we ensure that nothing has been left by the scan that might be a virus or similar."

"Captain!" the young ensign sitting at the secondary communications station called excitedly.

"Yes, Fox." John had had to think for a moment who the ensign was, cursing the fact that Ellen had been so much better at recognising every member of the crew while realising that Didier Fox was not a regular member of the bridge team.

"Captain, the scan's dataflow has reversed. It seems to have downloaded a large amount of information on to the pod's local storage."

John was now relieved that they had physically isolated the pod and its associated hardware rather than relying on software-based firewalls.

"Get the computer team on this. Now." Then an afterthought came to mind. "And contact Teri Larding. I think we will need her linguistic skills."

Over the next few hours, the systems guys worked with an EVA team to extract the hardware from the sensor pod, while replacing it with new parts. After completing the physical work, they began to analyse the data using a standalone computer.

In due course, they sat down with John and Teri to explain their findings.

"The amount of data looks to be around ten times the amount of first contact data we effectively made available. However, it may not contain the volume of information that that would suggest." Gordon Haysmith, the senior information systems researcher explained.

Teri broke in at this point. "The data is made up of nine packages. Eight almost identical in size with a ninth which is both smaller and, it seems, simpler."

John's thoughts went back to the message broadcasting a warning about the planet where an apparent bioweapon had killed all life. "We have had a message in multiple languages before or so we thought. Is this something similar?"

Teri continued to explain that she had already run a comparison and found some similarities. Then she dropped the bombshell with a grin.

"I think the ninth packet might just be a Rosetta stone. It contains various universal constants, numerically, alongside words or expressions. It's going to take some time to produce a translation but the positive is that this looks as if whoever is running the scan wants us to have an opportunity to understand as many as eight languages. That suggests there may be a group of that number of civilisations with space faring capability including, and this is a big assumption, faster than light ships. There is an alternative, of course, and that is beings that have an extraordinarily long-life span such that the time to travel between stars is not an issue."

"You don't think small, Teri, do you." John's comment broke the silence that had fallen on the group as it tried to absorb Teri's words. "Right, thank you all for such swift work. Teri, I'd like to sit down with your colleagues later. Say at nineteen hundred hours. There isn't a formal team at the minute but that will change and I want you to lead the group."

"Captain, thank you but I'm not as senior as some of the group. I'm not sure I should lead them."

"Teri, two things. Firstly, in a private meeting such as this we work on first name terms. Secondly, I have no doubt that you have the best overall knowledge and have already shown capabilities beyond your colleagues. That was why I asked you to be involved in the first analysis of the data. I am quite sure that you should lead and I will be happy to explain in straightforward terms why that is my belief to anyone who wishes to object." John smiled, feeling in charge of matters in a way that had not seemed possible a few hours earlier. "Now, how long before you can arrange a presentation of what you just told us? And outline the information which suggests a Rosetta stone."

Teri, looked a little subdued by the prospect but the sparkle in her eyes belied that and she was quick to respond. "Can I have a couple of hours, Captain, sorry John?"

"That's fine but I won't need you to do that until tomorrow morning. Take the time to have a break. If I am right you and the rest of the team have been at it non-stop for almost twenty-four hours and you will be fresher then to face the questions! Gordon, it would be best if you attended, so that you can explain the mechanics as to how you extracted this data."

"I'll be there John. I wouldn't miss Teri's presentation for anything."

With that the meeting broke and John returned to the bridge for a brief update before he himself went as off duty as he ever was able.

"Captain, Deimos has reported that they are on final approach to Abel. They intend to go radio silent and will cut power once blind side of the planet and on a gravity assisted flyby."

"Acknowledge their signal and then keep watch. Call me if anything looks out of the ordinary or clearly wrong."

"Aye, Captain."

6.   Selene strikes Eden

John left the bridge, but feeling the need to remain on call while the Deimos made its silent approach towards Cain, only went as far as the nearest dining area before returning to his ready room. Before he settled to rest there was a gentle knock. The door opened at his bidding and Judy slipped in.

"You look tired, John." Judy's concern was obvious as she crossed the short distance to embrace her partner.

"It's been a long day and somehow I doubt I will get much sleep. You're on duty now though, so I know I'll get some rest!"

"I'll try and make sure Tung-Mei doesn't interrupt you." After a long embrace and kiss, Judy headed back to the bridge to take over at the helm where she did expect the next few hours to be quiet.

"Lieutenant, you're a little late." Cheung's admonition was softened by her smile as she was well aware where Judy had been.

"Sorry, Lieutenant."

Judy dropped into her seat swiftly reviewing the various situation reports of the ship's state of readiness. Her fellow helmsman, Miguel Sanchez, brought her up to date with the progress of the Deimos and the Selene probe which was continuing to orbit the moon but, now in less of a search pattern following its discoveries earlier, it was monitoring the strange light closely. After watching a few minutes of the last overflight, Judy frowned.

28

"Miguel" she quietly asked, "What are those changes in the light intensity?"

"Not really, Judy, though it does give the impression of a flicker effect. Alejandro thinks that must be caused by imperfections in the surrounding rock."

"Is the Captain aware of that?"

"I don't know. He wasn't on the bridge when I came on duty and he only asked about the probe and the Deimos. Nobody mentioned the light."

"Might I know what you two are talking about?" Cheung interrupted the discussion with a grin.

"Sorry. We were talking about the changes in the light beam." Miguel responded.

"What changes?" Tung-Mei's startlement at the news was clear. "Has the Captain been told?"

"I don't know. I think that the chief astronomer doesn't feel it means anything, just a side effect of the surrounding rock."

"Right, Lieutenants. I want the probe's orbit adjusted such that it can be slowed as it goes over the light. Judy, you do that. Miguel, contact our senior astronomer. Suggest that he should be ready to join the Captain in his ready room shortly. Judy, you have the com."

With that she left the bridge and after a pause pinged the Captain's communicator before seeking entrance to his room.

A few minutes later Tung-Mei had briefed a tired John after apologising for disturbing him. As she finished there was a knock on the door and Alejandro entered.

"Thanks for being so quick, Alejandro."

"Not sure why I'm here though, Lieutenant."

"I have a concern. When we first saw the light beam emanating from Selene it was, it appeared, a coherent beam. Not a laser light but very similar and unchanging."

"That is correct. That is why we felt it could not be natural."

"Then why did you not bring to my attention the fact that the light has developed a flicker?" John felt he needed to raise the issue. "Surely that is a significant issue?"

"I did look into it but it seems that the surrounding rock is simply bouncing a part of the beam around and adding an inconsistency to its coherence."

"It didn't occur to you that the changes might be caused by something using the beam as a message carrier?" John's frustration was beginning to show. "And, as I understand it, the beam's location is such that it is always missing the planetary surface?"

Alejandro paused. "Well, not always. It seems there are two points on the surface which the beam hits during each orbit, John. We just don't understand why."

John's fatigue did not help and his temper was close to breaking point. "And it didn't occur to you that this could be important enough to brief me? Just where are the contact points? Or has no one thought it would be a good idea to find out?"

"One point is on the side of the planet opposite to Yablon." Alejandro's voice disclosed his increasing nervousness. He could not remember Ellen or John being so angry.

"And the other? Don't tell me that it is the settlement itself."

"No, it isn't. It appears to be a valley on the mainland the other side of the mountain range from the town."

"So, within a few hundred kilometres of the town?"

"Yes, though we don't think it is because of the settlement."

"Alejandro, please tell me that nothing else has happened that I haven't been told about."

"Nothing really. Shortly after the probe made its second pass over the light source for a brief second or two the light dimmed and then flashed brighter. The time periods were so short that we only saw this when we ran the recordings in slow motion a few hours later."

"I really don't know what to say. Alejandro, are you and your team completely oblivious to the potential dangers we face? There are clearly alien devices now active, even if they weren't when we arrived in the system, and they have already scanned the ship. These changes could be directly related to our probing them and we have a manned ship approaching what seems to be a key communications point. Now we may have to abort that approach rather than risk losing them due to a misunderstanding as to our intentions. You had better get back to your team and reinforce my message. ANY changes to be reported to the bridge team preferably direct to me. And they need to provide some detail behind what you have just told me."

"Yes, Captain. Sorry, Captain."

It was a very subdued astronomer that left the room. John considered the situation for several minutes before resigning himself to having to forget about his, much needed, rest for the minute. Before leaving his room, he contacted Judy via his communicator and asked when the probe was next due to reach the light source.

"Captain, it is about twelve minutes away. I have slowed it as much as possible by raising its orbital path blind side of the target."

"Good, can you lift it into a geostationary orbit above the target?"

"Not this orbit but it should be possible on the next pass."

"Good, do it."

"Aye, sir. It will be in position in around forty minutes."

After some discussion after Alejandro had left, John's next question was one that Tung-Mei cursed herself for not having checked first. It took a moment to ask Miguel how far out the Deimos was from Cain.

"About thirty-two hours based on the last update, Lieutenant."

Turning to John, Tung-Mei said. "John, I estimate that we have about twenty hours before we need to make a go no-go decision and then, if necessary, order the ship to abort and divert away from Cain."

"I agree. Now let's have a closer look at the Selene point."

They left the room moving on to the bridge and taking their stations.

"Bring the feed from the probe on to the main screen. Let's see what we have found."

As the probe made its last orbital adjustment, Judy was totally focused on her remote control nudging the attitude motors to ensure the its final position was in a stationary orbit above the light source.

"In position, Captain."

"Well done, Lieutenant."

The view had settled into an unchanging scene for the moment. The moon's surface remained a dull grey lit only by a setting sun. At the centre of the view, however, was a strong blue white glow. At this point there was no change in the light's coherence and the flicker seen earlier had vanished. After a few minutes John had a thought.

"Are the probe's reverse sensors good enough to get a view of the planetary surface in line with the original beam?"

"They can, Captain, but the beam would miss the surface at the moment." Judy thought for a moment running a few calculations on her tablet. "I estimate that the orbital changes mean that the light could hit the surface in about seventeen minutes."

"Can we tell where?"

"It's rather odd but for a brief time it would, or will, hit about two hundred and forty kilometres from Yablon." Judy sounded confused by the fact that instead of a strip of surface it seemed to be a point contact. "Of course! The location isn't directly above the planet but almost on the edge, as it would be seen from Selene. Even so I don't understand how."

"I wonder." interposed Miguel. "That far from the town is a range of mountains. Could the beam in fact be hitting a tall peak, rather than at sea level?"

"Good thinking, Lieutenant. Lieutenant Cheung, please get the monitor team on it, see if we can fine tune the target point on Eden."

Shortly afterwards the countdown came to an end. As the moment arrived the light brightened many times over and for a fraction of a second outshone the sun. Even though the computer dimmed the screen in response the team were left with serious afterimages. The screen view wobbled a second later before slowly returning to the previous dimmer light. Then to the startlement of those watching the light vanished.

"What? Are the probe's sensors still working?"

It took a moment before Judy was able to confirm that the probe was still operating normally and this was supported by the view of the reverse cameras which showed a piece of the planetary surface glowing white with heat.

John responded instantly. "Comms. Send a message to the Deimos. They are to adjust their course using their directional jets to increase their apogee to five thousand klicks or more on their final approach to Cain. Then get me the administration office in Yablon. I need to talk with Admiral Bayman urgently.

"Captain, I have sent the message to Deimos but haven't yet had a response?"

"Watch for a very short burst acknowledging. They're running under radio silence so we may have to wait to see their course change. Tracking. Keep a close eye on them."

"Aye, Captain."

7.   Rescue Mission

John headed back to his ready room, asking for Ellen to be patched through to him once she had answered the ship's call.

He had had only a few moments to freshen himself up before his terminal pinged with an incoming message.

"Ellen!"

"John, I hope this is urgent. It's the middle of the night down here."

"Sorry, Ellen. You are right, of course. Though if you were to look eastwards you might feel that dawn was early."

"I haven't had reason to look outside yet. What do you mean?"

It took John a few minutes to bring Ellen up to speed with what had happened. He finished. "I can't be sure but I suspect that the glow from those mountains must be visible from the town. They are only a few hundred klicks away."

By this point Ellen was fully alert. "John, I may need your help. We have a lander and drones with a team in that area looking for metal deposits. Can you get a shuttle on standby in case we need to launch a rescue mission?"

"Certainly. We'll be ready to launch in twenty minutes."

"We will start looking to contact the team. Hopefully they will have left someone on watch but if there is no immediate response I would rather not wait and you can reach their site quicker than we can."

John thought for a moment before replying. "I will have tracking try and find their location. I assume that they are the only expedition out at the moment." Ellen's nod was enough. "In which case their tracking signal should be easy to locate."

"Thanks, John. We will get back to you." Ellen broke the contact.

Waking the rest of team, although Jing had already been woken by Ellen's departure from their bedroom, took a little time but trying to raise the expedition proved more difficult. The glow over the horizon had started to fade, though that was partly as a result of the approaching dawn.

The decision to call in the Einstein's lander was not a difficult one and Ellen called the ship.

"Captain, have you managed to trace the team?"

"We think we have, Ellen, but we can't be sure. The strike from Selene seems to have had an effect similar to an electro-magnetic pulse. We cannot find the tracking signal but we think we have found them visually. I have a lander prepped and ready to go with a medical team on board. Now I assume that you haven't managed to raise them either, so we're on our way."

"Thanks, John."

Breaking contact, John switched to an internal channel. "Lieutenant Cheung, you are cleared for launch. Your target landing zone is east of the mountains that the beam hit. Use the apparent location of the images that seem to be the expedition but make sure you are not closer to the strike point than fifteen klicks and make your approach from the east. Play it safe."

"Acknowledged, Captain."

Five minutes later the lander lifted away from the landing bay dropping out of the Einstein's orbit in a powered descent.

"We can't waste time taking a full orbit to land so I am going to drop down flying away from the target site eastwards. Once we are down to around five thousand metres, we should be around a hundred klicks from our landing site and can make a turn ready to come out of the sun." Tung-Mei smiled as she spoke to Judy and the medics sitting behind the two pilots. "Judy, you take the final approach."

"Are you sure, Tung-Mei?" Judy's nervousness was clear. "I've only flown landers a few times and that was during the transport programme to land the settlers following a regular marked approach."

"All the more reason to handle a landing with an uncertain terrain. We all have to do it eventually and you've got what it takes. Switching control to you, now!"

Despite her nervousness, Judy was quick to respond. "I have control."

Although aiming for a rapid powered descent Judy was able to keep the lander high enough and on a sufficiently shallow entry into the atmosphere to avoid the hull overheating. As they lost height, she slowed their velocity steadily until they were making the approach Tung-Mei had indicated.

Shortly after making the final turn towards the range, now to their west, they were shaken to see the entire side of one mountain seemingly burning with a white fire. Checks on the external sensors confirmed that the outside temperature was normal and there was little wind.

"That doesn't feel right, Judy." Tung-Mei's comment simply confirmed her co-pilot's own thoughts.

"I'm slowing our approach. Let's see if we can spot the expedition before we need to land. Launching drone one. Tung-Mei, you control the drone, I suggest you accelerate it to maximum. That will take it several klicks ahead of us and we can avoid a faster approach. That fire is not what it seems and I don't want to test our ability to avoid any side effects just yet."

As they slowed Tung-Mei switched the sensor screen to relay what the drone was seeing. For several minutes the view from the drone mirrored that visible to the pilots from the lander's windscreen. Then a range of low hills became visible and finally, after the drone had crossed these the expedition's camp came into view. It was a scene of devastation with the shuttle lying tipped on its side with the undercarriage completely wrecked and tents collapsed on to themselves. At first sight there seemed to be no movement but as the drone approached a figure could be seen waving.

"How far are they from the fire?" Tung-Mei's underlying question was obvious, was the camp nearer than the fifteen klicks limit they were not to breach?

Judy, clicked off her mouthpiece turning off the flight recorder. "I make it about ten klicks but that fire is a moveable feast and it could be fifteen. We can't land five plus klicks away and then trek that far." She suddenly made a decision and without waiting for Tung-Mei's agreement, accelerated the lander towards the camp.

"Judy, what are you doing?"

"Getting the medical team to the site as fast as possible. I'll drop them and you off and, if it turns out we are too close, I will lift off again and drop back.

Depending on what you find, we can decide if it is safe for a longer landing nearby. You can also check if the shuttle can be used while the medics do their job."

"John's not going to be happy if his orders are ignored." It was indicative of Tung-Mei's agitation that she had lapsed into informality.

"Everything we can see suggests that there will be injured people. We have to take a risk in order to get in close quickly. Those orders were made, from orbit, without full knowledge of what we would find. We're on the scene now and we must adjust accordingly." Switching to a general hail, Judy continued. "Everyone, get ready to disembark fast. It looks as if there are injured but the camp may turn out to be closer than the distance we have been ordered to avoid. So, quick landing in five minutes. Everyone off and I will shift the lander back to a safe point, unless it is further from the fire than we think."

Those few minutes passed quickly and as they reached the edge of the camp Judy brought the lander to a hover before rotating to allow for a swift exit. As soon as they touched down the team cleared the craft in a matter of a couple of moments. Tung-Mei hesitated before her own exit.

"Judy, take care. Back off far enough, then report back to the ship. I will let you have an update as soon as possible."

"On my way. Now jump, and you take care as well."

Shortly after, having flown a good ten kilometres back from the camp, Judy dropped the lander down and braced herself to report back to her Captain. She knew his initial professional anger at his orders not being followed to the letter would be managed but expected an emotional response to her actions, having placed herself at risk, as her lover would say. She knew why he'd be angry but as she had to remind him from time to time, she could not avoid all dangers just because of their relationship.

As she expected his formal response was calm if cold, his simple admonition being that they should have cleared their intent before their final approach and, an unexpected question, why was she flying the lander and not Tung-Mei. Given that their conversation could be heard by most of the bridge crew, he kept it short, simply reminding Judy that she and the team needed to keep him up to speed and quite coolly stating that they would discuss the matter further, after their return to the Einstein.

"Yes, Captain." Judy finished the conversation meekly. She then contacted Tung-Mei for an update.

"You can bring the lander back, Judy. There's no danger to it now. The damage here was, it seems, simply a side effect from the original strike. It should have been worse but some form of barrier focussed the energy into the mountain. The side effect was something of a localised gale which caught the shuttle trying to take off. We have injuries but none of them life threatening. We are going to need the lander to transfer the injured back to Yablon, the shuttle is out of action. So, come on back."

Judy duly flew the lander back to the camp, updating both the Einstein and Ellen back at the town.

"Ellen, the shuttle is going to need a fair bit of work before it can be flown again. I don't think that the damage is irreparable. I suggest you try and get a team of engineers and mechanics ready and I can bring them back as I look to pick up the rest of the team and my colleagues."

"Right, we're on it and we'll have a lander en-route shortly So best if you stay on site for the moment. Take care, Judy." Ellen's informality was a warm reminder that her former Captain was also her cousin.

The following hours passed quickly. The lack of communication from the expedition proved to be the result of the strike. Although the physical sense felt by the humans had been that of a brief gale force wind the underlying impact seemed to be, as guessed from the Einstein, a localised electromagnetic pulse which had knocked out the electronics including the radio.

Surprisingly, the injuries suffered by the team were, happily, no more than minor cuts and bruises except for one broken arm. Tung-Mei expressed her amazement as she reported back to the Einstein.

"All my understanding of the effects of an EMP burst is that its effect should have covered an area well over a hundred square kilometres. The camp should have been flattened and the injuries serious. Yet despite the strike hitting their side of the mountain the damage seems to have been extremely limited. I want to approach the edge of the damaged zone and try to get an understanding before whatever controlled the fallout collapses."

John considered the idea for several moments while listening to suggestions from his science officers. Finally, he nodded.

"Take the lander in closer but don't take any unnecessary risks. Keep your approach low and walk the final stretch. If in doubt get out, no heroics, Lieutenant. Understood?"

"Yes, Captain." Tung-Mei was careful to reassure John that they would follow his orders to the letter, despite wondering if it would be possible to do so. A quarter of an hour later the lander took off with her in command, Judy in the co-pilot seat and Stefan as the one scientist on the spot.

8. The Mountain that didn't Melt

Back in Yablon, Ellen and Jing were busy preparing a second lander to take an engineering team out to the expedition's site. They gave the team a simple task.

"We need to get the shuttle back in flying order. You'll have two problems. The undercarriage suffered some damage which should be repairable. But the electronics will be the bigger issue I suspect. Despite something reducing the effect of an apparent EMP, they have been knocked out if not completely fried. See what you can do." Ellen's words to Alan and his colleagues summed up everything they knew at that point but she continued. "Alan, I should warn you. Judy is one of the Einstein's lander pilots, so you may well bump into her!"

Alan and Megan had not seen either of their daughters for several weeks, apart from the party to celebrate the harvest, and were conscious that once the ship left orbit both of the girls would be gone, possibly for many months, with no contact after the ship went ultralight. When Alan told his wife, Megan was adamant.

"I have to join the team and," she went on before he could interrupt. "not just because I might see Judy but I need to find out what has happened. There is something odd going on around that site. If it was an EMP nothing should have been able to control it, at least nothing that we know of, and that suggests advanced science way beyond our understanding.

"Megan, love, I understand but you had better clear this with Ellen and I think that we should also let John know that we will be looking to investigate the alien location. The Einstein has already had some contact with whatever alien technology we are up against and we need to liaise with the experts in orbit." Alan knew better than to argue with her decision to join the expedition, knowing that once she had decided on a path it was unlikely that even an EMP would stop her.

Thirty minutes later the lander lifted off from the town and headed south before turning eastwards to avoid the need to fly over the mountain which was still glowing with heat. While on the flight they received news from the Einstein.

Alan summed up the information. "They've managed to slow down the recording of the beam from Selene. As you know the initial belief was that the light was some form of intense laser. Now we know that it wasn't. The slow-motion pictures show that it actually accelerated a solid object on a collision course. When this hit the mountain there was an explosion, not nuclear as far as we can tell but it appears to have been a dense focussed pulse of heat. That looks as if it is what we thought was an EMP. It explains why there was no apparent radiation fallout but doesn't answer the question as to how most of the energy produced seems to have been restricted to a very small area."

"You said most of the energy. What escaped?" The question came from Gino Russo, one of the mechanical engineers on board.

"Some heat, dawn temperatures at Yablon were around ten degrees warmer than usual and, on the impact side, a brief gale force gust of wind. That was strong enough to damage the shuttle's undercarriage. The other reason we believed the impact resulted in an EMP was that all the radio equipment at the campsite and the shuttles electronics have been knocked out by some form of electronic surge. An EMP appears the most likely source but we just don't know."

"Alan and I will be joining the ship's team to investigate, if we can, the impact point. Whether there is anything left to find, with what looks like half the mountain in meltdown, we can only wait and see." Megan's contribution, she had been quietly thoughtful, drew an unexpected response from Gino.

"I'm not sure that there will be nothing to find. If the impact, explosion, whatever, had completely destroyed whatever facility was located on the mountain, then what has kept the barrier in place? If it is some form of forcefield where is it getting its power from?"

Suddenly everyone was trying to speak at once before Alan called for their attention.

"Gino is right, it does look as if destruction of the site cannot have been one hundred per cent. It does mean that we need to be extra vigilant when we get there. The system appears to be designed to minimise collateral damage from a, shall we call it, self-destruct operation but we can't assume such beneficence, should we go poking our noses in where we aren't wanted. Now we have another four hours before we reach the camp site so I suggest that we all get some rest. We are going to be very busy."

9. Silent Approach

Time passed slowly on the bridge. Various reports kept John occupied but his thoughts were never far from the monitors watching the Deimos as it closed on Cain. Although there had been no response to the instruction to adjust course the tracking team had been able to confirm that the ship had changed its angle of approach in line with his order.

With the ship still twenty hours from perigee John left the bridge for a brief break before the possible pressures of the close approach. For once, he left his own quarters for a stroll to one of the nearer eating areas still operational with the slimmed down occupancy of a ship designed to hold nearly five thousand crew and other teams but now with less than a thousand in total on board. Also dining, he found Miguel Sanchez deep in conversation with Teri Larding. They were clearly quite excited and John guessed, correctly, that it was about the alien languages.

Deciding that there was an opportunity to hear, informally, about the linguist's work with the data received from the alien scanner, he interrupted, asking if he could join them. Miguel, guessing what John really wanted, moved to leave the table excusing himself until John gestured for him to stay. Leaving them just long enough to get his own food, John settled down to hear from Teri how she and her colleagues were progressing.

"It is exciting, Captain, the ninth packet has given us an opportunity to decipher seven of the languages and the different packets each provide a good basic course in a single language." Teri had difficulty restraining her emotions at the opportunity to use her own linguistic skill. "And the courses also provide an audio version of the words and that is even more fascinating."

Then, to John and Miguel's amazement, Teri spoke in a guttural tone half a dozen words that were clearly not of human origin.

"Gyftthog hraf harvd Zeders, Sfrunq, gyftthog."

"What on earth, or off Earth perhaps I should say, was that?" John's quizzical eyebrow emulating another fictional hero of his childhood.

"Welcome to our home, Zeder, Captain, welcome." Teri grinned. "If I have got it right that is. We still have a lot of analysis but those words are from the first packet and relate to a civilisation whose home planet seems to be called Zeder. I hope we can develop our translation programming to enable us to use English because, as you can guess, it is not designed for the human larynx. There is one problem, Captain. The eighth language is in a form that is almost impossible to translate, if I had to guess it is ancient in the extreme, yet it seems more advanced than the others. We are focusing on those we can work out but that one will take a lot more analysis."

"That is remarkable, Teri, and you have got that far in what, less than a day? Have you slept?"

"No, she hasn't John. The rest of her team packed her off her to eat and she is going to bed down for a good sleep as soon as she has finished here." Miguel gave Teri no chance to use the meeting as an excuse to avoid much needed rest and his words nudged his Captain in the direction, he wanted him to go.

"Miguel is right, Teri. You should get some sleep so that you are well rested before the Deimos makes its approach to Cain tomorrow. It would be good to have you on the bridge then, say at seven in the morning."

"I will be there Captain, sorry, John." Teri rose and then had to lean on the table, suddenly showing her complete exhaustion. With a nod from John, Miguel was quick to support his friend and indicated that he would ensure Teri made her quarters without falling asleep en-route.

***   ***   ***

"Captain on the bridge." It was six the next morning and John took the command seat from Miguel telling him to grab something to eat but to be back at the helm by eight.

A brief series of questions to his comms and tracking teams confirmed that the Deimos remained on course to pass Cain in a little over three hours and he settled down to review the ongoing status reports as to the ship's readiness should it be required to react to external factors.

An hour later the Lieutenant standing in at the first officer's station.

"Captain, there is something happening on Cain."

"What is that?"

"We are seeing a green spot forming, something like Jupiter's red spot. As you know we have been monitoring the planet in detail since the messages that we intercepted but the ship's computer was also programmed to watch the planets as an ongoing development of our knowledge of the system. During the time we have been in orbit the atmosphere of Cain has appeared very similar to that of Venus. Cloaked in clouds, we assumed a greenhouse effect run wild despite it being further from the sun, with minimal changes in appearance. Then about an hour ago a vortex started to develop and for reasons unknown, at the moment, the atmosphere is being twisted into a whirlpool almost a hundred klicks in diameter."

"Your analysis, Lieutenant?"

"Cause remains unknown. Location is over, what we estimate, is the equatorial region. The astronomy team is trying to come up with ideas. All we have is that there is a significant increase in atmospheric temperature in and around the edge of the spot."

"If the Deimos continues on its current heading will it cross it?"

Tracking were definite in their response. "Not on the first pass, sir, but if they decide to use the planet's gravity to complete one, or more orbits, they are likely to. On the first pass the anomaly will be on the other side of the planet."

"On their approach are they likely to spot it?"

"Possibly." The team were studying a variety of simulations. "Sorry, captain. We can't be sure."

"Then we must warn them. Comms! Get ready to compress the following message and send a burst transmission to the Deimos."

John thought briefly then dictated a short message to Pawl indicating that they needed to be aware of the events on Cain and warning him that he should adjust course to avoid an over pass of the storm.

This time there was an acknowledgement from the Deimos confirming that they intended a short burst from their manoeuvring jets to adjust the final approach, having spotted the apparent storm, themselves.

10. Meeting with a Watcher

With the shuttle having left, Ellen and Jing settled down to catch up with more domestic matters. Most items were straightforward and were dealt with quickly. Jing kept the issue of communications and a computer network for the town until the end of the discussion. Having passed over the minutes of the earlier meeting, she summed up her own view.

"As I said at the time, I was upset that the needs of our children had not formed part of the proposals put to me. In fairness both sides responded well and we do have Anton and Anita waiting to meet with us both. I suspect they may have tried to come up with a compromise."

"Let's get them in then."

Jing proved partly correct in that the two specialists had a compromise but Anita was clearly still unhappy at not getting all that she was seeking.

It was left to Anton to explain. "It was Jing's reprimand to both of us for not considering the children's educational needs beyond what has been happening in small groups. My colleagues, and myself I must admit, are focussed on ensuring that we can withstand a future attack by the machine ships to the exclusion of other projects. But we have had to accept that that is, in the short term, wrong. However, we were correct in stating that we do not have enough fibre optic cable nor do we have the source materials or, for that matter, the manufacturing capability to produce additional cable."

"It's the same excuses again." Anita exploded. "Always we haven't or we can't! I thought we had intelligent capable people."

Anton rolled his eyes in frustration. "Administrator, I have a compromise proposal but…."

"Tell us then." Ellen was intrigued, having some knowledge of the materials side she had sympathy with Anton.

"We can't yet cable the whole town but with the help of the Einstein's stocks and its on-board capabilities we can produce enough cable to reach a set of given points within the town, just not every house. Those points should allow the local area to have access to the central network by local wi-fi links. It will take a little time to manufacture enough routers but it would allow everyone to gain access within a matter of weeks."

"Wi-fi routers! And how fast will the dataflow be? Not fast enough I'll bet." Anita's frustration continued unabated.

Jing smiled, a little ruefully, but it was Ellen who responded.

"Anita, I understand that you would prefer the convenience of a cabled structure but there are times when we must deal with what is possible, not with what we really want. You have to remember that this is still a young settlement and, despite the wonderful start provided by the stores from the Einstein, there are limitations on how fast we can develop."

"If you are saying that this compromise is the best option, then I must accept but I still think the current projects need to be reviewed." Anita commented grudgingly.

"Believe me. We regularly review all our activities. For the moment, our biggest restriction centres on raw materials which is why Stefan and a team headed over the mountains in a search for metal deposits, ores at least."

Anton interrupted. "I know they took a shuttle two days ago but I saw a lander lifting earlier and heading in that direction. Have they made a big find?"

"That might depend on how you define a big find." Anita replied. "The lander included a medical team. There has been some form of "event" which means that there are injuries. There were a couple of mechanical experts and both of the Pipers were on board. I don't know exactly what has happened though."

Ellen, feeling that being secretive was senseless, explained the events as far as she understood them. "And that's the cause of the glow." she finished.

"I can understand the medics and the engineers, but why the Pipers?" Anton sounded perplexed.

"They're going to try and see what they can find out about the location. Or at least get an idea of how the force field, for want of a better description, is formed."

"I have a different question." Anita sounded concerned. "How did we miss them? Surely the surveys, when we were considering landing, should have found them or is this just more incompetence?"

Ellen gritted her teeth. "You would think so." She continued, not allowing Anita time to say anything more. "Well you can guarantee that John Lees and his team are trawling the data to see if they can work out why we saw nothing. If you want my opinion. I think that the system must have been dormant. Somehow our presence has triggered it into taking some action. I should say that nothing suggests it is aggressive."

"I guess that we can only hope that it has no relationship with the Machines." said Anton, expressing aloud the underlying fear that all of them were conscious of.

Ellen was certain. "Now, please keep it to yourselves for the minute. I would rather have a full report back from the expedition site and an update from the Einstein before releasing the news in full. But everyone will be informed as quickly as we can."

With the agreement of everyone, the meeting broke up and Ellen went back to her office to contact John and to hear the views of the specialists on the ship.

***　　　***　　　***

John's news of the events on Cain stunned Ellen. From John's point of view the plans of the Yablon team to investigate the mountain came as positive news and he immediately sent a message to Tung-Mei to stop their approach and wait for Alan and Megan.

It was a message that the Einstein team received with mixed views. Tung-Mei and Stefan were both irritated by having to wait while Judy, naturally, was delighted that they would be joined by both of her parents. Tung-Mei's response was heated.

"Why should we have to wait? I know Megan is brilliant and Alan really clever but this is the unknown? How can they support us?"

Judy thought for a moment. "Look, I know they are my parents and just seeing them is good enough for me. But there is a good scientific reason why they can help. Mom's background has been in analysing the unknown and Pop's engineering knowledge may well help."

"Sorry, Judy, we're just a bit fed up with the delay. I know your Dad and he is the best of our people and we all know we wouldn't be here without your Mum's work. Tung-Mei, we are just going to have to be patient." Stefan was quick to soften the atmosphere. "And we could all do with a rest, I guess."

In the event their wait was quite short as Megan arranged to be dropped near their lander before the town's craft continued to the expedition's location. With the Pipers on board, the combined team set off again towards the edge of the site.

Tung-Mei kept their speed down and they took over an hour to cover the eight kilometres to the edge of the area apparently destroyed by the Selene based laser.

As they came to a stop the view was not what the orbital photography had suggested. While the scene was hazy due to what appeared to be a barrier of some form it seemed that there was little, apparent, damage visible. What, from orbit, had appeared to be the scene of a blazing fire or even a complete meltdown of the mountainside now looked as if nothing had happened at all.

"I don't understand. I've seen the video of the impact and the whole area erupted in flame. Now if it wasn't for the haziness, you'd be hard pressed to identify this as the same location." Megan was stunned and mystified.

Tung-Mei was desperately checking her instruments. Equally amazed, her first thought was that she had made a mistake in navigation. "Judy, have we gone wrong somehow?"

Judy checked and could not find an error but as a double check she signalled the Einstein and asked if tracking team could confirm the location of the lander. The answer came back almost instantly as John replied.

"Lieutenants, you are exactly where you should be. Why the doubt?"

Alan responded first, explaining that all they could see suggested that nothing had actually happened. To his surprise John reiterated that the view from the Einstein remained indicative of a major fire or meltdown, albeit he admitted, the glow was fading.

"Look, Alan, we are clearly getting different views. Your first test will be the force field but, even if you can get around that, be prepared. Both views cannot be right and it is possible that the field is hiding the reality at ground level."

"Don't worry, Captain. We are going to go at this a few metres at a time. We'll stay in touch."

The next few hours were spent trying to find an end to the force field without success.

During a break for food and drink, Stefan voiced their collective thoughts. "We are going to have to try and pierce the field and see if we can get through it directly."

"Do you really think that it will be that easy?" Judy asked her parents.

"No. In fact, I think we may have to consider trying from the other side of the mountains." Megan's comment was a surprise.

Judy said, "We can obviously fly high enough to get over the range itself but, even then, landing is going to be an exercise in extremis and we'll need to fly at least a hundred klicks south, first. When you came from Yablon your course must have been at least that far to the south. We've tried a good part of that distance without success."

"Let's hope we can find a way through then." Megan's brow was furrowed with concentration

The team decided to see if anything happened if they walked slowly closer to the field. As they crossed a flat grassy area they came on a startlingly straight line. On one side greenery, on the other the vegetation simply vanished leaving what appeared to be bare earth. There was no apparent damage but nowhere did the local foliage cross that line.

"It's like the edge of a garden patio which has just been built and before the lawn can spread at all. It's weird." Tung-Mei voiced concern that she did not understand what she was seeing and no-one could provide an answer.

Stefan and Alan were talking quietly together. Megan interrupted them asking what they were thinking.

"This barren zone measures about twenty-five metres across and there seems to be some darker growth the other side which reaches the edge of the force field. We feel that we should test two things. Is it safe to cross such a barrier, if that's what it is? Equally how solid is the latter?" Alan's answer summed up the questions they would need to answer before risking any further approach.

Stefan continued. "We do have options and I propose that we use one of our miniature drones to first survey the road or patio. We can use a second drone to fly slowly into the field. In effect we can find out if it bounces!" He smiled.

"I have a better idea." Tung-Mei's own thoughts had gone back to the days when she had been involved in tactical war games and drones could be disabled by electrical screens. "We can try using rope first. There is a catapult on board. It's there in case a tow is needed and you can fire the rope into a secure spot in advance of the lander or any other vehicle for that matter."

"That's a good idea, Tung-Mei." Alan was quick to reply. "Let's try it."

Their first experiments involved testing the barren surface by throwing a clump of grass on to it. That produced a first surprise. The grass did not actually touch the surface and the breeze, that had been an ever-present draft of warmish air, blew it back across the barrier. The rope, once thrown at the soil also seemed to hover over the surface and then, slowly at first, was also blown back towards them.

"We are running into constant mysteries." said Megan. "Somehow there must be an invisible covering which is also smooth and frictionless. But we can feel the wind coming from that direction so there can't be a solid wall." She saw a movement in the corner of her eye and reacted with a cry. "Judy, what are you doing?"

Judy had decided that sooner or later they were going to have to try and cross the line and had stepped on to the surface. Her initial concentration was broken with an equally startled cry.

"I thought it would be like stepping on to an ice rink but it isn't. The surface isn't solid but more like a moving walkway. I can feel myself going to the left, slowly."

The others could see her working to keep her balance as she turned in the direction of the movement.

Alan called out first. "Step back in this direction."

Judy tried to turn again and make the step and then her face whitened as she found her movement failing. "I can't, there's something blocking me and I'm moving faster."

Stefan, running alongside, swiftly threw the rope towards her. To his horror it appeared to strike a solid surface falling short of the now desperate Judy. Without hesitation, he then jumped across the edge expecting to hit the same wall but to his amazement he found himself on the same moving surface as Judy and travelling in the same direction despite having jumped at an angle opposite to her own movement.

Megan yelled to Tung-Mei to get back to the lander and move it ahead of their two colleagues as she and Alan began to jog along the grass to try and keep up with their daughter and Stefan. Unfortunately, the speed of the walkway had steadied at a lot more than walking pace. It seemed unresponsive to movements by the two captives though Stefan had caught up with Judy.

While they ran along, Alan's mind was racing. Foliage and other inanimate objects were repelled by the machine. He had little doubt that that was what they were dealing with, and none of the local wildlife had been seen near it. So why had Judy been able to trigger it and how could it have differentiated between Stefan's rope and Stefan himself. It couldn't have been their weight. Animals would have been as heavy and the rope was not light. He recalled a quote from Sherlock Holmes, *"When you have eliminated the impossible, whatever remains, however improbable, must be the truth"*. You haven't eliminated the impossible he told himself but the improbable seems to be the only logical solution. Somehow the machine had recognised that Judy and Stefan were sentient, even though it could not have come across humans before. Or could it have? he puzzled. Whatever, he came to the conclusion that this was simply a way for sentient beings to travel quickly to a destination on the other side of the forcefield.

Pulling his radio out of his pocket he called Tung-Mei who was now a few hundred metres ahead of the group.

"Try and hover ahead and drop a rope ladder down to them." He gasped.

Tung-Mei acknowledged and Alan could see the lander rising and then moving above the surface. As it went into hover mode Alan could see that she had got far enough in front to give her time to drop the ladder ahead of her two colleagues. It was to no avail. As it dropped the ladder hit the same sort of barrier above them, as if Judy and Stefan were now inside a tunnel or tube.

"Judy, is your communicator's tracker operating?" Tung-Mei could be heard over the comms net.

"It's on, Tung-Mei. Can't you read it?"

"Just, but only just. It should be showing more strongly at this range. Better check it."

As the lander turned back on to a parallel path, Tung-Mei called Megan and Alan with the warning that they might lose contact should there be any change in the routing being followed by the walkway. It was Megan, gritting her teeth at the idea of losing her daughter, who responded first.

"Pick us up. We can't afford to lose them."

Almost to the minute it became apparent that Judy and Stefan were moving towards the forcefield itself. Stefan's voice could be heard on the lander as he spotted that the barren surface continued into the barrier and that the spread of foliage previously visible against it had stopped.

"It looks as if this walkway passes through the field although I can't see a gap or entrance at the moment. Wish us luck, guys. See you on the other side. I hope."

On board the lander Tung-Mei was bringing the Einstein up to date, while Megan and Alan could only watch, helplessly, as their daughter and Stefan closed with the field. John could only watch a screen showing the view being fed by the lander's camera fearing that harm was about to befall Judy. He was concerned about Stefan but watching his lover in such a position and being unable to help was providing him with difficulty in focusing on his own role.

Just at the last moment, Judy gave a shout. "The barrier is changing. It doesn't seem right but it looks as if it has hardened in front of us. Everywhere else the cloudy view of it hasn't changed but either we are approaching a door or a solid wall." She gave a nervous laugh. "I do hope it's a door and it's unlocked!"

John having recovered his normal demeanour, acted. "Lieutenant, drop off a drone in hover mode as near to the point where the walkway hits the field as possible. Leave it with camera running and transmitting to us. Then lift the lander until you can pass over the field. Our estimate is that you will need to reach an altitude of around six thousand metres. You can try sending a second drone into the field first but don't delay more than a few minutes."

"Acknowledged, Captain. Launching drones now."

The two drones launched successfully. With the monitor drone filming, they watched as the other drone crossed the walkway and reached the field itself. Ready for it to be destroyed by a collision they were stunned to see that, while it did not penetrate the wall, it remained in the air as if held by the field.

Back on the walkway Judy and Stefan were approaching the barrier. As they closed to within a few metres the door simply vanished leaving a view of a solid looking tunnel.

"Amazing, it didn't appear to open. If it was ever there, and now I wonder if it was, it simply dissolved." Stefan's curiosity was evident despite his obvious nervousness as to what might happen when they crossed the line into the tunnel.

A few moments later the two humans were taken into the tunnel with seemingly no effect from the field and what had been a little dark when they first looked into it became lighter allowing them to see walls that were apparently unchanging. With no idea of how long the tunnel was they both tried to contact the outside world without success.

"Looks like we are on our own, Judy."

"I'm sorry, Stefan. If I hadn't stepped over that line you wouldn't have followed me and…."

"Judy, no apologies. Sooner or later one of us would have had to try walking across that barrier. For the moment we can only wait and see. Now, if nothing changes in the next five minutes, I am going to try and touch the wall, see if it does anything to change our progress."

***   ***   ***

Back on the lander they had rapidly climbed to three thousand metres when the view of the forcefield changed subtly. Ensuring that communications with the Einstein were open and that the bridge could hear them, Tung-Mei said

"I think that we may be nearing the top of the field. Am I right that it looks as if it is curving from the vertical into a horizontal structure?" She was now pleased to have the two scientists aboard as the events, were way beyond her knowledge. That Megan and Alan might be as perplexed did not occur to her then.

Megan took the lead over her husband with a thoughtful comment.

"The Einstein thought we would need to reach almost twice our current altitude. That suggests that their sensors are being affected in some way that distorts their readings. I think we need to be very wary about what our instruments are telling us and what we can see with our eyes."

"Well one thing, we are definitely still below the level of the highest peaks and even the bulk of the range between us and Yablon. I have got to admit that I cannot see anything that suggests a fire or heat of any sort has been experienced here. Tung-Mei, can you bounce a radar signal against the

66

mountains in front of us? I know we can use dead reckoning, or Einstein's sensors to work out a number for us but, if instruments cannot be relied on, we must try other means to clarify our position."

It took a few minutes before Tung-Mei was able to provide an answer or, as she put it, to provide three answers.

"Einstein reckons we are just over five kilometres from the nearest of the range. My sensor array says we are six kilometres! The third answer is a little under half that distance and that is from bouncing a laser off the nearest mountain according to my forward sensor. As far as I can see something is disrupting how we measure the geography of the area but I don't understand or how. It does mean I am going to have to be extra careful as we get closer to the peaks."

"Very careful." Alan's dry comment provided a subtle lightening of the mood.

They moved slowly across the forcefield watching for any changes. With the mountains coming ever closer they were beginning to despair of finding an end to the field when the surface changed in the shape of a circle directly ahead of the lander. Tung-Mei did not hesitate, slowing further to a hover immediately above the circle. Turning to the Pipers she said,

"I propose to try and land on the field. I'm just not sure what will happen."

"Megan, I feel we must risk the outcome. Unless you can think of a better choice?" Alan expressed Megan's thoughts exactly.

"I agree but I'd go further and be ready for the surface to not be there. Tung-Mei, be ready to find you are landing on thin air and that you might find that you only lose altitude. Captain, can you hear us?"

John replied quickly. "I hear you. I agree with that. Be prepared to lose contact though. Since Stefan and the Lieutenant vanished into that tunnel, we have had no contact nor can we find them on our sensors."

"Right, Tung-Mei. Let's do this before I lose my nerve!" Megan, of course, knew that she would have jumped through the forcefield, if necessary, to find Judy. Nerves would have had nothing to do with it.

The lander slowly dropped on to the apparent surface and, to their surprise, stopped.

"What now?" Tung-Mei's plaintive words summed up the situation.

For several minutes they continued to sit on the surface with the power running at a minimum level just to ensure that they had control if the unexpected occurred. After ten minutes Alan made a suggestion.

"If we turned the engines off, cut power to a minimum. How fast can we restart if needs be?"

"Almost immediately." replied Tung-Mei. "You think cutting power might get a response of some sort?"

"I think it may and it is all we have left to try. I do not want risk forcing a breach as yet, even if it worked which I somehow doubt."

John interrupted. "I agree with Alan but, Lieutenant, be ready for a vertical take-off if the field simply vanishes and you drop without any apparent support."

"Noted, Captain. Vertical lift set to automatic. Will engage if we drop without resistance." Tung-Mei set her controls in a dormant mode and with a nod to her companions and a few words, intended for the Einstein. "Cutting power to engines."

Once again there was no immediate change except for the silence that followed the cessation of the engine sound, usually so quiet that it was rarely noticed, other than by the pilots. Then, with a suddenness that brought mutual gasps, they started to drop quickly down. Tung-Mei went to restart the engines but then realised that they were not falling out of control but continuing to sit on the surface which was itself dropping down a cylindrical column.

"It's like we were on the flight deck of a carrier before being moved to the below deck hangar. Only smoother and deeper." Tung-Mei had served in the navy and suddenly felt at home. "I wonder how far we will drop?"

They continued to drop until at one thousand metres altitude, something happened. No-one could tell what but suddenly they appeared to have dropped to three hundred metres without covering the intervening seven hundred, although it was apparent that the lift was slowing.

Megan realised that whatever had happened had taken some time. "We took a bit more than an hour to cover that distance."

"That's crazy. I was watching the altimeter and the change happened instantly." Tung-Mei argued.

"But I guess you weren't watching the clock at the same time?" Alan commented. "We have surely missed that amount of time. Though I have no idea how."

At fifty metres they came to a halt and the walls which had been unchanging became transparent. The scene, now outside the lander, was in complete contrast. A room of large dimensions with walls mostly covered in a variety of screens, each showing different views. Amazingly the lighting was not artificial but came from a clear roof through which sunlight cast shadows.

Despite this, efforts to contact the Einstein failed.

After taking the time to study their surrounds, the team decided that they had no choice but to explore and carefully stepped down from their craft. Megan made the first move crossing the room to what appeared to be a control point.

"Some of these screens are showing, what appear to be, live feeds from orbits around other planets in the system." Tung-Mei was almost whispering as the sheer scale of what they were seeing sank in. "This one shows the view of Eden from Selene and this one shows Yablon looking from one of the mountain peaks around us! I think we've run into a computer program running surveillance of the whole planetary system!"

"But why? We haven't found anything to suggest that Eden has ever had a sentient race of any form let alone one as advanced as this operation would require." Alan's own amazement mirrored hers and he also moved to join Megan who was studying an apparent touchscreen with what, she assumed, was the alien equivalent of a keyboard.

"I don't really know what I am looking at." she explained as the others joined her, "These might be individual characters or whole words. Until we can work out what it means or what it does, I'm not sure we should touch it."

There was a sudden change in the largest of the screens which was directly in front of the control point and an odd sounding voice began speaking. Although it was difficult to understand what it was saying Alan was the first to realise that it was speaking a form of English but pitched so high most of the words were lost. Speaking loudly himself, he replied.

"I am sorry but we cannot understand you. You are speaking words from our language but not in a way that conveys a message. We cannot hear all words at that high a frequency."

The voice responded and this time it was with a much deeper timbre.

"Can hear this?"

"We can, thank you. Who or what are you?" As ever Megan cut to the point.

"In language of you, I Guardian Two. I level ten artificial intelligence."

71

"What do you guard?"

"*I, with Guardian One, monitor system for evidence of sapience not of our designers. If designers were here, we would activate other ways.*"

"How do you know our language?"

"*Guardian One obtain basic language from vessel orbiting planet. Guardian One orbits planet one. Data transmitted this planet for analysis translation follow.*"

Tung-Mei asked an unexpected question. "You suggest that you have only just been activated? How long were you dormant or inactive?"

"*Guardians both inactive period four hundred complete orbits of star.*"

"That's nearly six hundred years!" Alan was stunned. "Why were you left here?"

"*Designers prepared planet for colonisation thirty thousand orbits ago. We were activated four hundred orbits ago by the designers' associated species, the Zeder. Guardian One despatching message drone home system. Seek instruction. Why humans here?*"

"Our home planet was destroyed by a fleet of alien machines. Only three interstellar capable ships escaped. Our ship named Einstein was one and the largest. We sought new home for seven rotations of this star. Home planet is one hundred light years away."

"*I do not have that data. My knowledge language yours still limited. What are light years?*"

"One light year is the distance that light travels in one orbit of our home around its sun. Approximately three quarters of a rotation of this planet around this sun. The speed of light is defined as three hundred thousand kilometres per second. This is explained in the data included in that extracted by Guardian One."

There was the briefest of pauses before the Guardian responded.

"*You exceed universal limit. How?*"

"I am unable to advise that information. At its simplest, we warp space. How did your designers' cross interstellar space?"

"*I do not hold such information. Such information may be held by Guardian One level twelve intelligence.*"

Megan could wait no longer before asking where Megan and Stefan were.

"*Two entities entered zone through land entrance. They subject to examination for disease.*"

"If so, why were we not subject to same examination?" Tung-Mei queried the inconsistency.

"*You were scanned during entrance process. Placed in stasis mode for examination.*"

"That explains the hour we lost." Commented Alan.

Tung-Mei continued "Are you able to explain how you were woken?"

"Guardian One activated energy source on satellite of planet. Energy store launched at outside of operation. Energy absorbed and routed to my power source."

"Why did our sensors read a fire or meltdown of mountain?"

"Energy matrix covers side of mountain."

As the Guardian completed its answer two people came around an unnoticed corner and the team were reunited. Megan's hug for Judy was only matched by her words of admonition.

"Don't do that again!"

"Mum, it's all OK. This place is amazing, how did we miss it?"

"Dormant operation was hidden from external instrumentation."

It was clear that the Guardian was refining its knowledge of English as the conversation went on. *"It is necessary that you leave this installation. No further contact will be permitted until response to message drone is received. You are not of the Seven nor related to the designers."*

Alan thought for a moment before asking. "Before we leave are you able to provide two things? A database of the designers' language. And any visual recording of one or more designers."

"*I have data relating to the Seven and have authority to release this to sentient species. I have scanned your vehicle and accessed its memory bank. The requested data is being transferred to that location. I may not supply visual recordings of the designers.*"

Judy asked a final question, conscious of the loss of Earth. "How long will it be before a response to your message drone is received? What if there is no response?"

"*I cannot provide that information. Only Guardian One has data and authority to override restrictions on contact. You must leave now. Deactivation of Guardian Two in ten of your minutes, that will cause location to be inimical to biological life forms until I am reactivated.*"

"Back to the lander everyone, now." Tung-Mei took command and, within a few minutes, the team had boarded the craft. Immediately the lift mechanism operated, lifting them at high speed.

"As soon as we reach the roof, I intend to start engines and lift us off the field surface. Judy prepare for flight manoeuvring." Tung-Mei was already trying to contact the Einstein without success.

11.   The Messenger Departs

Earlier on the Einstein, with eight o'clock approaching, Teri joined the bridge team and everyone settled down to wait with the Deimos now less than an hour out from Cain. With only a few minutes before the first pass Pawl broke radio silence.

"Do you see this?"

"Main screen." John did not need to say what view he wanted. As the sensor view of Cain appeared there was a gasp from the crew as a whole. The centre of the storm was starting to glow. Even as they watched, a beam of light, suddenly burst out of the atmosphere.

"Sir, there is an object at the front of that beam. It is being accelerated at, I don't believe it, over five gravities!" The young ensign on tracking was stunned by what he was seeing. "I don't know how that is possible."

"Clearly it is." John's reaction was mirrored around the bridge. "But I agree, the question is how. Commander, can you add anything to what we are seeing?"

The response was a few moments coming with the distance between the two craft still being several light minutes. Then Pawl responded.

"Not sure yet. The object is clearly a craft of some sort. We are turning to follow at maximum speed, though, if it can maintain that acceleration, we aren't going to be able to catch it. We'll stay on line and keep you updated. Just to confirm, we do not intend to touch that beam, our sensors suggest a laser of incredible power easily capable of cutting us in half."

"Stay well clear. A parallel course should be enough."

While his crew were centred on tracking the two craft John's own thoughts were split, with concern over the team investigating the anomaly on Eden who had now been out of touch for some time. Repeated efforts by his comms team had failed to raise any of the team and the longer they had to wait the more he worried.

Then to his relief and that of his team the voice of Tung-Mei could be heard calling the Einstein from the lander.

"Einstein, do you read? Einstein, do you read?"

"We read you, Lieutenant. What is your situation?"

"Clear of mountains at ten thousand metres. Captain, we intend to rendezvous with Einstein. We are carrying significant data provided by Guardian Two."

John responded first. "Agreed, Lieutenant. Who is Guardian Two?"

"Putting Megan Piper on, sir."

Megan kept it short and simple. "John, sorry Captain, Guardian Two is an artificial intelligence programmed to, I think, just below sentient status. May I suggest that you pull the linguistics team and the systems guys together."

"We'll see you in what, an hour?"

"Yes, Captain. Just under." Judy was busy adjusting the lander's climb rate.

Over the next few hours, as they expected, Deimos was left well behind as the sheer acceleration of the alien craft continued unabated.

Two hours later after taking the chance to freshen up, and in the case of Judy an emotional reunion with John, the team sat down with Einstein's officers and associated experts to explain their experiences of the previous twenty-four hours.

It was the video that drew gasps from the audience. It was short in length but showed three figures. All were humanoid with four limbs. Compared to humans their size and structure were very different. They were tall, Megan estimated around three metres for one and two metres plus for the second. Even the third was close to a metre and a half tall. Despite their height they were broad shouldered and had short necks. With colouring that differed between each.

"Do you think we are seeing them dressed in clothing that covers them fully?" Teri, present as head of the language team.

"I believe that is so," Doctor Carden commented, "but their faces suggest differences. The larger individual seems to be a dark red while the smaller is almost purple in skin tone. The child, we should not forget that we are imposing our own understanding of scale, seems to have a raspberry hue."

"You mean that we might be wrong to assume that the smaller adult is female. Surely the larger two are the adults? Assuming that this is a family unit, of course."

It was left to John to break the news of the events at Cain. "We are pretty sure that the message drone, the Guardian referred to, was launched from Cain this morning."

"What? Do we know, where it is headed?" Alan was conscious of the need to know in order to have some idea of when an answer might be received.

"Not yet. It is a little early to have a definitive course. The Deimos is tracking the craft but is losing ground as the alien continues to accelerate." John's calm tone did not hide his amazement that the laser appeared to still be able to provide such power. "Our science officers are convinced that the impact of the push must be reducing as the drone's velocity increases. If it is, though, we haven't been able to measure any change yet."

It was left to Teri Larding to provide the news that the language provided by the Guardian was the one that she and some of her team had already been working on. Her smile broadened as she explained that their research had still been given a boost by the Guardian.

"The language file uploaded to the lander includes a significant amount of direct translation. You told us that the Guardian's use of English had improved the longer you talked. Well he or it must have increased their knowledge and we now have well call it, a travel bilingual book. We will be able to advance our programming of our own translation software by months."

With that good news the meeting broke up with crew returning to their duties and the specialists deciding to reconvene after a break for refreshments.

Three days later the laser emanating from the planet switched off.

"There's no other way of describing it. It's as if someone or something has flipped a switch." Pawl was mystified and it showed in the tone of his voice.

"The team here agree but, Commander, did you realise the craft is still accelerating? Still around one g. We are still analysing the emissions from it but for the moment we don't know how. Keep tracking it, we need to be as close as possible should anything change."

"Noted, Captain." We'll keep in touch.

John turned to his tracking team with two questions for them.

"I want to know two things. Assuming it keeps to the current heading where is it going? And how fast will it be going, if it continues at one g?

The answers came back more quickly than he expected.

"Captain, there is nothing within the system and the nearest star, on that heading, is forty light years away. If the craft can keep accelerating it will reach about ten per cent of light speed in around ten days."

"Presumably then it must have some way of defeating that limitation or else it has a very long trip ahead of it." John thought for a minute. "Tell engineering that I want another probe despatched to Cain to get a close up of that site. Lieutenant Sanchez, you have the com." With that he left the bridge to try and gain a little rest.

Time passed slowly for the Einstein's bridge team. It was not that they had nothing to do, John kept them busy with regular test scenarios, but most of their attention was on the alien craft which was already approaching the system's warp boundary.

For the senior officers, conversations had begun to drag as the Deimos moved further and further from Eden and the time lag gradually became more apparent. Megan and Alan Piper had returned to Yablon for the time being but were in constant touch. Finally, John came to a decision and requested a meeting on board ship with both of them, Ellen and Jing.

That evening John, having left Judy in command, had the rare pleasure of hosting a small dinner on board Einstein. As the group relaxed over some Eden coffee, one of the first crops and better tasting than the machine coffee everyone had got used to during the journey from the Solar System, John raised the topic he had been spending time considering for some days.

"You all know that we are tracking the Guardian's messenger craft and it is still accelerating. Despite that, unless it changes course or has some form of FTL drive, the nearest star is forty odd light years away or close to a century travel time."

Ellen turned to Alan. "You are sure that the Guardian didn't give any idea as to the journey time?"

"None and it wouldn't even acknowledge that its designers had any way of defeating the light speed limitation. Having said that it knew we must have."

"What are you suggesting we should do, John?" Ellen raised her eyebrows in a quizzical comment that indicated that she already had a good idea herself of John's idea.

"I don't feel we should wait for the messenger. I think Einstein should leave Eden and make a start - heading for that system ahead of the messenger."

Ellen cleared her throat. "You had your orders to seek out sentience when you were promoted, John. You didn't need all of us here to discuss your proposed routing."

"Admiral," John replied to remind the others of Ellen's formal position, "that is correct. However, in the circumstances I believe that we need to approach this differently. That original task was a search of possibly many systems. Trouble was that we had nothing to point us in the right direction. No systems in the cluster are rich in the radio noise that would identify an advanced culture. Despite that we now know for sure that such civilisations exist and may be closer than we thought. It is inevitable that we will face a first contact situation sooner rather than later."

"And?" Megan asked.

"The team on board should be strengthened to include you and Alan as two non-crew who were present at the Guardian's location and Ellen, who is our leader, whether she likes it or not."

"What about me?" Jing's distress at the idea of being parted from Ellen, for any length of time, was clear.

"I had it in mind that you should be formally given the job of Administrator or Mayor, as I gather the people are referring to the role."

"John, how long do you expect to be away from Eden? Months or years? Ellen and I have only just got to be together regularly for the first time in a long time. I don't want that job no matter how important it is, if it means being separated."

Ellen intervened. "John, do you really feel that I should go? One reason I stood down was to be able to be with Jing and I don't wish to be apart either. Can we not both go or stay?"

"I feel it is imperative that you go, Ellen. If that means that Jing also does then we need to find someone else to take on the role of Mayor. The problem is that no-one stands out, who could spare the time to run the administration of the town. They are all up to their eyeballs in other development work." He paused. "Unless, I second one of my team to take it on. How would people respond to that?"

Ellen and Jing looked at each other and both shook their heads.

"Not well, we suspect." said Ellen. "As they had decided to stay with the Einstein, they would be seen, unfairly I must say, as outsiders."

"In that case what about Anita Pavel? She was an excellent member of the medical team here. Doc Carden spoke well of her."

"I suspect he did," Jing's dry tone perked interest, "but she's not the one for this role. She does not have the ability to see both sides of an argument and would almost certainly have the science and engineering sections up in arms quite quickly."

"Do you have any other suggestions, then?" John was struggling to maintain his calmness.

Megan had been thinking while the discussion continued.

"Why not split the role? Make it a two-person joint position, if we can't find one person."

Ellen and Jing both started to speak together before Ellen indicated that Jing should continue.

"That's a good idea, Megan, and I think I know who would make a good team. Helga Neilson and Anton Tyler have worked together well."

John raised an eyebrow in Ellen's direction.

"I agree with Jing. Helga is more on the farming and social side of things while Anton is a good engineer who can think his way around problems. I doubt if either would take the role on as a solo position. But sharing the job would probably be quite attractive to them and generally around the town. Both are well liked and respected. They would be a good team."

"Good. First thing tomorrow then we'll take a lander down and arrange things. You will all need to pack some things. I want to be ready to leave orbit in twenty-four hours." John finished the discussion with the suggestion that they all needed some sleep, arranging for an Ensign to show them all to their quarters. He, himself, headed for the bridge to relieve Judy and check on the latest news from the Deimos.

"Nothing to report, Captain. The drone continues to accelerate and Deimos is being left further behind. Should we recall them?" Judy asked the question that John himself had been considering.

"No, Lieutenant. We will be leaving orbit within twenty-four hours and will follow their course. We can catch up with them in a few days. Now look to get some rest, you'll be in command tomorrow while I am planetside."

Judy caught her breath. "Why not Tung-Mei?" belatedly she added, "Sir."

"She will be piloting the lander and it will do you no harm to experience the pressure that can be linked to that chair. You won't be sitting around as it is. I will expect you to have checked with all sections and made sure we will be ready to depart by seven o'clock tomorrow evening." John smiled. "Now go."

"Captain." Judy left the bridge heading to their quarters not sure if John would be able to join her for a break during the night.

In the early hours John handed over the bridge to another of his Lieutenants and headed off to grab some sleep which he did manage eventually. Judy needed time to satisfy herself that John's decision was about her own capabilities and had nothing to do with their relationship. His final words before they fell asleep calmed her nerves.

"Look Judy. I have the responsibility to ensure that the Einstein operates to the maximum. I will not put anyone in command that I do not believe is ready for it. And when it comes to you, I will always think twice. I love you and, given the opportunity, will always keep you safe. One because the ship is our responsibility, two because I will not put you, Judy Piper, in a place that might cause you pain or that you couldn't handle."

***   ***   ***

Early the next day, back on Eden, there were successful meetings with Helga and Anton individually and then jointly. There had been initial concerns as to how it would work but after a couple of hours understanding the demands both agreed to take on the joint role. Alan had spent time with his team briefing them as to what was needed, while Megan did the same. After dealing with the issue of the role of Mayor, Ellen and John turned to what would be needed in the absence of the Einstein.

Talking to Helga, Anton and Stefan, John highlighted the space-based operations that would need to be followed up on.

"We have a probe heading to Heira and a second is about to enter orbit around Cain. You'll need to monitor their transmissions. These should be received by our own satellites which we've programmed to then re-broadcast down to your comms centre. We will be leaving IPS Phoebe and a further lander to boost your off-planet capabilities so you can reach the satellites in case of instrument failure or for any other transport needs the town might have."

"Do we have any ideas as to what the probes might find?"

"Guardian One appears to be orbiting Heira while there is certainly a base on Cain. Will we get any reaction from probing them? I really don't know. From experience so far, I suspect that the worst case is that both probes will stop transmitting, blocked by the local alien operations. I would suggest that you do not take any action beyond transmitting a recall signal to try and get them back. Certainly, it is unlikely to be worth trying any physical recovery until they are back in orbit around Eden."

"John, we are short of pilots. Stefan can fly landers and, at a pinch, a shuttle but I don't believe we have anyone qualified to fly an interplanetary ship."

"I did wonder myself until I checked. However, one of your fellow settlers is Rob Jordan, Captain Rob Jordan to be precise. Not sure what role he has decided to take on here but, before we left Sol, he was an IPS pilot. The Phoebe was his ship when he delivered Ellen to the Einstein at Saturn. If I am not mistaken, I see him approaching now. I asked him to join us briefly."

Rob Jordon entered the forecourt of the building and, seeing both Ellen and John, came to attention.

Ellen smiled. "Old habits, Rob! Relax."

"Thanks, Ellen. Captain, you asked me to join you."

"I did, Captain, but enough of formality, Rob. To bring you up to date, Einstein will be leaving orbit this evening. Helga and Anton will let you have full details of recent events on Eden and around the system but I expect us to be away for several months, if not more than a year. We intend to leave some additional craft including your old friend Phoebe. We are hoping that you will agree to be the standby pilot, should it be necessary, to undertake any off-planet activities."

"I'd be happy to but I am a little rusty. Haven't flown since we left Saturn, apart from landers during the transfer to Eden. Is there nobody else?"

"Stefan, here, is technically qualified but only has experience as co-pilot. And, before you ask, Ellen will be leaving with the Einstein. You might not know that on handing over the captaincy she discovered that Einstein's core programming forced her to accept a promotion to Admiral. Given the strong possibility that we may achieve a first contact I convinced her that her place should be with the ship. That leaves you and, rusty or not, your record confirms that you have what it takes."

"All right, John. You make a good argument. I accept."

"Good, now you can get some practice. Phoebe is on board Einstein. We'll be taking off in an hour and there is a seat waiting for you."

"I had better let Jenny know. I guess, if push comes to shove, she is qualified as a co-pilot as long as we can get a baby-sitter!"

"Of course!" Ellen grinned. "She was Phoebe's co-pilot before. John, in the circumstances, I believe that we should file a promotion for Jenny. She would have been due that if she hadn't been caught up with us. I know it's only a technical thing now but still seems right."

"I concur. Rob, I will let you have the papers once we are in orbit. It might soften the blow when you get back with the news. Congratulations on becoming a father."

"Thank you, Sir. I will be back in the hour."

Later that day Rob, with Stefan as co-pilot, lifted the Phoebe out from the Einstein's docking bay and completed the short trip back to Yablon.

***   ***   ***

Shortly after the Phoebe's departure. John finally gave the order.

"Helm, quarter power, take us out of orbit." The Einstein moved slowly away from Eden, gradually swinging on to the same course as the Deimos and, beginning the long stern chase, that John expected to take some days.

"Lieutenant Cheung, you have the com. Once we are clear of Selene's orbit take us up to half power. I will be in my ready room."

"Aye, Captain." Tung-Mei sat down in the command seat alert but ready for an uneventful period.

An hour later, she was able to give the order to increase speed and confirmed that there had been no change in the drone's course.

"Helm, match course with the Deimos and hold steady."

With the ship underway, Tung-Mei sensed a change in the atmosphere among the bridge crew. She understood it. This was why they were here. The time in orbit around Eden had been well spent training and practising different scenarios, but there was nothing to beat the real thing and now they were looking forward to the journey. She settled back to enjoy that sense of purpose.

Time drifted and, as ship time reached early morning, John emerged from his room to relieve her.

"How are we doing?"

"Steadily, Captain. We are moving faster than the Deimos but it is still going to take time before we can catch them. Tracking have been following their progress and there is an oddity about their motion. They are cruising at about nine tenths full speed according to their reporting but our sensors suggest that they are moving faster than that in bursts. The Commander has checked their own systems but says that there is nothing happening so far as they are concerned."

"Have you raised this with the science team yet?"

"No, sir. It being the middle of the night I felt it could wait until this morning. It's not that we can do anything about it. Was I right?" Tung-Mei was unusually nervous.

"Quite right." John smiled. "Now get some food and then have a quick chat with Alan Piper and his team, before getting some sleep. I have command."

"Thanks, Captain." And Tung-Mei headed off pinging Alan's communicator to arrange a meeting.

John also sensed the feeling of purpose amongst the team which continued as changeover of the duty crew took place. He relaxed, confident that matters were as under control as they could be and waited for the feedback from the science team.

***   ***   ***

Time passed as the Einstein continued to slowly overhaul the Deimos. The changes in the latter's acceleration continued without any apparent effect on the craft.

The next day Alan sought access to the bridge. His perplexed look caused John to ask what the problem was. Alan explained that they could only come up with one possible solution as to what was causing the velocity "wobbles", as he put it.

"Tung-Mei told me that Pawl could not find anything on board Deimos to explain what was happening. He was sure that they would have been aware of changes. I only have one possible, and I admit it as only possible, answer. Deimos is running into some form of gravity-based anomalies. Again, I say anomalies, as there do not appear to have been any objects close enough to affect a spaceship in flight."

"We had issues around the Guardian's base on Eden, sensors showing the wrong data and so on. Could the messenger be causing these to happen?"

"Captain, I wish I knew. We just can't see how. It's several million klicks ahead of Deimos and getting further away all the time. Even if whatever powers its acceleration had such an effect, they should have been getting fainter with time. In addition, a scan back through tracking's data suggests that there were no such changes until a few days ago and they are now of a constant strength. One other piece of evidence that something has been happening is that the Deimos is at least a quarter of a million klicks ahead of where its maximum velocity would place them and, as I understand it, they have only been using ninety per cent power."

"Alan, that sounds as if they are being given a tow without realising it." John was now as confused as the scientist. Turning to his crew he asked. "Any ideas?"

Judy, on duty at the helm, turned. "Captain, I suggest we tell Deimos to cut their power. If they slow and the bursts continue then it almost has to be the other craft. They can't catch it anyway and if the affects fall away, it might still be the drone but it could mean that there is a local spacetime anomaly."

"Good thinking, Lieutenant. Comms send a message to Commander Jaeger. Instruct him to cut power to sixty per cent. Tell him we are trying to work out what is happening to his ship."

"Captain?" Judy's look caught John by surprise.

"Lieutenant?"

"We need to find out what is happening for another reason. If there is some form of gravity anomaly that our sensors can't see, then there could be a danger to Einstein when we go to warp."

"Agreed." John turned to Alan. "Look, we won't be able to go to warp for at least another three days at current speed. You and your colleagues need to work out what is happening and how we can sense such a danger. If anyone needs access to the bridge, science stations or tracking, they'll get it."

"We'll get on it, Captain. It is possible that this is a transient effect and for the moment we are too far from it for our sensors to pick it up. While we are in n-space, I mean."

With that Alan left the bridge, leaving a bemused captain trying to work out how their sensors might be used to find something that did not seem exist for more than a few seconds and was invisible as well.

A day later and the scientists were no further forward in working out what was happening. Deimos had reduced its power output but there were still more acceleration bursts, the same as the earlier ones. Apart from efforts by the bridge team to come up with an answer, little changed. In their search they too were stymied and then, just before duty shift, it happened. The Einstein had been speeding through the gap between two of the gas giants, running as smoothly as might be expected, when the entire ship seemed to shudder. Gasps of concern came from all parts of the bridge as the crew rapidly tried to adjust and identify the cause.

"Helm, cut power. Damage reports, all sections." John's orders came quickly, although the helm's team had already reduced engine power to a minimum.

Within a few minutes it was clear that there had been no damage. Although the engine room were complaining about misuse of their pride and joy, suggesting that the bridge should avoid such impacts. It was left to tracking and the helm team to identify the cause.

"Captain, we appear to have crossed some form of immaterial band. No mass that we could detect, or can for that matter, but it triggered the gravity sensors for a little under two seconds."

"Tracking, you say you can't detect anything behind us now?"

"No, sir. Whatever it was no longer exists."

"Helm, your position?"

"Nothing, Captain. As tracking reported, the gravity sensors triggered but they no longer show anything material other than the normal spacetime dips that emanate from the star and the planets."

"Captain!" Tracking interrupted with alarm in the voice of the young ensign on duty. "The Deimos, they seem to be drifting."

"Comms, raise them. Helm, take us on slowly. One fifth power."

The ship slowly moved ahead without any further upset but it was several minutes, longer than it should have been, before Deimos responded to the repeated hails.

When they did it was the voice of a clearly shaken Pawl that could be heard.

"Captain, did you see that or feel it?"

"We felt something, not sure what yet, but no damage here. How about you and your ship?"

"Badly shaken but no more than bruises as far as we can tell for the moment. It's just as well we had reduced speed. Whatever we hit killed our power. It was like hitting a brick wall. We've got power back and we're working on the engines now."

"Right, Commander. Once you are back up and running, keep to quarter power until we catch you. We're going to accelerate but not too quickly. Keep comms open, we'll be listening." With that John turned to the bridge with a smile. "Right, everyone. Firstly, well done. Seems the practical drills missed this type of event completely, but you all performed well. Helm, take us up to quarter power."

Tung-Mei entered the bridge heading to take over from Judy at the helm. John took a few minutes to brief her before handing over command to her. An ensign took over from Judy and ten minutes later John, himself, was able to leave the bridge heading for some food. For the first time in a few days he and Judy would have a few hours together, able to recuperate and talk over the events of their last duty period.

Halfway through their off-duty period, and not long after getting to bed, John's communicator chimed. "Captain to the bridge, urgent."

"Oh no! Can't they leave us alone!" Judy's frustration and dismay were palpable.

John's response was instant. "Bridge, on my way. Sorry love. You know it goes with the territory." John was already getting dressed. "Now look. Just to add to your unhappiness," his grin was a little forced, "I want you at the helm. If this is anything to do with these anomalies then I want my best team on duty and Tung-Mei will need to stand in as First Officer." With that he was gone, leaving Judy to reach for her uniform and quickly dress and follow him.

"Captain on the bridge." John was pleased to see that the only member of the team to move was Tung-Mei turning from the First Officer's station, having already vacated the command seat.

"Captain, apologies but this something you should see. Main screen."

"What am I looking at?"

"We don't know but sensors tell us that there is a massive gravity well in the centre. I have Alan and Alejandro coming to the bridge in the hope that they may have some idea."

The screen showed a swirling circular object of varying colours surrounding what seemed to be a hole in space, not quite black but visible against the background of the cluster.

In the centre, but clearly closer, was the image of the drone. Just near the edge of the screen the Deimos could be seen.

"Comms, get me the Commander."

"He is in contact now, Captain. We are close enough to them for minimal time delay."

"Pawl," John dropped the courtesy of titles. "I assume you can see this."

"We can, John. More than that we can feel its effects. It's pulling us towards it. If it hadn't just appeared, I would have said it was a black hole we hadn't registered. I have increased the engines to full power and we are trying to change course away from it." He paused and they could hear him checking with another voice. "John, it isn't working. Any ideas? I reckon we have about two hours before we are drawn in."

The bridge doors opened and Alan and Alejandro rushed in with Judy close behind. Both came to a stunned halt with Judy unable to avoid them. In the resulting mayhem, only Alejandro kept his feet but with a look of total astonishment on his face.

"I don't believe it. It's a wormhole! Somehow the drone is generating a wormhole. Captain, you wondered how the messenger could cross interstellar space. Well it looks like we now know how."

"Don't you mean we know what they use? Not how, at least not yet." John was still struggling with a mental image of the energies that must be involved.

"Captain, I'm not sure it is a wormhole, at least not in the form the scientists predicted." Tung-Mei interrupted.

"Why not Lieutenant?"

"We can see a starfield through the hole and I don't think it's the field that we could see before."

"Alejandro?"

Alejandro looked over to Tung-Mei with surprised respect. "Lieutenant Cheung is right, if we can see a starfield then we are looking through some form of gateway. Unless our past work is totally wrong then a wormhole should be opaque."

John thought for a moment then. "Alejandro, I need you and your team to tell me where the other side of the gateway might be and how far away. Hopefully there will be a stellar spectrum sufficiently close to identify the location."

"On it, Captain. Please have the live feed transferred to the astronomy team." Alejandro almost ran from the bridge speaking on his communicator as he went.

"Tracking, two questions. How far away are we? How large is that gateway?"

"Not sure exactly how far, Captain, but it must be around two million kilometres, maybe less. It seems to be pulsating forward and backward."

"And the size?"

"If it is that far then the gate must be about fifty kilometres diameter but again it is not stable."

"Large enough for Einstein to pass through then?"

"Just about, sir. At least at the moment, sir, yes."

John thought rapidly. "Helm, adjust our course. Target the centre. Tracking, what about the drone and the Deimos?"

"Drone is entering the gateway. Deimos closing with it, they are still trying to avoid but it looks as if their power isn't going to be enough."

Comms spoke up. "Commander Jaeger, sir."

"Commander, have you no more power?"

"No, Captain. We've pushed everything to the max and more. It's not enough. We're preparing for the inevitable entry into the hole. We hope we can transit through. If the drone enters then there is the assumption that there must be an exit. We just don't know what the side effects might be. Six or seven minutes, captain. Wish us luck."

"Pawl, we are trying to transit behind you but we are four to five hours away. Our view suggests it is a gateway not a wormhole. As yet we are not experiencing any significant gravitational effect."

"Good luck, Captain. Hope to see you on the other side."

Six minutes later Deimos's signal died as the craft finally crossed the gateway boundary and vanished. The whole team gasped as they lost contact but Tung-Mei's anguished cry shook them. Not all of them knew of her relationship with Pawl and John was quick to take her to his ready room before leaving her for a few minutes to recover her emotional state.

Back on the bridge John took a moment to talk to the team.

"Everyone, Deimos will almost certainly have transited through what is obviously an artificial structure. We may be out of touch for the moment but we need to hold ourselves together and ready the ship for our own transit"

His words were received with nods and a calmness filtered across the bridge as each of the team moved on to their roles in preparing the ship.

"Make sure the landing bay is clear and all craft tied down. We don't know how rough transit might be."

Thirty minutes later the entire ship was ready for the unexpected when duty tracking team called John back from his ready room.

"What is it?"

"Captain, the gateway is closing. We won't be able to enter it. At the rate it is closing we will still be outside when the diameter drops to less than two hundred metres."

"Are you sure?"

"Yes, sir. Sorry, sir."

John's dismay at not being able to follow the Deimos lasted a moment before he called the astronomy section with a request for an update on their efforts to identify the star on the other side of the hole in space.

"We are running computer analysis comparing the starfield with the data we collected when first searching for Eden. There is also the historic data brought from Earth. At the moment, Captain, we have no real idea where the system is." It was not Alejandro who had answered but his deputy Stephan Kolaski. "The best guess at the moment is that system forty odd light years from here. I'm not sure that that is correct as the starfield we could see does not match the field we can see now. Our problem is that we have to assume that the gateway is, effectively, a standard cylinder. If the reality is that it curves in some way then finding the system on the other end will take time, unless we are lucky. As soon as we have anything you will be the first to know. Sorry I can't tell you when."

John grimaced but faced with the inevitable delay, decided to leave the bridge in the hands of his team and conduct an informal tour of the main sections of the ship. While doing this it occurred to him that the developments of the past few hours meant that Eden would need to take a more proactive role in monitoring the planet's system.

Before continuing he requested his Comms team to arrange a link with Helga, Anton and Rob back in Yablon. During that conversation he suggested strongly that the settlement devote time to setting up one or more probes in or around the area where the gateway had opened with the object of having maximum warning should the aliens respond to the messenger drone by sending a ship back to investigate.

"You won't be able to resist them, if they prove unhappy with our taking their planet and, to be honest, we shouldn't try. But being ready to receive them on a friendly basis would seem sensible."

Rob, who had taken the lead, finished the meeting. "Those recommendations are fine, Captain. Hopefully you will find these people before they find us, as it were. I'd be happier if we had Einstein overhead, even if it isn't a battleship! But c'est la vie, we'll be ready. Safe journey."

***   ***   ***

Judy was on her way to the bridge to take over at the helm when she bumped into Megan rushing the other way with a worried look on her face.

"Hi, Mom. You okay?"

"I'm not sure, Judy. Molly was supposed to stop by for a coffee but didn't show up. It's not like her, so I buzzed her. You know I try not to interfere with her work, but she's not answering and the computer doesn't seem to be able to find her."

"But that's crazy, Mom." Judy used her own communicator to question the ship's computer to be told that her sister was not on board. "She didn't leave a message?" At her mother's shake of the head. Judy's heart missed a beat. If Molly was not on board then she had to be on the Deimos but how?

She paged John and asked if he knew who the team were on the IPS.

"Only Pawl and Hidecki Yamata. There was someone from engineering and a linguist but I gave carte blanche on his choice. Check with Scott."

It took only a few minutes to check and have her fears confirmed. Molly had volunteered to join the crew. Clearly, she had not left a message as she only expected to be away for a short period and would then have had a surprise for her family.

"Mom, Judy is on the Deimos and they entered the gateway. We are looking to find the system on the other side so that we can chase them." Judy was careful to use the present tense so that her mother's fear would be minimised. That the craft might not have survived was an even bigger fear for herself.

"Mom, I need to be on the bridge. I'll let you know as soon as anything happens. Will you tell Pop for me?"

"I will, love." Megan hugged her daughter trying to hide her tears just as Judy was doing the same.

12.   The Chase Begins

Identifying the target system took most of the rest of the day but in the end, as John admitted to himself, it could have been worse. The astronomy team had finally found a star whose spectra matched that of the system that seemed to be where the gateway reached.

"Can you give me a course? And how far are we away from it?"

"We are uploading the data to the bridge as we speak, Captain. The good news is that it is not that far, only about fifteen light years. The bad news is that we have been travelling away from that star and it is on the other side of our system."

"You mean that the gateway, wormhole, whatever, loops back on itself? How…no forget that. I was going to ask how that could be but that's a question for the future. You say that the starfield we could see is the same as if we had been looking over our shoulders?"

"In one sense, that is true, but there are subtle differences. It isn't the field directly behind Einstein's current course but only approximates to that, which is a good thing."

"Sorry, Stephan. Why is that?"

"If it were exactly the same, we would have to consider that we were not seeing through the gateway at all but simply looking at a reflection. Two things helped confirm that that was not the case. One, we could not see an image of the ship and, two there are subtle differences in the red-shift effects.

104

Unfortunately, it does mean we will need to cross the system before we can use the warp drive."

"Possibly, I will need to look at the logistics. Thank you, Stephan." As Stephan turned to leave, John had a second thought. "Stephan, wait a moment. What do we know about the system in question?"

"Not a lot, I'm afraid. Our original survey didn't reach that far in that direction. There are planets, we think, but we haven't been able to see enough yet to identify types. If it is occupied by an advanced civilisation, they are not using any identifiable energy."

"That seems to be something we will need to understand eventually. OK, let me know if you find out anything else. Thanks."

Back on the bridge, John found the team had already changed course. He was delighted to see that their proposed course would reduce the period before warp drive could be engaged.

"Explain your thinking please." John's voice indicated his pleasure at their pro-activity. "Why that routing?"

Tung-Mei responded. "We wanted to find a way that didn't involve having to stay in n-space to cross the system. It would take ten to eleven days even at full power but if we could reach the warp boundary more quickly then we could save most of that time." She continued. "The shortest way was to continue on our present course and go to warp in about three hours but that would require us to firstly cross the area where the gateway was and we would still be very close when engaging warp. With the gravitational anomalies that we have experienced, we did not feel that it would be worth the risk that we might hit another. So, I instructed helm to start a loop out of the ecliptic. At three quarters power we can cross the boundary in about ten hours. Well clear of the area that appears to have been the source of those problems."

"Excellent. Well done. Carry on with those changes."

"Captain, may I have a word? In private, please."

John's look showed his concern at Judy's request. "Of course, Lieutenant. In my ready room."

Once out of sight and hearing of the bridge team, Judy dissolved into tears and for the second time in a short period John found himself consoling and comforting one of his team. His quiet confidence did little to settle his lover or, if he was honest, his own concerns, but gradually Judy did calm and was adamant that she returned to her post for the rest of her shift.

Ten hours later Judy, having spent some time off duty with her parents and now focused on the task of catching up with the Deimos, turned from the helm with the words. "Captain, we are clear to engage warp."

"Thank you helm. Captain to all hands. We are about to go to warp." John then continued. "Warp five." He smiled at the gasps of surprise, the Einstein had never utilised warp drive higher than three before and that only for short distances.

"Everyone, warp five means that we can reach the target system in eighteen days or so. I would rather take more time but, all being well, the Deimos will be there waiting and we need to minimise that wait. The next two weeks will be very stressful, I recognise that but I am confident that you will all be able to handle it. The engine room is already aware. It won't surprise you that they did complain about the pressure on their beloved drives." He smiled at the chuckles from the team. "Now let's go. Helm, warp one and then increase to warp five."

"Aye, Captain. Warp one. Then to warp five."

***   ***   ***

Moments later the Einstein had disappeared from sight and out of the range of the sensor web leaving Guardian One as bemused as an AI could be. It was apparent that the great ship had a means to beat the universal limit but quite how was not clear. The question was - had the humans worked out where the gateway led? If so, the Guardian might have failed in its job to protect its designers nearest system from intrusion by a species not of the Seven. It could not change things and as its own messenger would certainly reach the system first and deliver the warning, the Guardian, not being programmed to worry turned its attention back to monitoring the system and the activities of the new species.

13.   First Contact

"Captain, wish us luck**.**" With those words Pawl turned to his team. "Right, everyone into suits. Let's not assume we will maintain structural integrity during whatever occurs. Leave helmets open for the minute."

While the four completed the process of donning their spacesuits and cross checking their colleagues' suits, the Deimos continued towards the hole in space. Pawl had cut power and was no longer trying to avoid it. The gravitational pull clearly too strong for the ship's engines.

With just a few moments before entry, Pawl turned to his comms guy. "Hal, please set up an automatic first contact message to broadcast as soon as we exit the other end. Did Teri send us the translation into the language of the Zeder? The language indicated by Guardian Two?"

"She did, Commander."

"Then make the broadcast in both languages. Let's try and show we mean no harm. Molly, monitor the engines for any changes as we continue. We may need to manoeuvre immediately or even within this tunnel or whatever it is."

"Ready, Commander." Molly tried to hide her mix of excitement in entering the unknown and her thoughts for her family, wishing now that she had told them of her intentions.

Then, with a suddenness that was beyond anything they could have expected, the Deimos was in the wormhole. The universe of n-space, and even of warp space, vanished in an instant and was replaced by a corridor that pulsed with light.

Pawl would later admit that it seemed somehow right that it did so but while at first the team could only gaze with awe at the sight.

After a few minutes, Pawl brought his team back to life getting them to check that the sensors were recording everything.

It was Molly who asked the question that had occurred to all of them. "How long will this take? I thought it would be an instant transition but we have already been in here for almost a quarter of an hour and the sensors suggest that we haven't moved at all! And, oh, the engines are starting to race. Commander, cut power now!"

Trusting his engineer Pawl cut power immediately. The noise associated with the engines died away and an unusual silence fell.

Hal responded to Molly's question first. "The truth is no-one knows. After all wormholes have only been a theoretical structure for a hundred years or more but, while the idea that it allows you to cut corners crossing the space time continuum was recognised as a part of Einstein's theories, how long it might take to go from A to B has never been considered."

"But the total time must surely be less than the time light would take to cover the same distance surely?" Hidecki was an astronaut first and foremost such that his knowledge of theoretical astronomy was limited.

"That must be the case. The technology needed is frightening and, even knowing it is possible, is still, I suspect, beyond anything we might imagine." Pawl was, himself, still wondering how long the journey within the artifact would take.

Time passed with no apparent changes to the external flashes of colour. Finally, after an hour Pawl decided that they needed to revert to a normal duty roster to allow the team to get well needed rest.

"This looks as if it isn't going to be a quick transit. Fortunately, there doesn't seem to be significant changes so we will switch back to a two on two off roster. Hidecki, Hal grab some food and rest. Four hours, then you can take over from Molly and myself."

With the others in the back of the ship Pawl took the opportunity to compliment Molly on her recognition of the engine issue.

"I should have spotted the change in engine noise more quickly. After all I have flown these beasts for many years. You spotted it and had the guts to simply tell me to act. You didn't ask me. You remind of your sister and that is a compliment."

Molly smiled and then her gaze dropped. "What is it Molly?" Pawl realised she was not that happy.

"I didn't tell Judy; she doesn't know I'm here. Nor do Mom or Pop. I thought I'd be telling them of an adventure and experience I couldn't have got any other way. Now I can't even tell them." Her distress bubbled up and tears followed.

It took a few minutes with Pawl helpless before Molly collected herself. "Sorry, Commander. Look I'll be all right. Just needed to let it out."

"Molly, just one point, while we are away from the Einstein and here. I did say first names."

Molly forced a grin. "Sorry, Pawl. Better get back to checking the systems."

In the end their journey within the cylinder, as Hidecki described it, lasted nearly thirty-six hours. The transition back into n-space was again instantaneous. The lighting and colours simply vanishing and being replaced by the blackness of ordinary space, black except for the light of nearby planets and distant stars.

Hidecki, at the controls, gave a startled cry. "I can see two planets but there is no star visible. It should be ahead of us, based on the planets' daysides."

"Change course towards the nearer of the planets, quarter power." Pawl dropped into his own seat at the controls having been off duty.

Twenty minutes later, Hal, monitoring his comms equipment jerked backwards. "Listen."

Over the speaker came a guttural voice speaking an unknown language repeating the same short phrase. Then it became apparent why they had not been able to see the local star, as a black shape started to eclipse the nearer planet followed by the bright flash of an explosion directly in front of the Deimos.

The message was clear and Pawl immediately cut the engines using attitude jets to slow his craft. As they drifted to a relative halt, Hal's translation software finally identified the language and cut in converting the intelligible phrase to English.

"Stop. You entering <restricted> area. Stop. We <boarding> you."

Teri's work had proved helpful, although Hal had to explain that the software was qualifying some words as the available vocabulary was still limited.

Pawl's reply was somewhat dry. "I think it's pretty clear and that missile emphasised their warning." As he spoke the spaceship moved across their course and the system's star appeared having been hidden by the sheer bulk of the other craft.

"Oh my, that must be a kilometre or more in length. That is some ship." Hidecki's voice was low as he almost whispered, seemingly worried that he might be overheard.

"I wonder what happened to the messenger drone. Presumably it would have had some form of recognition software to ensure it wasn't destroyed by accident." Molly was using the sensors to try and find their original quarry but without success.

"Hal, any response to our first contact message yet?" Pawl was trying to prepare for what was certainly going to be a first contact.

"Not yet. That ship must have received it since it used wavelengths that we could read but it seems to be ignoring it. Unless they are waiting to board us and identify our species."

"That won't be long. It looks as if that is a shuttle heading this way." Pawl was considering his next move when Molly came to the rescue. "Pawl, perhaps we should open the outer airlock door.

If we don't then they might just try and force entry. They might have a suitable docking link but if they haven't…."

"Good thinking, Molly. We'll do that but we keep suits on for the minute. Helmets open but ready for sealing, just in case they don't wait for the airlock to cycle. I don't like automatically having to think of another species being antagonistic but we came through their wormhole and within minutes find a warship waiting. I hope that this is a security approach rather than that we are in a warzone."

"I agree, Commander." It was Hal's turn to be formal. "It does look as if they are curious, if cautious. With the firepower that ship presumably has they could simply have blown us apart with that warning shot."

There was the sound of the shuttle touching on to the Deimos and using some form of docking process to latch to their airlock.

"Right, everyone. A word of warning. No sudden moves. Try not to flinch if they should be, how can I put it, unattractive."

"Someone is in the airlock." Molly said. "Humanoid at least if the camera isn't lying to us. They seem to be waiting."

"Operate the airlock cycle. They will know that we left the outer door open. I suspect that they are expecting us to cycle the lock and open the second door rather than risk them hitting the wrong button." Pawl ensured his voice demonstrated confidence that, if truthful to himself, he did not feel.

The screen showed that there were, in fact, three individuals in the lock, each of a size that meant no one else could have entered. As it could cope with five, or even six, humans at a push, Pawl thought, these were either very large beings or wearing massive armour. Somehow, he felt, he would rather that they were naturally big.

"Airlock has cycled, Commander. Opening inner door."

"Okay, Molly. Let's make them welcome. Hal, open the bridge door and stand back."

A moment later, the first of the aliens came through the door. With a gesture it halted its companions as it realised that the room was already crowded with the four humans. It looked around the bridge before reaching for its head and undoing its helmet. It was clear that he or one of his colleagues had analysed the air and decided that it was breathable as it opened its own visor to reveal its face. It was humanoid although broader and its skin was a dark red.

Pawl took a breath and said "Welcome aboard, Commander." The speaker produced a short burst of incomprehensible sound and the alien seemed startled but responded speaking, it seemed, slowly and carefully.

The speaker was silent for a moment before: "You not one of Seven but you translate our language? I not commander. I deputy commander. I need you come me. Now."

Pawl responded as would any commander. "What about my ship? And my crew?" A few moments passed again before the software generated a translation. Again, the alien seemed startled and, it was obvious, was trying to understand what the words it had heard really meant. Pawl added a few simple words. "I am sorry. Our system is still new and the words may not be right."

This time the speaker converted his words more quickly and, this time, the alien officer gave a nod of recognition. At least that was how Pawl read his expression and the words from the speaker supported this. "You and crew with me. Our ship pull you craft into dock. Now follow other to airlock." With that he indicated that the humans should lead the way.

Pawl nodded and motioned his crew to lead. On reaching the airlock they found that the aliens had overridden the safeties and both lock doors were open allowing for an easy transfer to the adjacent shuttle which was sealed against the Deimos' hull. As he passed the inner lock Pawl paused and with a careful movement triggered the closing of that inner door. The alien acknowledged the sense of Pawl's action and the two crossed to the larger vessel where Hidecki and Hal were struggling to adjust to seating that was, even in zero gravity, for them, clumsy and too large.

Pawl and Molly were pointed to two more of the seats and left with no choice but to make the best of it. Within a few moments the shuttle had broken the link with the Deimos and was rapidly heading toward its mothership. Looking through a side window, it was difficult to call the large square of transparent material a porthole, Pawl could see a second small craft, with some form of grappling arms, moving towards the Phoebe.

A few minutes later, their transport reached the large ship and using an access much the same as that on the Einstein landed in a docking area. Here, though, there were differences. There was no apparent atmosphere in the docking area as the aliens all locked their helmets down and indicated that the humans should do the same. When they exited through an open airlock, Pawl and his team suddenly realised that they were still in a zero g environment, as Molly would say later. "You don't realise how valuable the artificial gravity on Einstein is. And then we found ourselves with no means of gripping the floor."

As the humans started to drift the aliens reacted quickly and each took the arm of one of the team, towing them, in effect, to an airlock in the side of the bay. Once through they were give some foot covers that had coatings that gripped a similar coating on the floor. It took some time to fix these over their own boots but, once on, they were able, with a little practice, to walk along the passageways to a room. There their hosts, for want of a better description and better than captors, Pawl thought, indicated that they should remove their spacesuits and wait. A check of the atmosphere confirmed that it was breathable and Pawl indicated that they should comply.

Molly asked him. "How long do you think it will take the Einstein to find us?"

"I don't know, Molly, we have no real idea how far we have travelled through the wormhole. I do know that they will be working non-stop to track us and the captain will undoubtedly be as fast as he possibly can."

"At least these aliens do not seem hostile to us, just curious, if I had to guess. Or maybe they are waiting to learn what information, about us, the messenger might have brought." Hal mused.

"But I couldn't find the drone and it should have been in range, at least until we were hailed by this ship." Molly was a little perplexed.

That drew a thoughtful comment from Hidecki. "You know. Just as we entered normal space there was a jerk, a small jerk, in our motion. Everything happened so quickly I didn't think anything of it but, I guess, we could have been pushed on to a different course away from the drone. Molly, where were you looking?"

"Oh lord, straight ahead. It didn't occur to me that we wouldn't be on same course."

"Easy with hindsight." Pawl smiled. "I'm guessing now that the messenger was sending an ID signal which allowed it clear access. We weren't and so the system twisted the exit through an angle to send us into a safe zone while alerting a planetary defence ship."

"They feel the need to keep an active defence operation? What have we walked into?" Hal exclaimed.

"We can only wait and see."

14.   Distress Call

Back on the Einstein, the bridge had become a focussed zone of stress. With the ship travelling at warp five, the sensors, and therefore the crew at the helm had little time to identify and avoid any objects large enough to harm the ship. After a few hours, John decided to shorten the time anyone was on duty. He cut the normal four-hour stint to two for the helmsmen and reduced other on-duty times as well.

The offset was, of course, that the team were all expected to handle more shifts. Fortunately, there were enough crew available to still allow for a full eight hour break each day ensuring that everyone got a chance to properly rest and recover.

The first three days passed without serious disturbance then, early on the fourth, bridge alarms sounded and the forward sensors dropped the ship out of warp automatically. As the team searched for the reasons, John, who had been in his ready room constantly, when not on duty, rushed to the command seat.

"Report."

"We haven't hit anything nor is there anything large enough to trigger the automatic systems, sir." The young ensign at the helm sounded as mystified as he looked.

Lieutenant Sanchez, at the comms station, looked up with as much surprise as anyone.

"Captain, we appear to have intercepted a signal that is repeating. Somehow it seems to have been able to trigger our systems to react as if there were an object in our way. I don't understand it, sir."

"Tracking, carry out a widespread scan. See if you can see anything unusual."

"Helm, take us forward at quarter speed."

Sanchez called out. "Sir, the signal appears to be coming from a star system ninety degrees starboard. It sounds like a voice. Not human. Language appears to be a match to one of those supplied by the Guardian. Teri Larding is on her way to the bridge, sir."

"Good. Put it on speaker."

The voice could be heard clearly and, again to their surprise, the bridge crew all felt the apparent desperation in it, even though they could not understand the words. John sensed that there might be a need to respond.

"How far from the system are we?"

"Just under half a light year, sir."

After a moment's thought John made his decision. "Helm, warp one current course for thirty seconds. Tracking, Comms, as soon as we drop into n-space try and get a triangulation on the signal's source. Helm, engage."

It took the teams only a moment to confirm that they had a close estimate for the source, just as Teri reached the bridge moving swiftly to the Comms station. As she worked, tracking confirmed that the source was on the near side of the system on its extreme edge. Further checks also showed that the Einstein could use warp drive to within a few thousand klicks. Before giving the order to move in that direction he joined the discussion at the Comms station. As he reached the group the speaker changed from the alien language to English.

"This starship, <Anthezedo>. Damaged, star drive lost, drifting. Position edge system 18497. Warning. Warning. Pirate craft in zone. Engaging stasis field. Message repeats."

"Teri, two questions. That language is not that of the Guardian's designers? How accurate a translation is it?"

"Captain, it is not the designers' language. As far as we can tell. It is one of the other seven. Fortunately, we have someone working on each language with the help of the Rosetta file. I would estimate that it is ninety per cent accurate. Luckily the individual speaking used short phrases."

"So, we can accept that they are in trouble and that there is a risk of coming up against, what we must assume are, armed ships."

"Captain," Tung-Mei intervened, "that is true but whatever happened to disable the Anthezedo did so at least six months ago. Would the pirates stay that long? On the other hand, can we assume that the crew of the starship are still alive?"

Before answering her, John asked the comms to contact Alan Piper and Scott Bailey and get them to join him in his ready room. "Lieutenant, you are right on all counts but the simple answer is we don't know. So, we cannot ignore such a cry for help or the warning. We need to be careful, so we will plan accordingly. You have the comm. I will be in my ready room."

Back in his room John took the opportunity to finish the meal he had been eating. A short time later Alan and Scott arrived together both wondering why John had asked for them. After explaining what had happened, John asked them a question neither was prepared for.

"How good are our defensive capabilities?"

"I'm sorry. Our defensive capability?" Alan was struggling with the concept, forgetting that the ship was fitted with torpedo type bays.

"Yes. If we move into rescue the Anthezedo, it is possible we may be faced with an attack by "pirates"."

Scott took up the challenge. "As you know, when we were running from the attack on Titan, we did check what we had in the way of offensive material. The original design included small missiles intended to destroy inanimate objects that posed a threat of collision. As I thought at the time, given the fears of the Earth governments, the missiles we have were significantly upgraded for use as offensive weapons. We do only have four bays, from which to launch them and they are all at the bow. Alan, I think, has forgotten we have adapted some of the warheads to utilise exotic energy. We haven't been able to test them but if fired within the warp boundary we should get an effect similar, if less powerful, than the implosion of a starship."

"That means that we could launch an attack ourselves but we have limited ability to withstand incoming missiles?" John was continuing to wonder if he dared risk the ship for a rescue that might be too late anyway.

"Almost none." Scott sounded glum until Alan suddenly smiled.

"John, you said that the ship that needs rescuing is on the edge of the system and, I think, you also said it was outside of the warp boundary. If so, why not use the warp drive to dodge any incoming weaponry. Scott," he continued, "if the warp engines are in standby status how fast will they put us in warp?"

Scott thought quickly before. "About ten seconds before warp fully engaged. Dodging is possible but remember even at minimum warp, a five second burst would mean that we would move over a million klicks. We'd certainly dodge any n-space missiles but it won't be easy to manage and you'd also want to know that there was nothing in the way!"

"Have all the missiles been converted to exotic warheads?"

"No. I'm not certain I know how many missiles we actually have on board but we only had sufficient material to upgrade a small number."

John finally made his decision. "Right, we are going in to try a rescue. Scott, I want three bays loaded with standard warheads. Bay four loaded with an exotic torpedo. Thank you both."

Scott's final comment. "I need fifteen minutes to get bay four switched, the other bays have always been ready. Let's hope we don't need them."

Returning to the bridge John briefed his team. "Cheung, check your board. You should be able to find a missile firing program." As Tung-Mei nodded, he continued. "Helm, adjust course for the current location of the Anthezedo. Warp three until we are half a million klicks away. As we drop out of warp, divert course ninety degrees port at quarter power. Leave warp drive on standby and set autopilot ready for a five second engagement at one tenth of warp one on my command. Tracking, if you see anything while we are still in warp I want to know, but otherwise, as we drop out of warp, I want visual on the starship and the positions of any other ships you can find, visual again if possible. Comms, Teri, I want a message responding to the distress call ready to be transmitted as soon as we are out of warp. Teri," thinking for a moment he went on, "are we able to transmit in the language of the Anthezedo?"

"We can, Captain. I'm on it now, how long do I have?"

"About twelve hours, so take your time. Keep it short and succinct. As simple as possible so that we have the best chance of getting it right."

Teri nodded as she left the bridge to join her colleagues. John turned back to the comms board and asked them to contact the bridge crew currently off-duty and instruct them to report back two hours early. Tung-Mei raised an eyebrow, providing John with another wry thought about how she could on occasion remind him of that Vulcan.

"I know, but chance has it that I have almost all of my first-choice team on duty now and I will want you all back here fully refreshed and ready for what might be our first contact with a living species. Now everyone, let's get checking all our systems are ready to go."

The next couple of hours passed quickly as the teams checked everything was at peak operational status. John spent time at each station. Not expecting to find anything wrong but looking to add his reassurances and support where needed. None of the team had ever been required to deal with the pressures that might happen and there was understandable nervousness.

With the crew changeover complete after thirty minutes of briefing, John passed command to Lieutenant Sanchez and retired to his ready room only for Judy to almost drag him back. "Captain, we are going to need you fully refreshed. Staying in your ready room will not allow you any relaxation. Come on, we'll get some food and chat. Then, if you feel you need to be back there, so be it."

John nodded reluctantly but allowed himself to be taken to one of the nearest eating areas. As they sat down, Ellen appeared, to Judy's irritation.

"Captain, might I ask what is happening? I didn't command the Einstein for six years not to be able to feel changes in power."

"Sorry, Admiral." John had noted Ellen's use of his title off-duty. "There has not been a lot of spare time. We are about to eat. Will you join us?"

"I'd be delighted to, John, with a course of instruction included, please."

Over the meal, John briefed Ellen as to the events of the previous few hours and what he planned.

"Strikes me, you are having all the fun!" Ellen commented after he had finished. "Now tell me, who's got command at the moment? Sanchez, excellent. It means you can fully relax as nothing new is likely to happen until we reach the area of the stricken ship."

"I wish he would, Ellen, but he'll be back in his ready room as soon as we are finished here!" Judy exclaimed.

"Rubbish. John, Judy is right you need a few hours away from the bridge environment. In any case in your own quarters you are still only a few minutes away if you should be needed."

"Ellen, I just feel that the bridge team relax knowing I am close by." John stuttered a little.

"More rubbish, you can't live there so take my advice and spend a little time together, both of you. And, unless you object, Captain, I will borrow your ready room for the next few hours. Of course, that might just make them nervous, having an Admiral present!" Ellen grinned.

"I give in." John said, although he clearly did look as if a few hours alone with Judy would get him ready to fire on all cylinders.

***   ***   ***

Down in engineering Scott and Alan were deep in discussion with their deputies.

"Look, we know how the ship can dodge incoming fire or a missile, the question is what happens if we drop out warp close enough that a hostile ship could fire and hit us in that ten second delay before the warp engines fire up."

"Actually, they would likely have more than ten seconds." said Pierre. "They would have the time it would take us to identify them and then activate the drives."

"Surely tracking will be able to spot them before we drop into n-space?" Simone asked.

"Probably, but it might depend on what size they are or if they can shelter behind a natural object, perhaps the local equivalent of a Kuiper belt body."

"What do you suggest then?" Alan wondered.

Pierre suddenly banged the table they were sat at. "Got it." Then after a second, realising that the others were looking at him in astonishment. "Well, maybe."

"Go on." grinned Scott.

"If the ship changes its course and instead of a direct approach swings around to make a flying pass. As we close with the system, we drop out of warp for just a few seconds and launch a shuttle into a parallel course on the blindside."

"Manned? Armed?"

"Not sure. That would be the captain's decision, I guess, but we could use an AI. The aim is to draw fire or provide targeting data as Einstein drops out of warp after making a loop round to drop out close to the original point."

"Can we arm it? At least allow it to respond to hostile fire and counter incoming missiles?" Simone, thinking about the pros and cons of arming an AI, was concerned.

"For a purely defensive mode, I believe we can." Alan was well aware of his deputy's worry. No one wanted to arm a robotic craft which would have to have some autonomy. "I will take it up to the captain. Scott best if you start prepping the AI and shuttle, good practice even if John decides against."

"Alan, I'll do that, but don't trouble the captain until the next duty changeover, I gather he's been encouraged to take a proper break before the action." Scott replied. Turning to Pierre, "Come on lad, we've work to do."

A few hours later as he returned to the bridge, after the most relaxing break he had had since the Deimos had left on its mission, John found himself being waylaid by Alan.

In his ready room, John listened to the proposed idea. It took a few moments before he called in Judy and Tung-Mei to get their views on how feasible the logistics of the Einstein's own movements were. It did not take long before the decision was made.

"Alan, we have about ninety minutes before we will reach the suggested drop point. Will Scott have the shuttle ready?"

"He will, we decided to make the preparations a few hours ago. We just thought we should avoid disturbing you before you were due back on the bridge. There was always going to be enough time to adjust course and so on."

"Right, let's do it. Back to your stations, Judy, Tung-Mei."

An hour later, Judy announced that they were starting the curve that would change their course into the fly-past routing. "Twenty minutes to drop zone, Captain."

John nodded before contacting Scott. "You have twenty minutes. Have the shuttle dropped outside the docking bay. As we discussed, program it to fire its engines at ninety degrees to our current course as soon as Einstein is out of warp. We need it to clear the warp bubble as fast as possible."

"Aye, Captain."

"Helm, as we drop out of warp, full power on the n-space engines, ninety degrees starboard. I want us far enough away from the shuttle, to be able return to warp, in no more than ninety seconds. The moment sensors tell you the shuttle is clear engage warp."

Judy and her colleague both drew a deep breath. "Aye, Captain."

"Tracking, anything on long range sensors yet?"

"Nothing yet, sir."

A few moments later, with tracking still not finding anything, John gave the order.

"Cut warp drive."

Everyone felt the change in drives as the Einstein returned to n-space and then started a fast turn as the shuttle's engines accelerated it in the opposite direction towards the starship's calculated position. Tracking were also working flat out checking sensors for anything out of the ordinary. Tung-Mei filling in at the First Officer's station had focussed on one set of sensors, looking for the distressed craft, was first to raise an alert.

"Captain, long range visual on what seems to be the Anthezedo."

"On screen."

The view on screen changed to show what at first seemed a collection of rocks. Then as Tung-Mei brought the picture into better focus a terrible vision of disaster appeared. A spaceship of an unknown type could be seen drifting amongst a group of rocky bodies and clearly badly damaged.

At that moment, Judy warned. "Shuttle out of bubble range. Engaging warp drive. Warp one. Commencing loop."

John's response was as expected. "Continue as planned, helm. Lieutenant," turning to Tung-Mei, "did we get enough on that visual to get an idea of the size of the ship?"

"We should have but I'm not sure I believe the numbers." Tung-Mei was clearly confused. "If they are correct, the ship is no bigger than one of our shuttles. I know we sent a shuttle back to the solar system with a warp drive but that was exceptional. The rear of the ship has taken a beating as you can see but the forward areas seem to be in one piece."

"Captain, we have found what seems to be debris from a second ship, if so, it seems unlikely that there would be any survivors." The tracking team were still reviewing what their sensors had found in the short period before Einstein returned to warp.

"Comms, is the distress call coming from the ship on the screen?"

"It is in so far as we can be sure, sir."

"Helm, adjust approach. I want us within a thousand klicks of the ship. Engineering?"

"Yes, Captain." Scott had clearly been listening in to the conversation.

"Scott, the ship is small enough to fit in a docking bay. As the message suggests the crew were going into stasis, we have to assume there will be no help or easy access without some form of code. So, I want to get close enough to be able to fire cables across and winch the ship into bay four. Secure the bay, just in case. How near do we need to get?"

"Captain, you don't ask easy questions, do you? I wouldn't want to take Einstein in that close. We'll get a shuttle ready to take cables out and loop them round the ship, or grapple it, if there are any suitable points. It can tow the ship in one way or the other. Probably quicker and easier."

Time dragged until. "Cutting warp drives, switching to n-space engines." The helm team were in full mode as they changed course towards the stricken vessel. "Captain, we are closing on the ship. Two thousand klicks and slowing rapidly. We should be alongside in eight minutes. Warp drives on standby."

"Tracking, anything in our way. Any other ships out there." John was on the edge of his seat ready to take the Einstein out of the area in warp if there was any obvious danger.

"Nothing yet, sir. Our own shuttle is coming in but is still thirty odd thousand klicks away. No sign of anything other than the natural objects you might expect to find."

The comms team called out. "No change in the message from the Anthezedo but it is definitely coming from the ship we can see. Have contacted the shuttle. AI reports no hostile action."

"Engineering. Scott, you are clear to despatch detail to bring the Anthezedo on board."

"Aye, Captain, we're on our way." John cursed under his breath. I should have ordered him not to be a part of that team, he thought, should have known better.

"Bay doors on screen."

They were able to see the shuttle, towing a long cable, heading for the other ship. By dint of some smart manoeuvring the cable was neatly looped around the midships and then on a second circle snagged on a projecting arm of some sort. With the ship snared the shuttle slowly started back towards the Einstein.

The bridge tensed as the most difficult part commenced, guiding the vessel safely into the bay and then securing it. They were starting to relax as the front half entered the bay doors when…

"Captain, incoming vessel astern! Closing at high speed. It's firing some form of missile set. Looks like a net!"

John reacted instantly. "On screen. Fire missile, bay one, target other missiles. Helm, warp one now. Five seconds. Scott, hold on, we're going to warp!"

"Captain, we're not on the ship!" Scott's anguished cry was followed by a gasp. "Oh, my! That's incredible!"

A few seconds later the Einstein dropped back into n-space almost a million klicks away from the other ship. Scott and his team were still alongside having been caught in the bubble of spacetime that, he had forgotten for a second, extended outside of the main ship when in warp.

"Tracking, the other ship?"

"Seems to have cut power, Captain. The mesh of netting appears to have been shattered by the impact with our missile."

"Right. Engineering, get the Anthezedo into the bay and your shuttle back. I want everything secure in fifteen minutes. Helm, turn us towards our other shuttle, quarter power, but warp on standby. I assume it is all right, Tracking?"

There was a chorus of "Aye, Captain" as the different sections got to work. Tracking confirmed that the AI operated shuttle had not been affected and had changed course to follow its parent. Shortly afterwards the Einstein closed with the smaller vessel and took it back on board.

The apparently hostile ship remained in position and ignored hails After several attempts John decided that enough was enough and the Einstein engaged its warp drives moving back on course for the system that, they hoped, Deimos had travelled to.

"Well done, everyone. Lieutenant Cheung, you have the com. I will be down in engineering." Leaving the bridge, John headed for the lift and the docking area, calling Will Carden as he went, and asking him to join him. He was not surprised to find that the doctor and a medical team were already on their way.

When he finally reached bay four it was to find a perplexed chief engineer and his team struggling to find any point of access to the Anthezedo.

"Scans show that there are multiple life signs on board, Captain, although they do not appear to be active. How we can gain access to the ship itself baffles me. There are no apparent points of entry at all. Which might explain why the ship was still in one piece. If you are aiming to rob a ship you need to get access. If the pirates could not do so then maybe they were planning to destroy the ship when we turned up."

"Commander, you might want to see this." John almost responded before realising that it was Scott who was being addressed. The young engineer using his formal title with the Captain present.

"What's that, Raab?"

"Round here at the stern."

The party all moved towards the stern to discover that the damage that had disabled the ship was spread intermittently across the stern and the rear quarter of the superstructure.

"If I were a betting man, I'd say that that netting we saw being aimed at us caused this. Large numbers of holes as if a set of giant pins has penetrated deep into the engines. The only thing that I can say is that they can't possibly have realised how large the Einstein is. Yes, a net that can do this would cause damage but I doubt it would have been fatal to our engines." Scott looked on with a degree of grudging respect. "Got to say that it is a clever means of disabling smaller ships with a low likelihood of destroying the cargo or, if they want them alive, the crew."

"That's all very well." Will Carden interceded. "But if it isn't possible to gain access to the ship without forcing entry through the hull itself …."

John was thinking. "If there is no visible entry forward of the damaged area could it be that the airlock was in the stern, along with access to the cargo hold?"

"There is nothing obvious but it is a possibility. Leave it with us." Scott gestured to his team and a further examination of the ship started. He went to join them but then hesitated. "Captain, there is a possibility that it was not an attack.

Netting like that could have been intended to capture small rocks and even asteroids. That ship could be no more than a mining vessel."

"Now that is a thought. You mean they may have hit the ship by accident. Their instruments simply identifying a metal rich rock. I guess it is possible but equally I doubt we shall ever know the real reason." Looking at his medical team, John could see that they were somewhat bemused.

"A problem, Doc?"

"You mean, apart from not being able to board the ship?" Will laughed but then his expression turned serious. "Captain, it is the sensor data showing life forms. Yes, they appear to be in some form of stasis or possibly artificial hibernation. No surprise there then, given the message wording. But if our scans are correct there are at least forty entities and maybe fifty!"

"How many?!"

"I know, it seems impossible in a ship that size. Our shuttles can only hold five and that at a push. As far as we can see their species must be very small in size, perhaps less than a metre tall. If you had asked me, could such a species have become a space faring one, I must admit I would have said probably not."

"Assuming they are in suspended animation, would it be reasonable to assume that they should be able to survive for another fifteen days or so?" John decided that it might be more sensible to leave well alone, if possible.

"They must be able to. Their distress call was strong enough to reach other systems eventually but it would still take a number of years to do so. If you want to wait until we reach the system where we think the Deimos will be found, I would suggest that that will not be a problem." There was a sense of relaxation in the doctor's voice as he had not looked forward to, perhaps, having to administer medical support to an unknown race.

"In that case. Scott, a word please." John called over to his engineer. "Keep studying the craft and see if you can identify any entry points. If you do, I want to know before we try access. Since the crew seem to be safely in suspended animation, I am happy enough to leave them in place until we find Deimos. But I want the ship monitored twenty-four seven. I do not want to find the Einstein being invaded should they wake."

"Understood, Captain."

With the decision having been made to do nothing more, John returned to the bridge.

Back in his command chair, he decided that a second look at the events would benefit his team. Giving them the task of finding ways in how they might have improved matters kept the team busy. John's own feelings were that anything they did identify was likely to be of nominal value but practice was never wasted. He settled down hoping that the next week would be uneventful.

15. Eden Prepares.

Summer, at the settlement, was well underway with warmer weather and only light rain showers allowing for outdoor relaxation especially in the evenings after the day's work was over.

On one evening, shortly after the birth of their daughter and a couple of days after Einstein had warped out of the system, Rob and Jenny were enjoying an evening picnic on the edge of the town.

"Is it silly, Rob? That it's little things about Earth that I miss?"

"No, it isn't, what do you miss most? Apart from those we lost."

"You know, it's the blue skies. I mean, I know the sky here can be bluish in the early mornings but most of the time it is a shade of, well, lilac. So different from the way the planet looked from orbit."

"I know what you mean, the scientists will tell us that it is partly because the sun is slightly cooler than Sol and the atmosphere also has a different mix of trace gasses. If I got it right the reason that the planet resembles Earth from orbit is that the upper atmosphere is much more like Earth's and so it has a higher degree of blue in it."

"Yet everything else is almost as if the planet had been planned for us!"

"True though there are subtle differences. Nothing to compare with the monkeys and apes of Earth, for example." Changing the subject Rob continued. "You know, Jen, we really need to come up with a name for little one." He was holding his daughter who was gurgling happily away, having just fed.

"I know, Rob, it's just that I can't make up my mind. You wanted to call her Ellen, but Sinead beat us to that name and the Chans have called their daughter Liu. Nothing else seems right."

"I have been thinking, what about Ellie? I looked it up and like Ellen it derives from Helen. I mean, I know we owe our lives to Ellen. She decided that we should stay with the Einstein after we delivered her to the ship back at Saturn. But I don't want to give the little one the same name as another of the first Eden born children."

"Rob, you can't call her Ellie! It sounds too much like ELE, you know, extinction level event. Not after Earth." Jenny was on the edge of tears, the memories of watching Earth destroyed by the machines flooding back.

Rob gently pulled her into his arms. Wife in all but name, I must get round to making it more official, he thought. "Sorry, Jen. I wasn't thinking. One more, then it's back to you. What about Evie? Not Eve, it has too many direct connotations with Eden and, even if we did, you can bet that everyone will start calling her Evie anyway."

Jenny took a few moments to recover her composure, gazing at the little wonder who was continuing to gurgle,

139

blissfully unaware that she was the subject of their conversation. "I think I like that. Yes, let's call her Evie."

"Jen?"

"Yes."

"You know I love you, don't you?"

"Rob, of course I do." Jen grinned up at him. "I love you too."

"I know it's rather late. I mean it's been nine years since we met. And now we've got Evie and I know it's rather old fashioned these days but will you marry me?"

"No down on one knee and here's a ring romantic question then." Jen grinned. "The answer is yes, of course I will."

Their embrace lasted rather a long time before Jenny said. "Let's get back home. I think little one will need changing and then I think I would like to gently work on making babies again!"

***   ***   ***

The next morning, over an early breakfast, Jenny commented.

"You never got round to telling me what you are working on, now, with Stefan and the team. Is it really all that hush hush?"

"Not really, Jen. Though we aren't going to be broadcasting it. Not everyone will approve but the team and I believe it will be an essential part of our development in the coming years."

"So, what is the project?"

"I guess the easiest way to explain is to talk about the phasers that were used by ships in Star Trek, you remember the programme?"

"Of course, I do. Even if none of us easily admitted it, I suspect most astronauts watched old recordings when they were kids if not as adults. Phasers?"

"Well, some day we are going to have to go after those machines and stop them before they destroy other civilisations. We've got torpedoes or missiles with exotic warheads and Alan Piper and his team had developed a mini warp driven equivalent that could be used inside the warp barrier."

"You mean in the way Earth used the unfinished starships to destroy most of the incoming alien ships?"

"That's it, on a smaller scale but they hope such a missile could effectively hit several targets in one go. The project we're working on would be to find a way to store exotic energy and then release it in a directed stream, a bit like a laser or phaser. Did you know that the first time the team at CERN discovered the energy it escaped in a ball of immense heat travelling at thousands of klicks per second?" Jenny shook her head. "Well the ball actually hit the lunar surface barely an hour after leaving the Earth."

141

"You mean that that new crater wasn't caused by a meteor?"

"No."

"How did they keep that a secret? Never mind. There were lots of secrets in those days. I must admit I don't like the idea that we have to spend time and effort developing new weaponry. I mean why must we go after those machines? Surely the other species around this part of the galaxy must have plans?"

"I hope you're right but that assumes they know of the fleet and, in truth, it doesn't matter. Ellen and John found a message broadcast to the Europa as it fled the Earth, just as Armageddon was hitting. It was simple "God speed, Europa. Avenge us." I imagine we might have received the same message had we still been in the solar system."

"Why didn't they tell everyone?"

"Because, I think, they knew we would not be ready to do that for a long time. We still aren't but that shouldn't stop us preparing." Rob was now quite dead pan, knowing Jenny's emotions were already a little out of kilter.

"You'd better get on then." Jenny giving him a kiss. "I do hope the Einstein is back soon."

"Why?"

"Because Ellen will be the one, or John maybe, that marries us, silly!"

Rob headed across the settlement on his bike, feeling a bit guilty at not telling Jenny the full truth. The reality did include his work on the laser weapon, of course, but he was the only one dealing with that research as the project was taking a back seat with the need to develop sensor satellites that could be dropped in place across the system watching for a wormhole opening. Not that they could do anything about it but having some warning would allow the settlement to prepare for visitors.

Arriving at the engineering centre, he was surprised to find the rest of the team already around a table with one of several small metallic orbs.

"What on Eden are they?" he exclaimed; the term having replaced the old equivalent phrase from the past.

"That will teach you to take time off for baby arrival!" Grinned Stefan. "How are mother and daughter?"

"Very well, thanks. Now come on answer the question."

"We have managed to develop these sensor packs and tested one in orbit yesterday. Small, plenty of reach and with enough mobility, with their guide jets, to be able to hold position almost anywhere you want to put them."

"That's great, I thought it would take a lot longer. I guess that means we will have to set out tomorrow. Have you spoken to the powers that be?"

"You mean Helga and Anton? They will love that! Yes, of course, we have. In fact, here comes Anton now!"

Anton had been working with Rob on the weaponry project and had not been that involved in the sensors, an area outside his practical knowledge. After exchanging greetings, the three settled down to decide where they should look to place the sensor packs.

The difficulty, Anton made clear, was working out the relationship between the wormhole and the larger planets further away from the star. He was convinced that they must have had some role in sourcing the power generation needed to trigger the immense energies needed. That, he suggested, restricted where the wormhole could be generated. Rob disagreed.

"That assumption was probably true when the wormhole was opened to send the drone through but, if a tunnel or hole is being generated from another system the power would be coming from there. And, we should remember that it is perfectly possible since this is an artificial structure not a natural one, that there may be a hidden entry at the same spot relative to the star."

"Are you saying that when the gateway closed it did just that and is still there?" It was Stefan who expressed concern. "In which case why can we not see it?"

"I have no idea but there are theoretical bases to work on. Not visible because it is no longer drawing energy. Its physical presence is out of phase with our sensors. That's two guesses. I'm sure you could both come up with others. For me I just think there are limited times when it could be opened from this end but such limitations will not apply the other way around."

Anton, acting as a power-that-be, grinning at the thought, and made the decision. "How soon can we get Phoebe en-route?"

"Tomorrow." Rob and Stefan said together. Rob continued. "We need to give her a full check over and, of course, load the orbs, and other supplies. The trip is going to take at least a fortnight. We'll also need two additional crew members; I'm sure Jenny would have been one but in the circumstances."

"Have you told Jenny about the trip?" Anton asked.

"Not yet. I didn't want her worrying for longer than necessary and, in truth, I wasn't expecting to be going that quickly. I'm not looking forward to that conversation to be honest."

"I can believe that. She's too experienced an astronaut to believe you when you tell her you'll be perfectly safe. All I can say is that, as space missions go, it does look straightforward."

"Try telling Jenny that, Anton." Rob gloomily replied.

***   ***   ***

That evening, with the preparations for the mission completed, Rob made his way home. Funny, he thought, how easy it was to think of their house as home when they were a hundred light years from Earth. Arriving home, he took a deep breath and went in.

"You decided to come home then! You didn't just launch tonight then! When were you going to tell me?" Jenny greeted him with a flurry of anger and fury, pummelling him with her fists.

"I don't understand. How did you find out? I was going to tell you tonight. We only knew this morning we'd be able to launch tomorrow."

"You've been planning this but you hid behind the idiocy of phasers! Why? Why? Why?" Jenny was now crying wretchedly.

"Jen, you know why." Rob was as gentle as he could be. "If you'd known sooner you would have been just as mad and worrying for longer and I couldn't have that with Evie on the way."

"But you lied about what you were doing."

"No, Jen." Rob was trying his hardest to placate his partner. "I didn't lie. Yes, I didn't mention this aspect but the work on using exotic energy as a laser weapon has been my main work for months now. I just knew about the work being carried out by the rest of the team and I must admit that I didn't think that would be completed for weeks yet. It was as big a surprise to me that they were ready when I went back this morning."

"And now that Evie is here, you're going off planet for months! Do you think we don't need you now or something?"

Jen was struggling to hold her emotions in check and failing badly. "And don't tell me it's completely safe."

"Jen, it's as safe as can be these days. All we'll be doing is flying a loop round the system dropping off sensor packages and it won't be months. Two weeks at most. That's six days out, three days covering the locations we've identified as best and six days back at most."

"Only! And who's the idiot co-pilot? Stefan? You know he's not as experienced as I am."

"Jen, you only gave birth ten days ago. This isn't an emergency flight when you might need to risk the stresses involved. This is a routine flight for Phoebe but there is still enough physical pressure to slow your recovery and neither of us want to get in the way of that."

"Damn you, Rob. I know all that and I know that the mission can't be delayed. Helga told me that. I just don't want to be without you and neither does Evie."

Rob stared, mentally wishing Helga was on another planet or had had the sense to check with him first. Just at that point, the baby started crying and Jenny marched out of the room to fetch their daughter for a feed, still fuming both at Rob and at herself because, although she knew he was right about the mission, she didn't care at the moment.

Carrying out the necessary feeding and bathing of the baby took a while which allowed the atmosphere to calm as the two parents looked after her. Eventually Jenny allowed Rob to prepare some food and, with Evie now fast asleep, the conversation resumed in a more sedate manner over the evening meal. Before Jenny re-opened the subject.

"Rob, don't think I am going to forgive you yet but you can at least explain how you and those other idiots in the team have come up with the planned locations for the sensor packs."

Over the next hour Rob explained that much of the planning had centred on where they thought the most likely place that a gateway or wormhole might open were.

"Truth is, we don't really know where it will open but we are sure it will, at some point, when the designers react to the drone's message. All we can say is that we believe that the energy required will originate from the other end unless they have a way of sending a message through the hole before it opens and that triggers some mechanism here. When the hole opened up here, there were indications that some form of gravity field was being generated, possibly from planets six and seven. The question would be, do they need to be in particular positions relative to each other for that to work or doesn't it matter. Controlled gravity fields are beyond our knowledge at the moment, so we can't begin to calculate how far apart the power sources can be."

"So why those points for the packs?" A much calmer Jenny was now becoming more intrigued by the problem.

"For the moment the two planets remain relatively close to one another so we decided one pack in orbit around each planet. We're also going to drop two in the region where the hole first appeared, in case that point is fixed. We don't know but maybe it has to be a fixed distance from the star or possibly, like our warp drive has to be, a minimum distance away. I mean that last point would explain why the drone had to travel that far in normal space."

"And that is all you are going to do?" Jenny's tone suggested that any answer other than yes would be dangerous for Rob but as he was happy it was the truth he nodded. "We've no plans to do anything else. There is nothing we can do apart from scan the planets for anything odd as we flyby each and, even if there is anything, we won't be able to analyse the data until we are back."

***   ***   ***

The next morning it was a more sedate Jenny who, with Evie in a papoose, accompanied Rob to that part of the town, where the, rather grandiosely named spaceport, was active with technicians working on the ship.

Stefan greeted them but, on seeing the glare in Jenny's eyes, was probably a little more formal. Anton was present and, ignoring everyone, took hold of Evie, cooing to the baby and showing her off to the other engineers, as if she were his.

The junior members of the crew were introduced as Petra and Hans, both specialists in communications but both also having some experience in satellite maintenance.

"We are ready to go, Captain" Stefan then reported formally to Rob. "Cargo is aboard and pre-flight servicing is done."

Rob turned to Jenny. "I'll be back before you know it and we'll keep in touch."

Jenny's reaction was to grab him in a hug and whisper in his ear. "You'd better be back soon. I'll know you're gone every minute. I love you." With that she kissed him and warned Stefan. "If you don't bring him back in one piece, I suggest you head for another star!"

Stefan gulped at her obvious emotion. "We'll be back, no reason to be any longer than planned, Jenny. I am sorry it isn't you flying this time."

"Go, both of you, while I recover our baby."

A quarter of an hour later, after Rob had completed his onboard systems checks, the ship lifted from the ground and, as the pilots increased power, rapidly gained altitude, reaching a low orbit for final checks before heading away across the system towards the outer planets.

Six days later, after an uneventful trip, the Phoebe started its first flyby. As it looped around the planet, now called Har, for no good reason that anyone could come up with, Rob eased off the power to keep the ship in an orbit outside the furthest of the planet's three small moons.

"Right guys, one orbit for you to drop off the package and test it, okay?"

"Aye, Captain."

An orbit later, with the sensor pack safely dropped in orbit and tested, the Phoebe fired its motor and headed towards planet eight, now known as Vest. Thirty-six hours later they repeated the process, again with a single orbit before heading towards the area where the wormhole had first appeared.

Another two days passed with the crew only having to carry out routine checks and scans of the different bodies passed, mostly the equivalent of small asteroids. Finally, they reached their target without mishap and, having completed the placing of the remaining sensor packs, turned to head home back to Eden.

16.   The Gate Opens

A few hours later, with Rob resting and Stefan on duty, it happened. A shudder rippled through the craft causing several alarms to go off.

Rob covered the few yards to his seat on the bridge in almost no time flat, conscious that, the one good thing he knew was that, the loss of pressure alarm was not sounding.

"What happened, Stefan?"

"No idea, Rob. It was as if we hit something but there isn't or wasn't anything to hit."

Rob thought for a few moments, as they checked all the systems and could find nothing wrong. Then. "Einstein reported a similar event when they were chasing the drone and Deimos. A few hours before the wormhole opened."

"You mean…?" Stefan responded nervously.

"Yes, if that was a similar event then we can expect visitors sooner rather than later and I don't think I want to be this close. Buckle up everyone, we're heading back at full speed."

"Captain, we are still five days out from Eden. Will we be able to get back quickly enough?" Hans asked the question that Rob was wrestling with.

"Hans, I don't know. As I understand it Einstein's incident occurred around twelve hours or so before they spotted the wormhole but they were heading towards it. Best we can do is cut our journey time by a day or so by using full power. Looks as if our sensors are going to get a live test, so best to start monitoring all four for anything unusual."

Fourteen hours later the sensors located near to the presumed wormhole position started recording changes in the local gravity.

With the Phoebe less than halfway home, Rob started transmitting data to the team on the ground, warning them that it looked as if a wormhole was about to open.

Seven long hours were to pass with nothing else seeming to happen. Then the sensor packs gave the electronic equivalent of a scream as the local gravity strength went off the scale. Minutes later the screens on Phoebe were showing pictures of a large disturbance in the void close to Har and almost exactly where the earlier wormhole had been.

"Oh my god!" It was Petra who was looking directly at the spot when the hole appeared. "It's huge and it's growing. If the sensors are correct it is already twice the size of the first one and it is still getting bigger."

"First one was large enough to allow the drone and Deimos to transit but it was questionable if Einstein could have managed it even if it hadn't closed as fast as it did. I wonder what is coming and how long it will take to appear?" Hans was checking the original dimensions. "If this is bigger, then it suggests that a larger ship may be coming."

"We can only watch. We're still more than three days out of Eden and I see no reason to stop running." Rob preferred the idea that he would rather be with Jenny when whatever was to occur happened.

Three hours later and the sensor packs screamed again and the crew watched as a huge shape started to appear in the centre of the wormhole.

"Around two kilometres long, so smaller than the Einstein. But it's not a friendly looking giant, so black it's almost invisible to the naked eye. Helga, Anton best prepare people, I think that first contact may have come to us."

"Right, Rob. How far out are you now?" Helga responded.

"We are still around three days out. We are running at full speed and should be far enough ahead of it. So please reassure Jenny."

"Right you are."

Thankfully, Rob thought to himself, the alien ship was not apparently looking to accelerate towards the planet, yet anyway, nor did it seem to have located Phoebe.

"Captain," the dismayed voice of Hans broke in on his musing, "our sensor packages have been destroyed. All of them."

"What?"

"We still have passive sensor capability, Rob. As that ship came out of the wormhole they were attacked. Look."

Hans started a video running which showed the wormhole surrounding an image of the alien ship as it transited. As it did lightning seemed to strike upwards from the two planets closest.

For some time, the black ship seemed to hesitate about moving. It appeared to be waiting, on the edge of the gateway. It eventually started to move in system and it was apparent that it had identified the Phoebe as their sensors reacted to some form of scan. Moments later the engines died and, to Rob's horror, so did their communications link with Yablon.

"Ideas?" he asked his astonished crew. Not surprisingly their initial response was a set of stunned faces before Petra, who had been monitoring her comms equipment trying to find a way around the block, whatever it was, reacted.

"Captain, Rob, the scan wasn't a scan it was a simple radio signal. Somehow they have managed to override your systems authority and told the engines to shut down." Even as she spoke, the life support systems died.

Rob did not need to say anything. All their training kicked in and within a few minutes everyone was suited up and ready to switch to their suit oxygen tanks.

"How? I didn't think you could override a captain's authority on his own ship and how would they know the codes anyway."

"It's a guess." Petra was almost weeping with frustration. "I can only believe that the message must have included some form of virus."

Stefan interrupted. "Rob, perhaps we should shut down the computer systems and then reboot. Maybe that would allow us to restart the engines."

"That'll take time." Hans reacted.

Rob forced a smile. "Well it's not as if we are going anywhere, but let's try a few things first before we do that. I'd prefer to have some control when that ship catches us. My guess would be that we have a day or two, depending on how fast she can shift. Unfortunately, she looks built for speed."

"Best get on with it then." Stefan answered turning to his screen.

***   ***   ***

"Phoebe, do you read me? Phoebe, do you read me? Come in, Rob!"

Helga was getting more and more upset. There had been no contact from the craft for an hour now and she did not understand why.

"Helga, what's going on?" Oh no, thought Helga, how did she find out so soon.

"Jenny, please. We don't know for sure."

"I said, what's going on, Helga. I come over to talk about the prospects for using some of the embryos Einstein has and I find the place in uproar."

Helga gritted her teeth. "We have lost contact with Phoebe. They were downloading data when the link was cut."

"How long?"

"Sorry?" Helga's confusion over the ongoing situation was worsened by Jenny's indeterminate question.

"How long have they been out of communication?" Jenny's fears were threatening to overwhelm her but she wasn't going to let that stop her seeking answers. "Just what is going on?"

"Jenny, I am sorry. It's been almost an hour since the data downloads cut off without warning."

"An hour!"

"Look, Jenny. A few hours ago, Phoebe advised us that a wormhole had opened and a large ship was transiting into the system. Rob had already decided to make a run for home before the hole appeared, so they were only about three days away when we lost contact. Anton redirected one of the satellites to scan where Phoebe should be. It found her still heading towards Eden but it seems that they have had engine failure and are simply coasting along their original trajectory."

"So, what plans for a rescue mission?"

"Rescue mission?"

Anton came into the room at that point, just in time to hear Helga's response.

"Jenny, I guess you haven't heard the full story so far."

"Story?"

"Just about the time we lost contact with Phoebe, the ship they had reported started to move in-system. The sensor packs were destroyed but we can still use our satellites to monitor it. So far passive scans have been ignored. The ship is around a kilometre long, smaller than Rob's team thought, and built for speed. As things stand it will catch Phoebe in less than a day and easily sooner than any of our shuttles could manage."

"You mean we wait and see what happens to them without making any effort to save them? How can you? I don't understand you any more, Helga."

"Jenny, if the ship simply passes them by, we can launch a shuttle to match course with them and they will be that much closer to home. If it wants to take them onboard there is nothing we can do."

"I'm not happy, Anton. We should have acted sooner."

"And it wouldn't have made any difference, Jenny. You should know. Of all people, you should know. It was clear almost immediately that we could not match the incoming ship, that we couldn't reach Phoebe first. Please. We can only watch and wait. If you want to help, the team working on the shuttle need any assistance you can give."

*** *** ***

"Rob, there's something odd about that virus."

158

"Beyond the fact that it could override our most secure systems?" They had been working for an hour trying to understand what had happened to the ship's computer before finally taking the ultimate risk and turning their systems completely off. Then they would be reliant on a successful reboot. There were obvious risks and Rob had decided to delay until they were certain that they could not kill the virus first.

"I don't think it's a virus at all."

"What!"

"I've been looking at the message we assumed carried the virus and it seems to be in our own computer code. If I'm right it contains Pawl's override codes! Or what Deimos' computer would understand as them. His codes are senior to yours and could be used to carry orders to our computer which it would assume were valid. Somehow, our "guests" must have had access to the Deimos' systems." Stefan looked totally miserable.

Rob felt the same realising that simply rebooting the computer would not help, even if his own command codes worked and, dependent on the full orders transmitted to Phoebe, might even aggravate the situation.

He decided on one try. "Computer, restart life support and engines. Command code. Sierra nine whisky tango six four."

The computer responded, not with an audible response but simply a screen-based message. "***Command code not valid. Senior officer code overrides this command code. Captain has been relieved of command.***"

159

Rob and Stefan sat back stunned.

"Rob, I have looked ahead as well and it looks as if the satellites we put in orbit around Eden, are still ok, we just can't contact them." Hans was clearly nervous, feeling that he was out of his depth. "I wonder, we must just look like a rock to any sensor scan unless it could identify our heat signature. If we were under power, is it possible that we would have been targeted as well?"

"You mean that the message may have saved us?"

"I think so, yes." Hans was still stuttering, "and the sensor packs were not the only targets. As far as I can see the ship itself was hit."

"Has it been damaged?"

"I don't know. Looks as if it is too big to take serious damage or it might have some form of defensive shield. Look, the lasers or whatever seem to have bounced or been reflected."

Petra stuttered. "Captain, what do we do now?"

"We wait, Petra. We can only wait."

***   ***   ***

Back on Eden, the team could only watch the satellite data as the unidentified ship rapidly closed the gap on the human vessel. It had been apparent for some time that there was only one destination for the aliens - Eden.

17 Earlier - In an Alien System

Pawl was pacing the floor as their wait lengthened, not an easy task with only limited grip. As far as they could tell, the ship they were on was not moving and they were having to cope with a state of zero gravity in conditions that were far from ideal. As Molly had said the only saving grace was that they could breathe the alien air which gave them hope for the future.

"Commander, did you get anything from your scans of this ship before they intercepted us?" Pawl had the feeling that Hidecki was asking the question more to pass the time than expecting any detailed answer.

"Very little. It's about a kilometre in length and appears to be as black as spades. One thing which was not from those initial scans but more a feeling I got. This ship is designed for speed. Even for a spaceship operating in a vacuum it gives the impression of being shaped for manoeuvrability. I hate to say it but everything I have seen suggests that this is a warship. Certainly not a pleasure craft." He finished with a forced grin.

Suddenly there was a series of siren-like noises following which an alien opened the door and with a gesture indicated that they should strap themselves into or onto their seats before vanishing again.

"Looks like we are about to get underway. So, I suggest that we do as he indicated. At least as far as you can."

A few minutes later there was a further long noise and moments after that they began to experience a sense of up and down for the first time since boarding the ship. At first the direction of travel was such that they would have fallen towards one of the walls, if they had not strapped down, then the room seemed to rotate so that the seats were "down" and the floor also was below their feet.

"The whole deck must rotate to reflect the motion of the ship, that's amazing." Hidecki, who admitted to having limited experience of zero g, was finding the situation quite exciting.

"I believe that the original plans for the Einstein included similar arrangements for the bridge and medical facilities but that was before they found out about the side effect of the warp drives, even when in standby mode. Once you have artificial gravity in a single direction it becomes easier to handle ship motions. Of course, the Einstein and its sister ships were not designed as warships."

"I wonder how long we will be underway. I'm getting a little hungry to say the least!" Molly grinned. "There's water in our suit supplies but we weren't expecting to be away from food this long. Were we?" she asked a little plaintively.

"No, we weren't. Problem is that we can't get to our supplies."

"I wonder how long our captors can last between meals? Because that might colour their ideas about us." Hal looked resigned to missing a few meals and despite everything the others laughed.

"I wonder if we could leave this room." Pawl said, deciding to try the door. Slightly to his surprise it opened on to an empty corridor. "How observant are you guys? I mean, is this a different corridor to that that we came to the room by?"

"Sorry, Pawl. Different?" Now it was Hidecki who was bemused.

Neither Molly nor Hal could see the difference and that left Pawl wondering if his own memory was playing up.

"When we were led here the floor was a shade of blue but none of the surfaces in this corridor are blue. So, have they changed the colouring by some manner or….?" Pawl's voice drained away in confusion.

"Pawl, there is one possibility. Our room rotated as the ship got underway. Maybe that meant that the door opens on to a different corridor. I mean if the whole deck rotated nothing would change but if it was only the rooms that move then there would have to be different corridors. It must be very complicated but I guess it might or must be possible." Hal responded thoughtfully. "It might explain why there isn't a guard here."

"Though you'd think they would be aware of that." Pawl mused.

Molly suddenly smiled. "I think that that might be good news for us."

"Why?" The other three chorused.

"If they haven't taken account of the changes, then maybe they aren't used to having "guests" who need guarding. And that suggests we really are considered as guests rather than as prisoners."

"I see what you mean. Perhaps we should give them a little more time before we look to escape." Pawl was even more thoughtful now but then smiled again. "If you can fight off the pangs of starvation, Molly!"

"Oh lord, I am hungry. I do hope they come back soon." Molly's face was a picture and the others could not resist chuckling.

"We will give them an hour." Pawl decided, leading them back into the room. "But then we will look to find our way to somewhere more palatable."

In the event there were less than ten minutes of the hour left when the siren sounded again and the team quickly strapped themselves back into the seats. Fast as they were the ship's engines had died and they could feel the room starting to rotate back to its original state before they could complete their preparations and Hidecki and Hal found themselves starting to float upwards. Pawl and Molly quickly grabbed their teammates by their legs and pulled them back towards the new floor. As they completed the manoeuvre the door opened and a figure entered.

The alien indicated that they should follow him before speaking slowly. Hal brought up their translating tablet and they listened to an English version.

"I, Deputy Commander Adzly. Captain, follow me please. I sorry we had to leave you here. Please understand you are considered visitors not prisoners our system. We go to our planet now. Before we travel you require anything question."

"Deputy Commander, thank you. It would be good if we could go to our craft for food and other clothing. If we are to go planetside we should be dressed accordingly. Also, we have not eaten for some time." Pawl was careful not to rush his words and was glad to see the other officer nod. "Sir, what is the name of this ship?"

After a moment's delay while the translation was delivered. The other officer replied. "Ship is Defender Eeeedle. We protect system with fellow ships."

Moving carefully to allow for the zero g conditions the team followed their host out of the room and down a corridor that Pawl was glad to see now had a blue floor. Their journey seemed shorter than that from the shuttle which had landed them on the ship but, to their relief, they found themselves on a deck with a number of small vessels most of which were dwarfed by their own Deimos.

As they crossed the deck via a track which contained a textured surface, similar to the corridor and they found that their shoe covers still gave them a grip.

To Pawl's surprise the Deputy Commander waved them on to their craft with the words. "Quick. Please. We leave ship fifteen <darfs>." Realising that the time element had not translated he thought and then added. "Fifteen <darfs> like time you on our shuttle."

It was Pawl's turn to nod. "We understand." Turning to his team he said "That makes a darf roughly three minutes so we have three quarters of an hour. Better be quick."

Once onboard Molly turned and asked. "Pawl, you said clothing. What sort did you mean?"

"I guess, none of us have our dress uniforms." Molly and Hidecki both shook their heads.

Hal simply shrugged his shoulders. "Pawl, I don't even have anything like a uniform."

"Best to dig out your best kit. I just have a suspicion that we will want to make as good an impression as possible. Right. Move. We haven't much time and we should also grab some food to eat while packing some to take with us. We can't be sure that local cuisine will be edible, though given our experience of food produced from local crops on Eden, it is possible that we will not starve."

"What makes you think that?" Molly asked while diving into the galley supplies.

"We know, from the data sent to me by the team on Eden, that Guardian Two told them the planet was apparently prepared as a refuge, thousands of years ago. If so, you might expect conditions on their home planet to be similar. I hope, anyway." He added at the end.

With time to spare, the team were able to assemble outside the Deimos and were led to a second craft more the size of a human shuttle similar to that which had brought them onboard the Eeeedle. A few minutes later the shuttle lifted from the deck and, as the docking doors opened, departed towards the planet that could now be seen below.

The deputy commander turned as they all gazed through portholes. "Welcome to <Zent>. My home planet." He was clearly proud of the sight below them. The planet was not unlike the blue of Earth but, like Eden, there was a sense of lilac in the colours.

"It's not the same as Earth, or Eden, but it is beautiful, isn't it?" Molly's voice was loud enough for the translation software to hear her and, Hal not having thought to limit its range, her words were repeated a few moments later. And Pawl could see that they were being received in good spirit by the Deputy Commander and his co-pilot.

The drop from orbit took roughly an hour before the shuttle landed, at what was clearly a spaceport with several ships on the ground. "Welcome to my home, Captain." The Deputy Commander's words were translated quickly and Pawl guessed that was a reflection on the software's AI gaining more practice.

"As my officer said, it is a beautiful sight from orbit and I suspect it will be so when we disembark." Pawl was careful with his choice of words, being disappointed that this was not the home world of this species.

"I must now leave you. I return to my ship. You will be taken to our command centre. This is so we can understand how you came to pass through the gateway. My best wishes, Captain."

Pawl drew himself to attention and saluted. "Thank you, Deputy Commander. We appreciate your assistance. I hope we will meet again."

"I also hope this will happen." Turning to a fellow uniformed but smaller figure. "Captain, this is Officer Senior Adzly, my daughter. She will be your escort for this day."

"Officer Adzly, a pleasure to meet you."

"Captain, if you and your crew would follow me." The translation software was a little slower as it sought to understand the young woman's accent, subtly different to her father's.

She led them to a six wheeled vehicle which had seating for all four behind the driver and, as the vehicle's floor was over a metre off the ground, she helped them to board it.

"I think I can cope with the gravity but the sheer size of the equipment and furniture is going to make it hard work." Molly commented.

"What is apparent is, I think, that the home planet must have a lower gravity, otherwise these people would be shorter. The gravity here must be about one point three g and that is enough to affect how a species would develop." Pawl commented, pondering how matters might progress.

"I must apologise, honoured guests. If we had had enough warning, I would have organised a vehicle suitable for one of the Seven who are smaller than we Zeder." Adzly's daughter spoke.

Pawl decided to ask the question that had been worrying him for some time. "Officer, you talk of the Seven. Do you mean that there are seven species in co-operation in this part of the galaxy?"

The Officer looked a little uncertain, at least that was how Pawl read her features, somewhat blocky like her father and the other Zeder they had seen. The main difference being that her skin colour was a lighter shade of purple, closer to a lilac colour. "You are not incorrect, Captain, but I must ask you to wait until you have met our planetary commander to get more information."

Pawl nodded. "Sorry, I did not mean to ask you to say more than you are allowed to."

Silence fell and the humans took the opportunity to watch the view as the vehicle travelled rapidly along a fairly quiet road. Most of the scenery was forest but they did pass through a number of small villages and occasionally they could see what appeared to be small industrial units. There was little traffic and most of the vehicles they did see were travelling in the opposite direction.

Eventually, after some ninety minutes, they finally came to a much larger town and halted in an open area in front of a building, the biggest they had seen.

"Captain, if you would follow me."

Pawl and the crew crossed the area which had areas of cultivation with flowers and shrubs. "A bit like home." Molly whispered.

After entering the building, they were shown to a large room apparently set up as a meeting room and with what looked like a video link screen. It also appeared to be used by different species as the seating and tables were of different sizes and shapes. They were encouraged to take their seats being given the freedom to choose a set more appropriate to them.

They were offered water and some fruit which, after a little testing by smell and taste, the team decided would not cause them too much harm. Shortly afterwards a second door opened and an official in uniform entered accompanied by three other individuals, two of whom were clearly not Zeder, being similar in size to the humans but with a blue tint to their skin. Conscious that the leader of the group was probably a higher-ranking officer, Pawl indicated that his crew should all stand and he himself stood to attention before saluting the officer. Hidecki and Molly as officers themselves also saluted while Hal nodded his own acknowledgement.

The officer returned their salutes with a hand raised to his opposite shoulder though the others simply nodded once each.

"Captain, welcome to Zent. I understand that you are able to translate my language as you seem to have had experience of it. As you have not done so with the language of my colleagues, we will continue in that of Zeder as they can understand that. I am Uzbol and have the privilege of commanding this colony world shared with another of the Seven. My two colleagues here are of that race which is known as the Hokaj."

The two Hokajs nodded their agreement before one spoke. "We also welcome you who are known as <question>"

Pawl replied. "We are known within our own language as Humans or Terrans, Terra being one name of the planet that was our home world."

The officer intervened. "It may be that the translator was wrong. You speak of your home world as if it is no longer that. Is it that you mean that you and your colleagues come from a colony world such as Zent, a place that many of our two species would also call home?"

"Terra or Earth was the planet where humans originated. It was destroyed by a fleet of machine-controlled ships about seven Earth years ago. That would be about one million two hundred thousand darfs ago, I cannot translate into longer time units yet. We were able to build five starships before that fleet arrived in our system and three escaped. Our ship is the Einstein. We found a planet where we could settle two hundred and twenty thousand darfs ago, approximately. It seems that that planet was prepared as a sanctuary for your species in case you were attacked by another fleet. We learned that from a computer called Guardian Two." Pawl paused, realising that the others in the room needed time to absorb what he had just said.

The Zeders and Hokajs started talking rapidly to reach other in low voices before turning back to Pawl and the other humans.

"Captain, you speak of the ultimate tragedy. That another intelligent species might have been completely removed from the universe by this fleet of non-civilised beings. How many of your species escaped, may I ask?"

Pawl had already decided that openness was the only route he could take. It seemed clear that these people were inclined to be friendly but if they decided otherwise there would be little the surviving humans could do to stop them.

"Our ship is the largest and carried almost five thousand people, the other ships are smaller and would have had at the most two thousand each onboard. Each ship fled in different directions but they were all equipped to allow their people to settle a suitable planet if they could find one."

"You can have five thousand on your ship? I was told it is no bigger than one of our fighter ships." Uzbol sounded confused, not surprisingly thought Molly.

"No, Commander. Our craft is only a ship for travelling within a star system between planets. It is not a starship." Pawl continued. "We entered the gateway by accident."

"By accident! That is not possible. That gateway had been dormant for hundreds of our years, it cannot be opened by accident. We still do not believe it could have been opened, except by our ships here." Uzbol was clearly upset and questioning Pawl's words.

Uzbol's companion Zeder broke in. "Uzbol, did they not tell you? Before the Captain's ship exited the gateway, a messenger drone was identified and recovered."

One of the Hokaj also spoke. "We do not understand. We were not aware of this gateway until we were told that it had opened. Uzbol, please would you explain."

"I am sorry, Imlaq. When it first opened it was as big a surprise to us as it was to you. We had to search our records. It would seem that, when the Seven were preparing to fight the Pindat fleet, our ancestors found a system and built a gateway in secret. They meant it to be a hidden escape route. But the Pindats were forced to retreat, albeit at massive cost. With no need to escape, the gateway was shut down. I believe that they did expect to use it and colonise that planet eventually. But time passed and it seems the records were mislaid or buried." Uzbol appeared disconcerted at being challenged.

"Yet, Esbij, you found that information within a matter of hours." Imlaq's fellow companion was equally doubtful.

"That is because of the data included within the messenger drone. It was sent by Guardian AIs left in the other system. That allowed us to query the ancient records specifically rather than the search taking many days. You must understand that we would never have looked so far back in time, at least not at first. Without that messenger we would have had to refer back to the records on Zeder itself."

Imlaq began to nod. "I begin to understand. If my knowledge of the history of that time is correct you and the Bedev had only just started to colonise Zent a short period before the Pindat attack. We, Hokaj, would not have been involved with this part of the cluster until much later. I apologise for doubting you, Uzbol."

173

"Apology accepted, Imlaq." The humans sensed that Uzbol's response was rather stilted, before finding themselves the subject of his questioning. "If your ship is only for in-system work how did you enter the gateway?"

"We were following the messenger drone when the gateway opened. We were too close to avoid the gravitational pull caused by the opening process. In effect we fell into the wormhole. Our mothership was trying to catch up but it does not seem to have been able to enter the gate." Pawl decided to remain quiet, for the moment, about Einstein's ability to cross interstellar space.

"How large is your Inestiner?" Esbij's accent was not as clear as that of Uzbol but Pawl got the message.

"It is about twenty kilometres long."

There was a stunned silence on behalf of both the Zeder and Hokajs. Before Uzbol reacted. "That is almost fifteen times the size of our largest ships!"

Esbij gasped as well before letting a cat out of the bag. "The Guardians would not recognise a ship that size as being a ship, at least not at first. And craft from it would not be seen as a threat. Captain, you have, I think, been very lucky. The Guardian system was originally set up to protect our own ships from Pindat ships that might have found the system by accident. They would not have used a gateway. It is knowledge they do not seem to have but their ability to travel at close to the universal limit could allow small groups to reach star systems nearby without our knowing."

"Commander, under what circumstances might the Guardians decide to attack other ships?" Pawl was now concerned about those left on Eden.

"I am not sure how they would have been programmed all that time ago." Uzbol admitted.

"I believe I can answer that question." Esbij spoke again. "As the weaponry would only have been expected to be used when on a war footing the Guardians would only take action against unidentified craft at such time as the system's gateway opened. Without a disarm code they would strike at any such craft. They would assume that that craft was a threat to any ships transiting the gateway."

"You mean that if you send a ship back through the gateway, any ship, any human ships or even shuttles could be destroyed without warning?" Pawl's dismay was tangible.

"I regret that that might be the case but, now that the gate has opened, we must respond to the message we have received. If we do not it is possible that the Guardians might go to a war footing in any case. I have placed the ship, Defender Eeeedle, on standby to make that transit. But I must first communicate with my government back on Zeder. It is possible that they will be able to answer that question more rapidly than we can here on Zent. They may also ask you to travel to Zeder to meet our leaders. You will understand that we have not met a new race of beings for hundreds of years, except for the Pindats."

"I understand that. How long will it take to contact your leaders?"

175

"The journey will take the fastest of our ships, which is already underway, approximately five of your days. Its captain will wait for final instructions before transiting out of this system. After that it must make seven transits through different systems before it reaches Zeder. You must understand Captain that we are on the edge of our civilisation even though Zent was first colonised almost five hundred years ago."

Pawl was still trying to grasp the fact that his friends and indeed everyone on Eden might be at risk of being the victims of an ancient war machine left idle for hundreds of years.

"How will you stop the Guardians from reacting? It is likely that there will be another ship similar to the Deimos in orbit, if not elsewhere in the system."

"Captain, you must understand that we are having to look at security records that relate to a war that took place hundreds of our years ago. Finding these will take some time but it is necessary that we prepare for the journey back as a matter of urgency otherwise even the correct codes might be ignored by the defence system, if we delay. If it were my decision alone, I would look to send you back with the Eeeedle today but I must seek approval first."

It was at this point that the two Hokaj decided that they must leave the meeting and brief their colleagues. "We wish you well, Captain. And, should we not see you before you leave, to your crew safe journey."

Only now did Pawl realise that there was an underlying issue. If he was reading the faces of the aliens correctly, not easy he reminded himself and possibly completely wrong given his limited contact with them, then the Hokaj were very unhappy about the idea of, firstly, the secret world and, secondly, the idea that an old weaponry system might be still active. It was as if ancient sores had come back to haunt them. Somehow, he decided, I must learn more of these historical events and their aftermath but, first things first, he thought, we have to solve the issues in front of us.

With the departure of the Hokaj the two Zeder had been talking quietly together before they turned to Pawl.

"Captain, Esbij has instructed our security team and our various ships' captains to search their records for the necessary disarm codes. These are never deleted, so it should be possible to find them before the Eeeedle must leave orbit to reach the gateway in time. If we can find them, I will make preparations for a transit." Uzbol suddenly seemed much more relaxed.

"In the meantime, I hope you will accept our hospitality while we await instructions from my homeland. We will assign an officer to be your host guide. She will be able to help you see this world." Uzbol continued. "As you were able to live on the colony planet, it seems likely that you will be able to eat our food but may I assume that you will wish to return to the ship and your own craft?"

"That is correct, Uzbol. It will provide us with other necessities. Perhaps I could be taken to the Eeeedle and bring our ship back down to the planet."

"We will arrange that. You will understand that we would ask that your co-pilot be one of own pilots during the trip from orbit to our spaceport."

"Understood. I would have asked for that support anyway."

Esbij, who apparently had been conversing with someone else via a comms link, suddenly looked up at Pawl. "Captain, it occurs to me that you have expressed concern as to other craft similar in size to yours. However, you have not commented on the risk to your starship. Does it have adequate defensive screens to defeat the beam technology that the Guardians might use?"

Pawl considered his words carefully. "I do not have sufficient knowledge of the power of those weapons, so I cannot be sure. I did not comment on the Einstein as I suspect that it will no longer be in the system."

"What do you mean?"

"My colleagues were scanning the gateway and I am aware that they believed that they might be able to identify the star which is this system's sun. Can you tell me how far this star is from the other end of the gateway?"

"It is, I am not sure how you measure such distances but, using the definitions included in the contact data which was sent with the messenger, it would seem to be approximately sixteen of your light years. So, unless you can find a second gateway then it must take at least thirty of your years. Assuming that your ship has a top velocity similar to our old interstellar craft."

Pawl thought about that for a moment. "Molly, you are the maths wizard. What is your best estimate of the time it will take Einstein to reach this system?"

Molly had obviously been thinking on those lines already as her answer was very quick.

"My best estimate is between forty- and forty-five-days assuming John sticks to warp two or, maybe, three. If we take the middle and give an estimate, based on the time we took to transit the gateway, I'd say about eighty times that latter figure."

"Esbij, is the time taken to transit the gateway constant?" Esbij nodded. "Then our ship will take between seventy and eighty times that period. Unfortunately, we have no means of identifying gateways, we assumed that they are not natural phenomenon but built by you or another species."

To say that the two Zeder were astonished might have been overstating the impression that the humans got but there was no doubt that they doubted what Pawl had said.

"That is impossible! Only the Bedev ever developed a ship they claimed was capable of exceeding the universal constant and they are no more. They were never able to demonstrate that ship's capability. Unless somehow you found that ship and activated it?"

"We developed the process ourselves. Our ship does not exceed the universal constant. When at warp speed it moves within its own spacetime continuum. That allows it to dodge the light speed restrictions."

"Yet it will cover sixteen light years at velocities exceeding one hundred times the universal limit. I find it difficult to believe, though you seem certain."

"Uzbol, I am sorry that you find this hard to believe. You should know that our home world and its sun are over one hundred light years from here. Our home world was destroyed a little over seven of our years ago or a little more than that number of your years, based on the comparisons our mutual numerical translation systems have now generated."

"But if you could do that why did you not also make gateways?"

"I still find the idea as amazing as you find our starship. The energies required must be immense and I would need to understand how they can be generated. To me, that the gateways can be made at all is incredible but that you must be able to aim them in some way is equally almost unbelievable."

"You realise that your Einstein will be tracked and intercepted when it passes another of our systems five light years from here? It is necessary that I despatch a messenger to that system as well to warn them. The ship will be entering part of our defensive network and will be forced to stop."

Pawl thought about the Zeder's statement before deciding that he would only say: "I am not sure that you will be able to do that. A ship under warp drive is not strictly in our universe and will be invisible to your trackers. I am only saying that, as I would not wish your military to consider the arrival in this system without warning as a hostile action."

"I appreciate your candour, Captain. I must still report to my superiors and advise them accordingly. Now we must part. You will be escorted to the Eeeedle and your ship. I must go now to carry out my duties. We will meet again." With that Uzbol rose and left, almost at a run.

180

"I don't think that he is that happy." Hidecki commented a little drily. "Pawl, Captain, we cannot contact the Einstein but I guess that we should try and consider how we might warn the Phoebe, if she is operating off planet, when we return home."

While they waited for their escort the team discussed how that might be done but, having bounced a few ideas around, came to the conclusion that they needed more information on how the Guardians might react.

They were about to discuss their impressions of their host and the others in the meeting when a side door opened and the Hokaj, who had accompanied Imlaq, entered the room. Relying on the humans' translator he greeted them before swiftly handing Pawl a small computer chip and saying. "Captain, we believe you should understand something of the history of the Seven and the relationships between our different species. We obtained certain information about your systems from the staff on the Eeeedle and it should be possible for you to access the data on that storage element." He paused for a moment. "May I suggest that you do not do so until you are on your own craft. I must go now." He left the room as swiftly as he had arrived leaving behind a group of very bemused humans.

Speaking quietly, so as to avoid any microphones that might overhear her and translate her words, Molly commented. "I thought that I sensed a degree of tension between the Zeder and the Hokaj, could the relationships between the Seven not be quite as friendly as our first contact seemed to imply. Or have I got it wrong?"

"I think we all sensed that over the "hidden" planet and the new gateway. He didn't actually say "keep it secret" but that does seem to be what he was implying."

"You know, there is one thing. This was a first contact situation and it didn't go how I expected it to. They don't seem to be hostile even if their friendliness is a little formal at the moment. I felt that those we met on the Eeeedle seemed both more friendly and respectful." Hal spoke, equally quietly. "Could that be because they recognised us kindred spirits? I mean, as fellow astronauts."

"That is a very pertinent point, Hal." Pawl responded. "You may well be right. Unfortunately, we can't be sure. As yet we can only place our own preconceptions on to their emotions and views. Anyway, for the moment, we are reliant on the Zeder ship to enable us to return home quickly."

"We wait then." Hidecki said and wait they did. Despite earlier suggestions of urgency, it was almost two hours before a Zeder officer entered the room and asked them to follow him.

This time the vehicle they boarded had seating that was more suited to the human physique and the trip back to the spaceport was easier. Their escort was less vocal and, as Hal put it later, taciturn in the extreme. Eventually, they did arrive at their destination and the minibus, as Hidecki called it, pulled up next to a shuttle which was clearly prepped for an immediate take-off. Again, there were seats that the team could sit in but only Pawl was invited on board before the craft launched.

Forty minutes later he found themself back in the docking bay of the Eeeedle only a few metres from the Deimos.

As he and his pilot disembarked from the shuttle they were greeted by an officer, whom Pawl had not seen before. Indicating that he should activate the translator programme, he spoke.

"Captain, I am Flight Officer Ilgen. I am to be your co-pilot for the trip back down to Zent. If I may join you on the flight deck?"

"Certainly, Officer Ilgen. Please, follow me."

A short while later, after completing a thorough systems check, Pawl turned to Ilgen. "I am ready, would you signal your colleagues?"

With the Eeeedle's bridge clearing them to launch, Pawl gently lifted the Deimos and, after leaving the docking bay, took up a trajectory that would drop them swiftly from orbit. He smiled inwardly as Ilgen's face expressed shock at finding himself pulled into his seat by the artificial gravity. "Can make gateways but haven't found a way to make gravity itself!" Pawl thought.

A little under an hour later the Deimos landed safely. Once clear of the ship and having parted company with his co-pilot, Pawl was pleased to see his crew settled into a smaller vehicle with human sized seating, except for the driver's seat which was occupied by the same officer who had escorted them to the government building.

"Officer Adzly, a pleasure to see you again."

"Captain, I have been assigned to look after you and your team for the next few lights. Please join us, so that I can take you to your quarters. We will return here tomorrow before undertaking a journey around this part of Zent."

18.   Zent.

As they were driven away, Pawl raised an eyebrow in the direction of his colleagues to receive nods back. He had sensed that Adzly's daughter was not overly happy at her role of nursemaid and his team's responses confirmed that they agreed.

The journey to their quarters was shorter than the trip to the administrative centre and Uzbol, lasting only half an hour before they turned into a small development of buildings and stopped in front of one particular residence.

"Captain, this house is one that is usually used by Ush diplomats when they visit here. There is no-one here or due to arrive for some time. As they are similar in stature to yourselves it is the best place for you to stay. I will show you round but then I must leave you until next light."

The residence was not very large but was fully equipped and well stocked with various foods. Adzly's daughter took the time to recommend some foods while suggesting that they avoid others that were very specific to the Ush. By the time she had finished it was dark.

"Officer, thank you for that. Night fell quickly, how long is a day or light here?" Pawl was intrigued to know how long it would be before dawn.

"It will be one hundred and sixty darfs before dawn. At this season a day is three hundred and fifty darfs. Captain, I must go. I will return twenty darfs after first light."

After she had left Pawl turned to the team.

"That means days here are quite long. Around twenty-six hours, so not a lot different to Eden."

"Pawl, do you think the food will really be okay to eat?" Molly was her usual starving self. She had never fully understood the envy of the other females back home at her ability to eat without adding any weight. Food was for eating, not for worrying about, unless there wasn't any, of course.

"Our friend seemed quite comfortable that, if we could eat food grown on Eden, we would have no problem here. I guess I would suggest a degree of care. Don't overdo it, taste first, the difficulty might be deciding what needs to be cooked. It doesn't really resemble our own food but that doesn't mean it isn't edible."

Conversation died for a while as they tested the food and finally put together a meal over which they began talking again.

"I don't think our escort is terribly happy about being given this job." Hidecki commented. "How did the Deputy Commander describe her? Officer Senior and his daughter?"

"He did. Funny about her not jumping at the chance. They've admitted that they haven't known a first contact in hundreds of years. Being responsible for relations with a new species would have seemed to me to be a compliment from the powers to be, unless they are actually trying to distance themselves from us."

"I wonder." Hal quietly interrupted.

"Go on, Hal." Pawl grinned, it had taken a while before he had realised that Hal was quite shy and tended to hold back from giving his opinions.

"I wonder." Hal repeated. "This development has just five similar buildings. Which suggests that this is a diplomatic compound as it were, yet we are at least an hour's drive from the centre. It hardly suggests that diplomats from other species are treated well. Or am I just being over sensitive?"

Molly responded first. "I'm not sure you are being overly sensitive, Hans. We saw what appeared to be dissension when we met the Colony Commander, Uzbol. He was not at all happy to be questioned by the Hokaj guy. I'd hate to say it but if we were back on Earth," she took a deep breath, "it would seem that there was some racism going on. At the very least the Zeder seem to consider themselves to be above the rest. I feel we will need to be careful what we say but the Zeder here, at least, do seem to be the dominant species, even if they referred to the Hokaj as fellow colonists."

"So, we pick our words carefully." Pawl said. "What did interest me as we flew the Deimos into the spaceport was what I saw while entering the atmosphere." He paused.

"Go on," said Hidecki.

"Two very large ships rising from somewhere else on the planet. They made me think of bulk carriers, a bit like ocean-going cargo ships. It will be interesting to see what this planet produces as an export. I haven't seen much industry though you would expect some, if only to provide support for the defence ships, they keep talking about. I am looking forward to tomorrow. Talking of which, we should probably get some shut eye."

***   ***   ***

The next morning, after a brief breakfast of local fruit, the team were ready and waiting outside the residence when the officer arrived. Fortunately, she appeared to be more relaxed about her role.

"Good day, humans. Captain. It is a bright start to the light and the weather will be good for us." Her voice sounded as bright as her words and Pawl and Molly found themselves glancing at each other quizzically.

"Good morning, Officer Adzly." The team chorused.

Before she could reply Pawl added. "Officer, my first name is Pawl. As we are going to be together for several days, perhaps we could be less formal?"

The Zeder looked surprised at first and a little unsure but then gave a smile. "I think that would be good, my name is Calri."

"Good. This is Hidecki, Hal and this is Molly."

Molly intervened. "You have a lovely name, Calri."

"Thank you, Moolly." Molly laughed at the slight mispronunciation of her own name. "Now Pawl, are you ready to see a little of my home?"

"We are, Calri."

"Please board my vehicle and we will go."

Calri drove them out of the compound and, after a quick stop back at the Deimos to collect some essentials, proceeded to take them on a winding journey through several small settlements, villages as Hal put it. She explained how they differed from each other and, to the surprise of the human team, showed them the different skills each of which appeared to be unique to each location. Finally, they pulled into a village that looked much as the others.

"Do you need or wish to eat in the middle of the light?" Calri asked them

"Eat at middle of the day." Molly, naturally, was the one to answer first. "Oh, yes please."

"Please follow me then." Calri led them to a slightly larger house and opening the door invited them in. "This is my home. My mate and I prepared food this morning. It is our favourite meal and should be okay for you to eat."

She showed them through to a terraced area which was shady but still warm from the sun before leaving them to get the food. Molly decided it was a good opportunity to talk one-to-one and followed Calri, offering to help.

As they collected the plates and food, Molly blunt as ever and conscious that there was not much time before they would be back with the rest of the team asked.

"Calri, last night you seemed very unhappy at having been assigned to look after us. Is this job seen as one to avoid?"

"Oh no, Moolly. I am honoured to be assigned to you. It wouldn't be the same as having to look after others of the Seven, you are a new experience." She hesitated and then continued. "It was just that last night was my mate's time and I do not want to lose him."

Molly was, unsurprisingly, confused. "Your mate's time. Lose him? I don't understand."

Now it was Calri's turn to be confused. "Do you not have a mate?"

"No, my boyfriend was killed exploring a new planet and I haven't found or wanted anyone else. Not yet anyway."

"But you did have a mate. Are you that different to us?" Calri had to think about the conversation for a minute before continuing. "I must explain, I think. The male Zeder is only able to have full physical involvement four times a planetary orbit, I think you call it a year. If the female is not available, the male must seek release with another, unattached, female. I might have lost Binhal to another if I had not been back soon enough last night and I have great attachment with him. I am sorry if it was obvious that I wanted to be somewhere else."

Molly was astonished. "Gosh, there are really big differences between us and they aren't obvious. You mean that you can only have sex four times a year if you want to stay with the same mate! We can have sex any time we like. Well three quarters of the time. One quarter of the time isn't always seen as good." She smiled. "The idea that our men might be limited to four times a year, well wow!"

"I believe that all of the species in the Seven have slightly different physical attributes but I don't think any of them have such freedom as humans seem to." Calri continued to look bemused. "Physical linking as often as you want. I'm not sure if I'd like it or not but it might be fun to try it! Now the food is ready, we'd better get it out to the men. They are all men, aren't they?"

"Oh yes, they are. Very much men!" Molly laughed as she picked a tray of food and headed back outside. I'm going to enjoy that revelation she thought.

***   ***   ***

That afternoon they got their first glimpse of the farmlands. As the minibus reached the top of a hill the woodlands, they had been in ever since leaving the spaceport, came to an end and the view in front showed nothing but open fields. In the distance they could see what looked like giant harvesters steadily moving across the horizon.

"We help feed Zeder, our planet of origin," Calri said proudly. "and the other central planets."

Hal thought for a minute. "How do they pay for all your work, for the crops?"

"I'm not sure what you mean by pay but they provide us with protection and all the machinery and, of course, we feed ourselves."

"What are they protecting you from?" Pawl asked. "As I understand it, there has been no conflict since a war hundreds of years ago."

Calri was clearly angry. "I am a member of the space force. We protect the network of gateways. If a hostile fleet were to gain access then all the worlds of the Seven would be at risk and that nearly happened in that war."

"I'm sorry, Calri. I did not mean to cause offence. We are still trying to come to grips with the idea of needing such a defence force for so long."

Calri was a little calmer. "You need to understand that we lost whole systems to the enemy before we could stop them. In the end we cut a gateway trapping some of our own ships in an outer system at the mercy of the Pindats who had already destroyed the Bedev home world and its colonies. I hope you will meet one of my colleagues on the Eeeedle. He is a true historian and could tell you much more about those terrible times."

"Calri, when we met with Uzbol he said that the Bedev are no more. Did he mean that they were all lost in the battles for their home world?"

Calri was clearly upset at having to talk about that. "All of their race had to return to their system to defend their home. As far as we know they are no more. Please, may we talk of something else?"

"Of course." Molly replied. "Perhaps you can tell us more about how often you are able to harvest the crops and send them home."

Talk after that was much more mundane as Pawl gently indicated that they should, for the time being, avoid questions that might be contentious. Calri was pleased to be able to tell them that harvesting was a year-round process as the planet was close enough to its primary to have clement weather all year round. Space ships carrying crops, largely of a type of soya, wheat and similar grains, landed and departed every few lights.

They continued to travel along the tree line for a couple of hours during which time the landscape varied only a little until they reached a river. As they crossed a bridge, they could see locals fishing.

Molly could not resist. "Is the fish good, Calri?"

"Yes, it is very good. It is why I brought you this way. When we reach the village, we can get some of the morning catch which you can cook for your end of light meal."

"Would I be right that you only eat fish and crops grown here?" Molly's interest was, as ever, piqued by the subject of food.

"Mostly, occasionally the carrier ships bring delicacies from the central worlds but they are rare and hard to get. Mostly fruits that we do not or cannot grow here. My father does get some, because of his rank, and when that happens the family gets together for a feast." Calri's expression showed that she was happily thinking of such occasions.

They reached the village shortly after and Calri obtained a selection of fish. The people seemed happy and content and there was no obvious payment transaction until Hal noticed that Calri and one of the villagers touched wrists.

"Looks like they have smart watches here too." Hal said, identifying the process.

After that Calri took the next turn back into the forest and, to their surprise, Pawl and his team found themselves back at the compound in only a few minutes.

"Thank you, Calri, for an excellent day. It was both educational and enjoyable." Pawl said. You don't know the half of it yet, grinned Molly, to herself.

Pawl continued. "It would be good if we could visit the spaceport and have a little more time on board our ship. We need to get hold of more clothing and other bits and pieces."

"I am sure we can, Pawl. We will be going there anyway. I want to show you another part of my home and that will mean using a shuttle craft. Until next light." Before they could react, Carli was gone.

"Oh! I was going to invite her to stay for dinner." Pawl said.

"She might be off to see her mate." Laughed Molly, thoroughly enjoying her little secret and anticipating how the others would react when she told them, after dinner.

Calri had been as good as her word and the fish proved to be excellent washed down by some, for want of a better description, beer, Hal had found in a chilled drawer that they had missed the night before.

Appetites satisfied the team turned to the day's events. Spending some time discussing the Zeders' belief that they needed to maintain a military force across their network of gateways.

"I wonder how big the network is. In truth we only know of this system, another one five or so light years away and the fact that Calri referred to Zeder and its central colonies." Hidecki mused.

"Strictly, she referred to the "other central planets" which could mean planets of others of the Seven, as they call them." Hal corrected. "But that might just be the translation software not identifying such a nuance."

"I would like to get a look at that memory chip the Hokaj left and meet Calri's historian colleague." Pawl commented. "Still, that will have to wait. Now anything else before we finish for the day.

Molly chuckled. "I have something I learned from Calri while we were getting the lunch ready. It explained why she was pissed off last night and, well, you lot don't know how lucky you are!" After which she told them of the restrictions that nature had placed on the Zeder and how lucky humans might consider themselves. As she had expected the rest of the team were stunned by the news.

"Only every three months or so, and then it's a must! That must cause a few problems." Hidecki gasped at one point.

"I don't know," responded Molly. "Calri is clearly very attached to her mate and understands the nature of their bonding. My thought would be - what if there isn't an unattached female? I guess we won't be finding that out, not yet anyway."

Finally, they broke up to get ready for bed but Molly decided to take a short walk around the compound before settling down.

"It's a beautiful night and I want to take a look at the night sky. We are further into the cluster and I'm guessing it will be quite a sight." She explained to Pawl.

With that she wandered out into the open air. Unfortunately, security lighting came on, reacting to her presence. Cursing under her breath she decided to make her way around the back of the building. There she found a gate into what passed for an overgrown garden. Walking in, she was delighted that the lights went out allowing a view of the night sky. For a moment she stood and stared. Then she sat down, before lying on her back. "Oh my," she thought, "that is wonderful."

The sky was filled with stars across the whole area she could see. Now I know what it must be like to live in a star cluster. A little time passed then the lighting at the front came on dimming her view somewhat. "Damn!" she thought, not completely silently as it happened and then she heard Hal.

"Molly, where are you?" His voice was almost a whisper as if he knew he was disturbing her.

"Round the back. Come through the gate and let those damned lights go out."

A few minutes later, Hal came through the gate and found Molly still on her back.

"What are you doing?"

"Shut up and come lie down next to me and look upwards, then you'll know."

Hal lay down a couple of feet away and as told, looked up at the sky.

"Oh. Now I know why you wanted to come out here." Silence fell for a few minutes then Molly murmured.

"Hal, you can come a little closer if you want. I don't bite you know. Much anyway."

"Really, Molly. I didn't think you'd want to." Hal sounded as nervous as she could remember any of her earlier boy-friends back on Earth.

"Hal, you are lovely. Come here."

He rolled over and before he could say anything else found himself unable to speak for what seemed like forever. Eventually Molly allowed him to breathe again.

"Was that good?" she asked, it was her turn to sound a little nervous.

"Was that good!" he echoed. "Can we go again?"

It was a little time before they settled back to study the heavens above.

"Molly, I don't understand what I'm seeing. This is everything we might have imagined as to how the night sky might look but it's nothing like the sky at night that appears on Eden."

"That's true, Hal. The sky back at Eden should look more like this and I know that the astronomers have been saying that there is something not quite right. They reckon that less than half the stars in the cluster that should be visible to the naked eye are."

"How do they explain that? Could it be because we are only on the edge of the cluster? Or is it that the nebula is thicker in parts than we think."

"I don't know, Hal, and to be honest I don't really know much about you either. I mean, I know you're a linguist, and as good as Teri, but not how you came to be on the Einstein. Do tell me."

"Look, I am not as good as Teri. She is nothing less than brilliant. As to being on the ship, I was lucky, I guess. I graduated a few months before crew selection started and was approached by the NASA team. It seemed that someone at the University had recommended me. They knew of my late great grandmother and reckoned that I had inherited my linguistics and math from her. For the recruitment team that meant that I ticked two skill boxes."

"Your great gran was special?"

"I didn't know her, she passed away before I was born, but she was very special. They made a film about her and she was awarded the Presidential Medal of Freedom."

"Wow! Oh my, your gran was Katherine Johnson? No wonder you studied math but why linguistics, I mean it doesn't seem an obvious fit?"

"The best way I can describe it is that math is a type of language in itself and I had to pick a second string to my degree so linguistics was the way that seemed right for me. Why engineering for you, Molly?"

"I always wanted to follow my Pop but I didn't manage to get to study it beyond high school. I just fell into that area on the Einstein. I guess I got his genes." She smiled, "Judy got Mom's brains though."

Hal laughed. "You run yourself down."

It was rather late when they both went back into the residence. Pawl saw them both from his doorway and silently slipped into the shadows with a warm smile on his face.

Molly lay awake for a long time trying to get her emotions in order and wishing her sister was with her. For a long time, she had thought that she would never be able to get over the loss of Dennis. Dennis, who had been so forthright and supportive of her when she was trying so hard to impress Scott and worrying that her acceptance by the engineers might only be because of her Mom and Pop. Hal was almost the opposite, shy and reserved. Yet here she was in a turmoil at the thought that he might really like her. That those kisses and cuddles were really two-way and not just because she had dragged him into the first one. In the end, tiredness caught up and she drifted into a dream tossed sleep.

***   ***   ***

The next morning Calri was much later.

"I am sorry, Captain. There was some delay in getting approval for the shuttle flight. The Eeeedle is being prepared for the trip through the gateway and they claimed they needed every shuttle available if they were to be ready in time. It took a degree of persuasion to get them to release one for the light hours."

"Is the Eeeedle not always ready for such a transit?" Pawl asked as gently as he could, with the translator tending to be very precise.

"It's a fair question." Calri gave a smile. "Truth is ships such as her are rarely required to leave the system. It is why it is almost entirely crewed by those of us born on Zent. We do need to leave now or someone might decide it is needed after all!"

With that everyone climbed aboard the vehicle and settled down for the half hour trip. Pawl noted that Hal made a beeline for the seat next to Molly and was pleased to see her smile. He had grown fond of the young woman during the mission and, a little to his surprise, had found his original opinion of Hal change. He had demonstrated capabilities not immediately obvious and had been a good team player. A good pair, if it lasts, he thought.

Thirty minutes later they arrived at the spaceport and Calri drove across the tarmac directly to one of the shuttles.

"Binhal! You are going to pilot us today?" The team heard Calri's obvious delight in the tone of her own voice.

"I am, although the Commander is not impressed by your wish to steal the shuttle even for just a part of the light." The younger Zeder took Calri in a quick hug before becoming more formal.

"Captain, welcome. I am Binhal Hullint, Officer Senior from the Eeeedle. I am tasked with flying you to our manufacturing zone, if you would like to board."

Once everyone was on board and finding seats Binhal continued. "Captain, if would like to join me upfront, my colleague will take the engineer's seat behind us."

"Thank you, Officer."

Calri giggled, rather a strangled sound in a Zeder. "No need to be formal, Pawl. Binhal, we have been on informal names since we started two days ago."

"Sorry, Pawl. As my friend says, I am Binhal."

A few flight checks and the shuttle lifted for what proved a swift flight the equivalent of northwards as Pawl calculated. Just over thirty minutes later they landed at a much larger spaceport where several massive ships could be seen settled on the ground.

Hidecki's comment echoed the whole team's impressions. "They are huge. I'd hardly have expected such ships to be capable of landing planetside. How do you power them? I mean the lift energy requirements must be immense."

Binhal's own pride was apparent "They actually take off as if they were planes. They have powered wings attached before take-off. The wings lift them into low orbit before releasing them and returning to the landing area. I'm sorry, our direction of landing meant that you did not see the take-off lanes. They run for about six kilometres."

"That is impressive." Pawl replied.

"Now we go to see how this all works. Binhal, are you able to come with us?" Calri's question disclosed a sense of anticipation.

"I can, I'd only be sitting in the shuttle waiting if I didn't!" Binhal grinned. "But you're going to have to do the work."

Molly watching the side play had recognised that there was more than a professional aspect to their relationship. One for later she thought.

There was another minibus vehicle waiting for them and Calri duly took the driving seat while the rest settled down. "We are going to show you the food processing factories followed by a mid-light meal. Then one of our metal processing units," she announced.

The morning passed quickly as they toured two factories. The first was converting wheat and similar grains into what appeared to be cereals. When questioned the factory manager explained that what they produced would be treated again when it reached the planets they were supplying, but the types of produce ended up being lighter than the harvested grain and used less space.

Hal would later express surprise at that idea, feeling that it was an inefficient use of resource. He was however as amazed as the rest at the fish processing plant.

"Does this factory work non-stop? Where do all the fish come from?" Hal's questions seemed to cause surprise among the Hokaj who made up the majority of operatives.

"Why would it stop? The fish are grown in pens across the seas all over the planet and whole pens are transferred here by airships. The process cannot stop." The Hokaj manager told them. "Now, Captain. A mid-light meal has been arranged."

After a good meal, again with fish the main course, they boarded the minibus again. As they were taken on to the last place, they were to visit, it was Molly who expressed their feelings succinctly. "I struggle with the sheer scale of those two production lines. One single factory handling the output of ocean sized fish farms and another a world's harvest of wheat crops."

"If I were setting this up, I would be concerned that there seems to be no backup. What happens if there is an accident which damages the production line?" Pawl was trying to understand why an advanced civilisation would set up a system with no apparent fail safes in place.

"We are here." Calri suddenly announced as they came to a stop outside a set of buildings from which steam and some smoke could be seen rising from vents and chimneys.

"We could be back on Earth at one of the steelworks." Molly whispered.

"Not really," Hal murmured, "I don't think we ever had such large setups."

Calri took them to an entrance which led into a reception area. After donning protective clothing, they were introduced to the operations manager, a Zeder called Haltet. He happily took them on an extensive tour of the factory, explaining that each factory handled a different metal process.

"Which metals do you have available on Zent?" Hidecki's secondary skill was metallurgy and this part of the tour was his forte.

"There are many but we only use three in large amounts which are <Aluminium27>, <Platinum195> and <Copper63>."

"You have large amounts of platinum!" Hidecki gasped.

"Why is that important?" Hal asked.

"If the translation is correct and Haltet's names included what appear to be the atomic weights so it is probably right, then they have significant amounts of one of the heavier elements. Unless this is one of the older star systems in the cluster, I would have expected it to be rarer than back on Earth."

Binhal came to the rescue, sort of. "There is a mountain range about two thousand kilometres from here which has large deposits of an ore which contains, perhaps twenty different metals but mostly platinum. I was told our scientists do not fully understand how it is possible and the local Guardian was not programmed with anything that helps. I mean, we had hoped that those who had discovered it might have recorded ideas as to its origin."

"We know how they must feel. There was a similar anomaly found on another of the planets in our solar system which helped us to develop the star drive our interstellar ships use."

"You mean that you don't need to use gateways to go between stars!" Calri looked absolutely stunned.

"We have to admit that artificial wormholes or gateways are beyond our science at the moment. They must have been an amazing development so long ago."

Binhal joined them at that moment. "All I know is that after the war we never made another gateway and we closed down many of them on that side of the network."

"How many are there?" Pawl asked.

"I am not sure, several hundred at least. Most systems have more than one and the central systems have as many as ten. That includes Zeder, our planet of origin."

"What are the three metals used for?"

Haltet answered. "Mostly in the building of the defence spaceships. We send them to Corty, one of the central planets. Other materials are produced on other colony planets. I think that it just depends on what the local resources are."

"That is a remarkable process. Thank you for your time." Pawl replied, nodding to Calri who took the hint and brought the tour to an end.

"We must head back to the spaceport, Binhal will need to be back with the shuttle by end of light." She explained to Haltet as she also thanked him for the tour.

A rapid drive back to the spaceport was followed by an equally fast sub-orbital flight back and after parting with Binhal, they spent a little further time in the Deimos collecting fresh clothes and a heavy-duty tablet before Calri drove them back to the compound.

This time, she agreed to stay for the evening meal insisting on helping prepare it and after a good meal, which benefitted from her expertise in the local cuisine and the find of some bottles of a local wine, they settled down to discuss the day's events.

Molly started things off with a question. "Calri, how many people live on Zent?"

The answer was unexpectedly low.

"Roughly one thousand thousand, I'm not sure how you would count them. Roughly two thirds Zeder with the rest Hokaj."

"Only a million! I thought you had first settled here hundreds of years ago."

"We did but our birth rate is not very high. That is balanced by the fact that we expect to live for almost three hundred orbits of Zent around its sun. How old do you think I am?"

Pawl thought for a moment. "It's difficult but, if I try and compare with human aging, I would have said mid-thirties. Now I am less sure."

"I will be one hundred and twenty years old next wintertime and I am only now becoming ready to have young. I must wait until my first term in the space force is complete, in nine years' time."

"Can you tell us something about Zeder, your planet of origin?"

"Only a little, you must understand that I have never seen it. We are a long way from the core planets, even with the gateways."

Over another glass of the wine they learnt that Zeder was much the same size as Zent but not as dense, as a result the local gravity was lower. Recorded history suggested that her oldest ancestors had first appeared more than a million years ago but the initial Zeder were not sapient. That was much more recent, perhaps as little as forty thousand years ago. Venturing into space had come only around two thousand years before.

"You have been space travellers for much longer than we have. When did you work out how to make gateways?"

"That was, I think, about one thousand years ago. I don't really know, it never formed part of our education until we applied for the space force. Even then we are not told much about it."

"I'm a bit surprised about that. It must have been such an exceptional point in your history. Opening up the galaxy for exploration and to find other civilisations." Hidecki mused.

"I believe it was and we were able to build a network and bring together the Seven but then we went too far and found the Pindats. You must understand that all the races of the Seven are basically peaceful and friendly. I know that, in the early lights, there were stories about how we might be invaded through the gateways or that other warrior species might make their own. For hundreds of years there was nothing but prosperity and excitement."

"And then the stories came true?" Molly asked gently, unable to grasp the sheer age of the Zeder she was feeling was now a friend.

"As I understand it, we opened a gateway into a system ninety of your light years away, one of the furthest except for the one that linked us to the Bedev system. It was an empty system, planets but no life, then our ships found the Pindat fleet."

"They were not native to that system then?" Pawl asked.

"No. They came from outside this star cluster, we think. Huge slow ships travelling between systems looking for worlds to colonise, we think. There are some pictures, taken by our ships, in museums. As our explorer ships approached, the others launched smaller ships, fighters, fast and armed with missiles. We had never faced such hostility before. One of our ships was destroyed. Its captain placed it between the smaller ships and our second ship which managed to escape back through the gateway. As it returned to the system from which we had opened the gate it managed to shut it down before the hostiles could complete their transit."

Calri went on to explain that the hostiles had managed to identify the nearest systems with intelligent life and, although it had taken many years, they found and destroyed a small Aash colony, threatening other systems close by. The Zeder had developed ships with battle capabilities in the time they had, although not as good as, for example, the Eeeedle.

"The Pindat ships manage to travel at about half the speed of the universal limit and the systems in that part of the cluster are very close. All of the Seven worked to produce a fleet that could defend us and after the second meeting, when the Aash colony was destroyed, all the gateways closest were closed except for the one leading to the Bedev system."

The Seven's fleet was deployed into the Bedev system when it became apparent that it was the next system to be attacked. Almost three hundred warships were in the fleet, most crewed by Bedev themselves. It was their home world and there were over five thousand thousand thousand of them.

"Five billion? Almost as many as Earth."

Calri looked astonished at that information but continued. "The Bedev are, were I mean, a very small species. Perhaps half your height, Pawl."

"Go on," said Hal. "What happened?"

"We don't know the full story but the others had a much larger fleet than we had supposed and the Seven were heavily outnumbered. Our history tells us that there was a battle for several tens of lights. In the end the survivors had to retreat to defend the gateway in an attempt to rescue as many Bedev as possible. We failed. Every ship that launched from the planet was destroyed and, although many of the Pindat fleet were also destroyed, they were able to launch a set of massive bombs that split the planet in two. The remaining Bedev ships launched death attacks in revenge. One of the last two Zeder ships escaped while the remaining one held the gate as long as possible. Some of the hostiles managed to enter the gate but most were destroyed when the surviving Zeder ship closed the gate before they could complete the transit. Those who completed the transit were defeated by reserve ships of the Seven held back in case of the disaster that did unfold."

"What happened to the crews of the hostiles?"

"All but one of their ships exploded when they knew they were cut off. On that one they killed themselves before they could be captured. No-one has ever told the full story as to what the team that boarded the ship found but legend has it that it was a species very different from any of the Seven. That it was not a mammal, nor a cold-blooded species, but that it had a body with multiple legs and arms and armoured skin."

"That sounds like an advanced form of insect." Molly shuddered.

"I don't know, but we have maintained warships ever since in case they should find us again. Now you know why the Bedev are extinct, it is still the stuff of nightmares and not just for our young. I am sorry to end on such a sad note but I must leave you now."

"Until tomorrow then," said Pawl, "thank you for telling us so much, Calri, safe journey home."

"Pawl, I will not see you tomorrow. I am afraid you will have to stay here for the light. I have to attend a briefing about the transit to your system, if it is approved. I am afraid there is no-one else to fill in for me."

"Don't worry, we could do with the rest. We will see you in two days then." Pawl replied, not unhappy to have a break from the pressures of working with the translation software.

When Calri had left, Pawl turned to the team.

"In the circumstances and as it is late, I think we should leave our debrief until tomorrow morning. Does anyone have anything that can't wait?"

With all his team shaking their heads, Pawl suggested that they retire to bed and talk over breakfast the next morning.

***   ***   ***

Hal had taken time to get to sleep but was well away when he was woken in the early hours.

"Hal, are you awake?" Molly was next to his bed trembling.

Deciding that a white lie was the way to go. "Yes. What is it Molly?"

"I can't sleep. Every time I drop off, I keep having nightmares about those insects and wake up again. I've always been scared about some insects and to think that there might be intelligent ants or beetles or something."

"I don't like the idea either. Look, come to bed, I'll make sure you are okay."

Molly slipped into Hal's bed and cuddled up before immediately falling asleep in his arms. He grinned in the dark, so much for my irresistible charm, he thought.

The next morning Molly woke first and slipped back to her room, leaving Hal still asleep, not sure if she was more embarrassed by her fears or by the fact that she had fallen asleep without even giving him a kiss.

***   ***   ***

Over breakfast Pawl decided that they should discuss what they had learned the day before and then have a look at the data stick the Hokaj had provided. On that latter point he admitted that he did not know if they had sufficient vocabulary within the tablet, he had brought back from the Deimos, to allow for a full translation. Hal too was not sure but was happy to spend some time working on it after some fresh air.

"I don't know about everyone else but I think that that wine was stronger than we are used to and I have one hell of a hangover."

"Me too." said Hidecki, and Pawl and Molly also had to admit to feeling the worse for wear.

"Okay," said Pawl. "Let's leave work for a bit and take a walk. The forests around here seem unoccupied and, I guess, we would benefit from a gentle walk. Not too far though, don't forget that the increased gravity will tire us more quickly than we might expect."

"We've hardly had any exercise when you think about it." Molly commented. "But I do sort of feel that I am getting used to feeling so much heavier."

"Right, breakfast over. Let's not go out mob handed though. I suggest that we split into two pairs. Hideki and I will head across the compound and over that way. Why don't you, Hal, head out the backway with Molly. Just short walks and don't split up. Be back here in two hours maximum."

As Pawl and Hidecki walked through a small gate on the other side of the compound they found a wide path through the woodland and set off at a steady pace. Hidecki took the chance to ask.

"Pawl, am I missing something or did you split us up deliberately?"

Pawl grinned. "You probably haven't seen what I have. It's my feeling that our two colleagues have struck up a close friendship over the past few days and I thought it would do them no harm to have a little time to themselves."

Hidecki's own smile was warm. "It's not been the ideal time for a budding relationship has it? The four of us have really been on top of each other since we were picked up by the Zeder."

213

For the next hour they kept up a steady pace through woodland surroundings that showed little evidence of life. A few birds and, once, a small mammal stood still almost within touching distance.

"They clearly have no fear of us or, presumably, any other humanoid creatures." Hidecki spoke quietly. "But there must surely be some predators or these woods would be overrun by creatures like that."

"You would think so, wouldn't you?" responded Pawl, "Yet Calri implied it was safe to be around here, I am sure she would have warned us if there were any dangerous animals."

"We've been going over an hour, I guess we should be turning back." Hidecki's words caught Pawl by surprise.

"This has been so relaxing, even with the gravity drain, that I had forgotten the time. You're right we need to turn back. I suspect we'll be late as it is." With that they turned back for the compound.

***   ***   ***

On the other side of the woods, Molly and Hal had also headed out along a path but, to their initial disappointment, it ended, after about half an hour's walk, in a woodland glade with no apparent exit other than back along the path they had been following. After an initial search all the way round, Hal suggested that they could sit and watch the wildlife for a while before returning.

"That would be nice," said Molly, "though I can't say I've seen much wildlife or, for that matter, many birds. A rest

214

would be good though, even if we have to make our own wildlife!" She grinned as Hal's face reddened. "You weren't thinking what I'm thinking were you, Hal?"

Of course, he was and it was rather a dishevelled pair that entered the residence much later than planned. Ready with apologies and excuses, to their surprise they found nobody around.

"I don't understand," said Hal. "I was expecting to get a dressing down for not sticking to the two-hour deadline Pawl gave us but they don't seem to have got back themselves."

"We're half an hour late. I don't like it. Pawl has always been a stickler for timeliness. Judy told me. Five minutes late on duty and you can expect words from him. Look, two minutes to freshen up and then we grab the first aid kit and go find them. Something must have happened."

True to her word, two minutes later they headed out in the direction their colleagues had taken. With only a little hesitation in case there was another path they followed the same route. Twenty minutes later they spotted the other two in the distance and could see that Pawl was struggling to support Hidecki who was clearly hurt.

"He's been bitten on the ankle." Pawl responded to their questions as he released his burden and helped him sit on the ground. "It was a small squirrel-like animal that had sat watching us earlier. We thought it was harmless and even wondered if there were any predators. Then as we turned for home it ran across the path and, before we could avoid it, it bit Hidecki. One hell of a bite too."

215

Molly was getting antiseptic out of the first aid bag she was carrying and, having removed the temporary bandage made with a piece of cloth, started coating the bite with the ointment.

"It has taken a big chunk out of your foot, Hidecki. Pawl, we could do with some of the kit in the Deimos. The stuff we have here will work for a temporary fix but there isn't anything to do more than reduce the bleeding. I take it Calri didn't tell you how we could contact anyone?"

"No. I suggest we get him back to the residence and into bed with his leg raised. That and the coagulant that I think is in my personal first aid case will help."

"Right, let me lift you, Hidecki." Hal moved in to help and with Pawl also helping they started back.

The journey took nearly three quarters of an hour. For the first time they all really felt the impact of the higher gravity but, in due course, they managed to get Hidecki into bed. Using pillows and cushions they managed to raise his foot higher and applied a coagulant coated dressing.

"I don't know how he stayed conscious for so long," Pawl said, "the pain must have been awful but he managed to put himself in a semi-trance which helped him to ignore it. That didn't help with walking though because the bite has damaged part of the ankle muscles."

"We seem to have been dogged with bad luck this mission." Hal lamented, oblivious to the smiles of Molly and Pawl.

"Perhaps we should do our debrief now." Molly said. "The kit included some heavy-duty painkillers so Hidecki should sleep for the moment. If we leave the door to his room open, we will know when he wakes."

The others agreed and spent the next hour or so debating the various things they had learned the day before. In the end Pawl summed up their collective thoughts.

"We seem to be involved with a group of different races which has the Zeder in a dominant position through its ability to develop gateways or wormholes between different star systems. There is a degree of, possibly understandable, paranoia regarding the Pindats but there is also an odd structure to their trading. I cannot escape a feeling that the trading has been built on a divide and control basis, almost feudal in its nature. The Zeder speak as if there is complete harmony between the Seven but we already have reason to question that."

"There is one mystery about this cluster though that we haven't discussed."

"Mystery?" Molly was first to respond.

"Why did we not find any occupied planets during our survey? We should have at least registered radio signals. I'm even surprised that astronomers back on Earth did not record such indications of intelligent life. The cluster should have glowed with radio communications and other signals."

"You mean you feel that SETI should have found evidence?"

"Yes, they have had advanced civilisations here for hundreds of years before we even had radio. If they were using some form of communication that didn't register, I could understand it but they used ordinary radio to contact us."

"Do we know what is on the memory stick the Hokaj gave us?" Molly asked before going to check on Hidecki.

"You know, I've been thinking about that stick. How did they find out about our hardware? The stick is a perfect fit for our USB link. They said they got the information as to how it should be from someone on the Eeeedle. That suggests that they gained access to the Deimos, which means that our security is not as secure as we thought." Hal's thoughts were by now mirrored by Pawl.

"I will be honest. I had thought about that but in truth accessing the Deimos would have been simple. We actually do not have that much security, never felt it would be necessary. I am impressed that they could get the info and produce a USB plug in only a few hours, and one that works!"

Molly came back. "I didn't see any Hokaj on board the Eeeedle, and sort of felt it was a Zeder ship but, I guess, we don't know enough about either yet."

"How's Hidecki?"

"Asleep, but he looks pale. I'm worried that he has lost more blood. We need to get him to the Deimos. If I remember rightly there is a stock of plasma in the medical stores."

Pawl looked up in surprise. "You're right, Molly, but how did you know?"

"Part of my engineering training has been understanding what is what on the shuttles and interplanetary ships. Still a beginner on starships though." She grinned.

"I wish we had a means of contacting Calri or Binhal for that matter. We do seem to have been left to our own devices but without any transport and the sooner we get Hidecki to the ship the better."

That night no-one slept well. Hidecki was restless and the limited painkillers that they had available could only dampen the pain. It was a weary group who ate an early breakfast and then waited watching for Calri to arrive.

An hour passed with no sign of their hostess who was now much later than had been the case the previous days and Pawl finally came to a decision.

"Hal, with me and bring the translator. Molly, do what you can to get Hidecki ready to travel."

"What are you going to do?" Molly said, even as she headed towards Hidecki's room.

"An old-fashioned approach. We'll have to try and hitch a ride."

With that he and Hal departed, swiftly covering the ground to the main road, a few hundred metres away.

While she waited, Molly helped a drowsy Hidecki to put some clothes on. Having checked his bandaged foot, she decided not to change his dressing. The bleeding appeared under control and she feared that taking the pressure off the wound might cause it to re-open. Instead she strapped a fresh bandage around the injured area to support the first dressing. By this time almost an hour had passed with no news or return of their colleagues.

"I wonder why it is taking them so much time?" she said to herself. "Surely they could have got a lift by now?"

A little more time passed before Hal and Pawl came back to the residence.

"No luck whatsoever." Hal said. "In fact, I think we were more likely to have been run down." As he explained they had tried to get a lift from eight or nine trucks and cars with no luck and two of the vehicles had even accelerated at them, missing Pawl by the narrowest of margins. In the end they decided that they were not going to succeed and waiting for Calri was the only thing they could do.

Shortly after, a vehicle pulled into the square and a uniformed officer got out. He started talking rapidly before realising Pawl could not understand what he was saying. Pawl shouted for Hal to bring the translation tablet out. With that working, he replied to the officer.

"I am sorry, I could not understand you."

Hearing the words in his own language startled the other man but he repeated his words.

"You are not of the Seven. You should not be here. You tried to stop lawful traffic. That is not correct. Where have you come from? How are you in diplomatic zone?"

"Officer, I am Captain Pawl Jaeger. I and my colleagues are human. We were brought here by Officer Senior Calri Adzly at the request of Commander Uzbol. Officer Adzly has not yet returned after leaving us two lights ago. One of my colleagues has been injured and we need to reach our ship urgently."

The officer looked disconcerted but went back to his vehicle.

"Police, do you think?" Hal asked Pawl.

"That would be my guess. If he was part of the space force, he would undoubtedly know of us. Looks as if he is radioing for instructions."

Whoever the officer had talked to, it was clear that he was not happy when he came back from his car.

"I am instructed to remain here until a member of the space force arrives. An officer has been requested. They should arrive in twenty darfs."

Pawl gritted his teeth partly at the continuing failure of the software to convert the time reference to hours or minutes but more because of the delay in getting Hidecki to the Deimos for better treatment.

"I understand. The delay is not your fault. May we provide you with a drink?"

"No, thank you. I must wait here." He looked a little less annoyed but it was obvious that he felt he could be using his time more productively.

Time passed and then just under the promised hour another vehicle arrived. This time the uniformed Zeder was from the space force. There was a brief discussion with the first officer who, having made it clear that he did not approve, drove away.

"Captain Jaeger, my apologies. I am Officer Gultior. I was supposed to be here earlier but did not receive the message from my senior officer until a short time ago. Officer Adzly is now on the Eeeedle and will not return until after the transit through the gateway, should that be approved. I have been assigned to assist you in the meantime. I am told that one of your party has been injured?"

Pawl explained about the bite and the need to reach the Deimos where plasma was available together with other medical equipment. Within a few minutes Gultior had assisted with moving Hidecki to his vehicle, similar to that used by Calri, and was driving at a high speed towards the space port. Barely twenty minutes later he was clearing security and driving all the way up to the Deimos.

"Captain, you and your crew are welcome to use your craft's facilities to do as you need. Can you give me an idea how long you might be?"

"I feel that it will be perhaps two hours," Pawl smiled as he heard the software convert the time into darfs.

"In that case, Captain, I will leave you and return in that time."

"Thank you, Officer. By the way, my first name is Pawl. If we are to be together for a few more days it would be good to be on informal terms."

"Yes, Pawl. My other name is Wytem. I will return." And with that he drove off across the port.

Pawl joined his team in the ship assisting Molly and Hal in getting Hidecki more comfortable before treating his foot. It was a slow process but a little over an hour later they had managed to replace the bandages and, having put him on an intravenous drip using blood plasma from the ship's stock, stitch the wound.

"I never thought that I would have to use all that first aid training in one go." Molly heaved a sigh of relief as they finished the task.

"You mean they gave you training? And I thought you were flying by the seat of your pants!" Hidecki, feeling better already, commented drily, then. "Thanks everyone. Now what has happened to our usual escort?"

"She's apparently in orbit and staying there until the gateway transit is authorised. I guess we may see her then." Pawl replied.

A little while later Wytem returned with the news that he had been instructed to return them to the diplomatic compound.

"I regret," he said, "that you will have to stay there until the courier returns from Zeder. That is expected to be in three or four lights time. I will visit you at least once a light but I am not able to stay with you."

Pawl was not totally surprised and was wondering if Calri might be in trouble for spending so much time giving them a tour.

"Understood, Wytem. If you will give us a little time, we will collect together fresh clothing and other things for our stay." With that, he re-entered the Deimos and explained the situation to the team. It took a little while but they were finally ready to make the trip back to their home for the next few days. Having arrived back in mid-afternoon they were able to part company with Wytem, who agreed to return the following light.

The next four days were uneventful with very little to do except check that their records of all that they had learned were complete. Hal was unable to do anything with the data provided by the Hokaj. "Unfortunately," he said, "we only have a few basic words of the language, I think that the team had not got as far with it, as they had Zeder."

Hal and Molly took what opportunities they could, to wander down to "their glade" and after the third day he moved into her room.

19.   The Journey Home

 On the fifth day Wytem arrived with the news that Pawl was asked to attend a meeting with Uzbol.

After the journey back to the capital, now known to them as Zenee, Pawl spent a brief time with Uzbol, who did not seem happy. It appeared clear to Pawl that the Commander had had an easy life and now he was having to operate in matters that were outside his area of expertise or experience.

The first news was as expected. The senior commanders on Zeder had decided that the Eeeedle should make the transit back to Eden. Pawl, however, had not anticipated that the Zeder had decided to appoint an ambassador to the human colony.

"Who will be the ambassador?"

Uzbol seemed amazed that Pawl had had the nerve to ask the question and stuttered a little in his reply.

"Deputy Commander Adzly, whom I believe you have already met, has been appointed. He is not trained in political positions and I do not know why he has been chosen. I have other people here who would be better choices. I do not understand why my superiors did not select a more appropriate individual."

There was surprising venom in the Commander's voice, and his words, made Pawl sit up and listen more closely wondering if there was an underlying reason for choosing an ambassador from the military and not a trained diplomat.

Uzbol continued. "The Eeeedle is ready to leave, Captain." He gritted his teeth or so it seemed. "I wish you a safe journey, Captain. I doubt we shall meet again."

"Good day, Commander." Pawl, still trying to grasp the meaning behind Uzbol's words and his final statement decided on formality. "I and my team thank you for your hospitality." With that he left an apparently angry planetary commander behind.

Wytem was waiting outside the building and within a few minutes they were travelling at high speed back to the space port pausing only to pick up the rest of the team on the way. In the half hour trip from the diplomatic compound to the port, Pawl took the opportunity to update the others on the ambassadorial appointment. Hidecki was similarly bemused by Uzbol's dissatisfaction.

"I must admit that such an appointment seems odd, if they really do have a trained team on Zent."

"Well I'm sure we will experience the deputy commander's skills in this area in due course. For now, let's leave it at that." Pawl responded, indicating with a glance in the direction of the driver that it might not be appropriate to discuss the subject further while in the earshot of Wytem.

As they arrived at the space port, they found that security seemed to have been tightened up since their earlier visit. Wytem was forced to leave the vehicle and could be seen arguing with someone in the checkpoint building before returning.

"I am sorry," he said, "but you will have to walk from here to your ship. The local officers have been ordered not to allow any vehicles to enter the port unless they have an officer of at least Deputy Commander rank on board. I do not know why."

"Presumably, we will be escorted to our ship?" Pawl asked, smiling so as to tell Wytem that he knew he was not to blame for the inconvenience.

"That is correct. The officer outside will be with you. Good journey, Captain."

A stony faced, if the term could be applied to an individual whose skin was a dark purple, officer indicated that they should follow him while a second officer brought up the rear. It was a quiet party that eventually reached the Deimos, only to find that two Zeder were guarding the access and refused to allow them to board the craft. Their escort promptly left and the stand-off lasted for almost an hour before yet another individual arrived.

His accent was so strong that the translation software struggled to produce sensible English. Eventually they understood that their ship had been impounded due to a failure to pay for maintenance and landing fees. As Pawl said later, he would have laughed at the idea but, faced with three armed Zeders and no back up, it looked as if they might miss their trip back with the Eeeedle. He tried to claim diplomatic immunity from the charges, one of which was, as he said, false since the port could not have serviced the ship, but this did not work.

"The charges were authorised only this first light." They were told. "If you cannot or will not pay then your ship is forfeit."

Pawl held his breath for what seemed like forever as he fought to control his response. Finally, he said. "In that case we will await the officer due to act as my co-pilot when we return to the Eeeedle. You may find him harder to convince."

"I am senior officer here. You will not be leaving on this ship unless you pay the monies due." His tone made it clear that he would brook no further argument.

Some time passed before they watched a shuttlecraft drop down to a landing spot alongside the Deimos. As its doors opened Pawl was pleased to see Deputy Commander Adzly appear. This could be interesting, he thought.

Adzly came across with a salute for Pawl who happily returned it, as did his team.

"Ready to go, Captain?" the cheeriness in his voice faltered when Pawl replied.

"Sorry, Deputy Commander. As you can see, we have not been allowed to board our ship."

"Why?" he turned towards the individual who was demanding payment.

"There are landing tolls and maintenance bills due. No-one is allowed to board until they have been paid."

"Been paid, Sir! When you speak to me!" Adzly's voice had not risen but the tone emphasised his unhappiness and seniority.

The other stuttered. "Sorry, Sir."

"Who authorised you to block the legitimate actions of these diplomats?"

"The central office in Zenee, Sir." His resolve to stop the humans was clearly waning.

"So, you, a senior officer in the patrol kowtowed to a civilian commander's irresponsible desires."

"Yes, Sir. Sorry, Sir."

"I suggest that you and these two make yourselves scarce. You will be hearing from Commander Meeax on our return and I recommend you get your answers well prepared, officer."

"Sir, yes, sir." With a gesture to the two guarding the Deimos the unnamed officer swiftly marched away followed just as quickly.

"Captain, my apologies. That behaviour was not forgivable. My wish to experience your craft has proven beneficial. Officer Ilgen was amazed and impressed and his report encouraged me to take his place on this trip."

"You are very welcome, Deputy Commander, or perhaps I should address you as Mr. Ambassador?" smiled Pawl.

Adzly nodded with what passed as a grin. "Either way is fine, Captain, but I understand that you prefer to be informal where this is right. In which case, I am Sugnay."

"That is good, Sugnay. I am Pawl. I will introduce my team once we are ready to launch. We need, I think, to move quickly after the delay."

The Zeder nodded. "I believe I know everyone's names. My daughter has briefed me well. Molly, Hal, Hidecki," he continued, nodding to each in turn.

Pawl carried out his pre-flight checks and shortly afterwards they were airborne and climbing rapidly into orbit. Like Ilgen, Pawl could see Sugnay's mixture of bemusement and amazement as he experienced the effects of the artificial gravity as it deadened the usual extremes of planet-based launches.

Forty minutes later they were able to dock with the Eeeedle. Adzly left them immediately as he was needed on the bridge. Final preparations were underway for departure from orbit and the journey to the gateway.

"I will leave you with Officer Ilgen, for the moment. Thank you, Pawl, for that experience. You have technologies so different to ours." With that he was gone.

Ilgen arrived a few minutes later. "Captain, Commander Meeax has instructed me to await you and she invites you to join her in her planning room. She wishes to discuss how we can try and protect your fellow humans from any adverse reactions from the Guardians."

"Officer, thank you. We will be pleased to meet with your Commander. We need some time to freshen up. Ten darfs?"

"Certainly, Captain."

***   ***   ***

The team quickly got changed and with half the time remaining, Pawl got the Hokaj chip out in the hope that the Deimos's computer could make more of it. As Hal had indicated, reading the file was straightforward but translating it was not.

"You were right Hal; I suspect we will need the linguists back home who will have been working on the Hokaj language to translate this. It goes far beyond anything we have managed. I don't need to warn you all to say nothing about this to our hosts."

"I am conscious that the way the "Seven" is emphasised I find myself mentally giving it an uppercase "S", anyone else feel that way?" Hal said thoughtfully.

The rest of the team agreed with Molly asking. "Pawl, I guess there is nothing to stop us asking questions about the other races?"

"Nothing, though I am not sure how we can approach it easily. Anyway, time up folks. Let's go and meet Commander Meeax. A thought, Hal. Does the translator record conversations?"

"It does, Pawl, but not verbatim. It records new vocabulary and, what you might call, speech structures. It is intended to make it easier for future translation, if the system can recognise similar word orders and so on. I could change it so it does record entire conversations."

"Do it, but if asked just say it does that as part of its learning a new language. Okay?"

"You have it, Pawl."

With that final exchange ending the conversation, they all disembarked the Deimos. A little more used to the zero g conditions they were able to follow Ilgen off the deck, without assistance, and into a lift which took them upwards. Shortly after they found themselves being led into a large room where a number of Zeder officers were gathered around a table. Officer Ilgen came to attention and addressed the one, apparent, female.

"Commander, this is Captain Jaeger, human officer in command of the ship we apprehended earlier and his crew."

Commander Meeax turned to them with an expression that had it been human might have been a grimace. "Thank you, Ilgen, that will be all for now."

"Captain, thank you for joining us. I apologise for my officer's term "apprehended". It suggests that you were guilty of some crime or misdeed. Being propelled into a restricted area without a choice was hardly your fault. It is how the defensive systems work with a ship that does not identify itself with current codes."

"No offence taken, Commander. We did wonder when we exited the gateway if something had happened as we could no longer track the messenger drone we were following."

"You are correct. The messenger carried codes which, despite being hundreds of years old, were still recognised by the gate systems. It was able to finish its mission without challenge. That was fortunate, Captain, as it contained information that indicated that the humans on Gyder, as our records referred to the planet, were of an advanced civilisation but did not appear to reflect any link with the Pindats. The mystery for us was how you had reached the system. We were not aware of another gateway in that location."

"Commander," Pawl decided to approach the matter carefully, only providing the minimum information at this point since it seemed that Meeax had not been fully briefed. "I cannot say if there is another such gateway since our interstellar ship does not use that means of travel. Are you saying that the gateways are a natural phenomenon? I admit we assumed that they must be artificial."

"No. They are artificial. Our records of that system are some hundreds of years old and it might have been that there were two gateways one of which had been left open. That would have allowed you to access the system without knowing of the gateway we must traverse until the messenger opened it."

"I understand. Commander, I apologise if my question is inappropriate. While on Zent we learned that the gateway had last been opened hundreds of years ago having been built as an escape route from a fleet of Pindats who were beaten by

233

you in a war. Now you refer to us as not being linked with such a species and you still seem to remain on a war footing even now."

"Captain, those are reasonable questions for the future but, Commander, we have little time to prepare." Sugnay interrupted.

The Commander responded with what seemed like reluctance. "Adzly, you are correct, of course. Captain, I am sure that we will have time to take this further but my Deputy is right. We must leave orbit for the gateway and we need to find a way to protect any of your craft that might be operating in the system. Your crew are welcome to remain here for the moment but may I invite you to join us on the bridge when we get underway?"

"I would be honoured, Commander."

"Good." She looked to another of her officers. "Leader Hafzen, please ensure our guests are made welcome, Perhaps, you and they can make a start on that second problem."

"Commander." The younger officer stiffened as he acknowledged the order as Meeax and the other officers left the room accompanied by Pawl.

Hidecki decided that a good start would be to introduce himself and the team as they had largely been ignored.

"Leader Hafzen, perhaps I should introduce myself and my colleagues. I am Lieutenant Hidecki Yamata, this is Ensign Molly Piper and this is our Communications officer,

Hal Thomson. That all sounds a little formal but we would be happy to be called by our first names."

"Thank you, Hidecki is your first name?" Hafzen seemed a little overcome by his responsibility for handling a part of a first contact.

"That's right. It's Hidecki, Molly and Hal."

"My informal name is Zaster." The translator struggled for a moment before reproducing the sound almost as it had sounded when the Zeder spoke.

During the next hour the four questioned each other about what was known about the human craft and how the Guardians might react.

When they were taking a short break from problem solving. Molly took the chance to quiz Zaster about the Seven. It seemed that Zaster was something of an expert in the history of the Seven and that was why Meeax had chosen him for the task.

"Zaster, we keep hearing your colleagues talk of the Seven but have only met your own species, Zeder and a second race, Hokaj. Can you tell us much about the other five?"

Zaster was eager to talk about the other races and explained at some length that the Seven had incorporated all the space travelling races known to the Zeder and each other. There were four warm blooded species including Zeder and Hokaj and two cold blooded ones. The other warm species as he referred to them were the Yyonsy and Ush while the two cold ones were Aash and Voin.

"But that is only six." Molly queried. "When we were with your commander on Zent we were told of a seventh, the Bedev?"

The young officer looked amazed. "No one mentions them now."

"But why, if they are one of the Seven."

"Because they are no more. In the war with the Pindat fleet their world was destroyed when they tried to negotiate a peace and failed. The Bedev are extinct."

There was a stunned silence on behalf of the humans before Hans said. "None of them escaped? How? Could no survivors be rescued?"

"Our history tells us that the Pindats had breached the gateway from the Bedev system and were only beaten when their lead squadrons were cut off by the Zeder commander destroying the gateway cutting the fleet in to two segments. Even then it took many years to completely eliminate the Pindat fleet that had transited the gateway. The Bedev system is or was the furthest from our cluster, nearly two hundred of your light years away. There were two Zeder ships in that system and they could only watch as the Bedev home was destroyed. The second ship commanded by the fleet admiral ordered the first to escape through the gateway ahead of the Pindats, giving just enough warning to allow the defenders to react. The second ship turned away from this part of the galaxy to draw the rest of the Pindats in the wrong direction.

So long has passed that either the Pindats were hurt too badly by the loss of so many ships to continue the war or the fleet admiral was successful or maybe both. In any case we cannot take the chance that they might return and every gateway is guarded by ships such as the Eeeedle."

"You have remained on a war footing for hundreds of years? Surely not in case an enemy you have beaten returns?" Molly was incredulous.

"I guess not really. We just have a navy with a few ships in each system. Not enough to fight but maybe we could cut the gateways to slow their progress if they attacked again."

The conversation moved back to trying to find a solution to the problem of the Guardians. In the end they had one solution. They did not like it but decided that it was all they had.

Shortly afterwards Pawl returned to the room, escorted by another of the bridge officers who indicated that he would leave them and that Zaster was also to leave. That surprised Pawl but, at the same time, it meant that he and his crew would be able to talk without being overheard, if they were careful.

Indicating that they should gather closely around the table he said.

"Let's keep this a quiet conversation. We may be alone but that does not mean there is no eavesdropping going. Have you come up with any ideas?"

Hidecki replied. "We have one idea but we don't know if it is feasible."

"Go on."

"Zaster suggested that the Guardians would be likely to target active probes and any craft that were under power. We can't do anything about the various probes already launched but, I thought, if we can spot Phoebe from inside the gate, can we send a message that would get them to cut all power and make like a rock."

"That's not a bad idea but it does rely on the crew reacting without question and that is something we cannot expect them to do. Having said that, and I wouldn't want our hosts to realise that it is possible, I outrank any of the crew likely to be in control. Using Deimos' computer, I may be able to use the security protocols to tell the Phoebe computer that its captain is no longer authorised to take any action until I order it to accept his or her commands. If I include orders to shut down the engines and life support, Phoebe turns into a rock. That only works, though, if the craft is in open space and not on approach to Eden or Selene."

"Why not then?" Hal queried.

"Emergency overrides would block the command since the computer would see the orders as placing the craft in danger of crashing."

"How long do we have?" Molly asked the practical question.

"We are an hour from entering the gateway and it will take around ten hours for the Eeeedle to transit. Quicker than our journey the other way but the ship will be under power. Now what else have you learnt?"

In turn the team explained about how the Seven were in fact only six civilisations and that the Bedev were extinct according to Zaster's knowledge of the history of the war against the Pindat fleet.

"Could this be the same fleet that attacked Earth?" Pawl asked.

"It seems unlikely." replied Molly. "Zaster appeared convinced that the Pindat ships were manned by organic beings similar to insects. He seemed genuinely horrified by the idea of a fleet of killer machines."

"Well, given that the Seven appear to have retained a war footing for hundreds of years just in case. I suppose he would be."

"If they really are maintaining their navy as a defence against such a return - it does seem a little paranoid." Stefan commented.

"I wonder how many gateways are in this system, we know about the one to Eden but there must be at least one more since it seems that none of the Seven has developed an FTL drive. They might have developed ships capable of reaching a significant percentage of light speed and in a cluster like this such journeys might well be feasible."

"When they built the gateways, I wonder how they managed it. Did they open a wormhole and then send a ship through with the ability to set up a gate at the other end? And if they did, how did they aim it?"

Deciding that that was also one for the future, Pawl went to the door and, not to his surprise, found a member of the crew outside. Calling Hal over with the translator he asked if they could visit their craft and then talk with Commander Meeax. The crew member nodded and spoke swiftly via a communicator before indicating that they should follow him.

A little while later they were back in the comfort of the Deimos. Pawl rapidly programmed the computer with a message to be despatched to the Phoebe. He had only just finished when Adzly appeared and asked if he could come aboard.

After exchanging greetings Pawl explained that they believed a message from himself instructing the crew of any craft to cut power and life support until they received a second message might work.

Adzly queried why they would do that, but when Pawl pointed out that he was senior to any officers likely to be piloting any craft operating off planet, he nodded his understanding. He asked Pawl to pre-record his message so that the Eeeedle's computer could be programmed to send it the instant they were near enough to the system for the message to reach into the system. His mission completed, he simply apologised to the other members of the team before inviting Pawl to join him on the bridge as an observer when they exited the gateway near Eden.

After he had left, Pawl indicated that food and rest were now priorities. "I'm sure you all have other questions that we may need to consider but, as we cannot do anything more at the minute, it is more important that we are fresh and ready for action once we get home."

***   ***   ***

In due course, Adzly himself returned.

"Captain, Pawl, we are approaching the end of the wormhole and it is bridge time."

With that the two headed off leaving the rest of the team on board Deimos to await news.

Hidecki made the point the others, though, had not thought of. "We need to activate our long-range sensors. They must be ready for the return to n-space and to try find Phoebe, if the craft is off planet."

"Do we need to find them? Could we not send a general signal rather than one targeted?" Hal, not a technical person, sounded quite confused.

Hidecki explained. "The message content is such that we need to send a narrow beam aimed at Phoebe if we can. If we don't find the craft, which, if it is off-planet, we assume will be somewhere between the gateway and Eden, Pawl has authorised me to make the decision, if there is nothing between the two, to switch format to a more general band width. There is one thing we can't be sure about. Will our sensors penetrate the docking bay doors! Let's hope it doesn't come to that."

An hour later, Hidecki's communicator pinged and he activated Deimos' systems.

Twenty minutes later the system confirmed that it had found Phoebe and Hidecki sent the message. "It will take another ten minutes to reach the craft, then another ten before we can know if it worked."

He had looked at Hal, who grinned. "It's okay, Hidecki, I do understand about the delays over the distances involved!"

"They are going to have one hell of a shock when the systems shut down!" Molly grimaced. "I wouldn't want that to happen to me."

Suddenly the Deimos shuddered. "What was that?" Hal cried.

"No idea, but looking outside it seems that the whole of the Eeeedle suffered the same impact."

Over the next hour or so there were several similar shocks and after the second one Hidecki ordered his colleagues to suit up. "Just in case."

Shortly afterwards Pawl, looking badly shaken, arrived together with another junior officer from the bridge who departed quickly.

"Is everyone okay?" Following affirmative nods, Pawl continued. "We were just completing our transit when the ship came under heavy fire from two of the planets closest to the gateway. Some form of energy beams."

"Serious damage?" Hidecki asked.

"Some, the ship has a form of defensive screen which is able to dissipate most of the incoming energy, but the first two strikes hit the Eeeedle's main weaponry before they could engage the screen and it no longer has the ability to fight back. Coded messages have been sent to Guardian One but it will only just have received them and, you can guess, it will take even more time before any stand down instructions can be delivered to the various stations around the system. Assuming, of course, that the codes are still valid."

"What is happening now?" Molly asked. "Are we still under attack?"

"Yes, though the initial attacks are lessening in strength as we move further from the gate. Commander Meeax is intending to get as close to Eden as she can before delivering us and the diplomatic team to the planet. If the attacks are continuing, she intends to return to the gate and transit back to Zent for repairs and to, I presume, return with a stronger and better prepared fleet able to hold off the Guardians while finding the correct codes to take them off a war footing."

"What about Phoebe? Our sensors found her and sent the message you asked me to send in case they did not identify that one direct from the Eeeedle."

"Good. One of the messages worked. We are closing on the craft now. It is still moving towards Eden but is showing almost no heat signature at all."

"I was thinking. This diplomatic team. They know that we don't actually have anywhere to put them up, don't they? I mean a mission, as it were." Hal had a practical attitude.

"I understand that the "embassy" will only comprise Sugnay and a team of five. I'm sure that we will be able to find space for six."

"I may be a little cynical but someone has moved very quickly back on Zeder. I wonder why we are seen as so important." Hidecki looked thoughtful.

"You mean why do the Zeder feel such a need to beat the other species in a race to gain a foothold here and a relationship with humans?"

"Something like that. Or is this the first stage in reclaiming the planet for Zeder itself."

"The thought had crossed my mind. Truth is, if they want to do so, there is little to stop them from kicking us off the planet. Rightly or wrongly, I got the impression from the Commander that Zent is still only sparsely populated and the Zeder really don't want another system to defend. Her words not mine!" Pawl seemed rather depressed at the thought.

"That seems rather odd." Molly mused. "Eden was prepared, to use their words, some hundreds of their years ago. If that was the position that long ago, why has Zent remained so lightly populated?"

"That's a good question. Apart from what Calri had to say about it we don't know enough. I wonder how many systems are linked via their gateways. Are there more than they can properly colonise, perhaps?" Hidecki commented.

"Maybe but there are six potential species as far as we know and, presumably, that excludes any non-space faring civilisations. How would they handle first contact in those cases?" Hal interrupted.

"It strikes me that we have more questions than answers at the moment, so we'll leave it there. We need to be ready to assist with the recovery of Phoebe." Pawl drew matters to a close and the team settled down with a meal as they waited.

***   ***   ***

Back on Eden, Helga and Anton looked on in horror at recorded videos from the satellite long range sensors which showed the attacks on the sensor packs and on the alien ship as it made its exit from the gate.

"What is going on? I thought the gateway was generated by the local system presumably by the Guardians. Surely the returning ship has to be friendly?" Anton became more confused the longer they watched.

Sitting behind them Jenny came to a conclusion she did not want to make. "If this ship is not of the designers then maybe it is a hostile. Those beams clearly packed a punch but the ship does not seem to have suffered any significant damage. At least not enough to stop it. I think we should evacuate the town. Get people to scatter into the fields and woods. At least until we know more."

"What about Phoebe? We need to be here in case they contact us." Helga highlighted one concern.

"I will stay," said Jenny. "You were right, Helga, you couldn't have launched in time and it looks as if it is going to be dangerous enough up there. Now go, clear the area."

***   ***   ***

On board Phoebe it was quiet. Lack of life support had meant that all were suited up with helmets closed. Although communication via the suit radios was easy enough, Rob had deemed it wiser to rest and use less oxygen. "It shouldn't be a problem given how fast that ship is catching up but we have to accept that it might not be interested in helping us."

Eventually Stefan stirred. Closer to one of the monitor screens he had a better view of the external sensor feedback which had suddenly stopped showing the surrounding starfield.

"Rob, I think they have caught us. Something is blocking our sensor scan."

"That is faster than we might have expected. Everyone, get ready. I suspect we can expect a boarding party of some form."

He was correct, of course. What they did not expect to see was a single entity in a human spacesuit.

"Who are you?" his startled cry over the radio brought the unexpected sound of Pawl's voice answering.

246

"Permission to come aboard, Captain?"

"Not sure I have the authority to stop you, sir. I have been relieved of command. By you, it seems. I mean, it is you, Pawl, isn't it? The last we saw of the Deimos was as it fell into that wormhole."

"It is me and we are all okay. I will tell you more later."

"So that message relieving me from command really was from you?"

"Rob, sorry about that. We were warned that any craft in action off planet could be a target for the Guardian's defence systems should they activate as we started to complete our transit of the gateway."

"Defence systems? Activate? Attack systems more like. They took out the sensor packs we placed to check on the wormhole location and the two planets closest too it. We'd picked the right place all right. Then the hole opens and soon after but before the alien ship arrives - wham! No sensors."

"Tell me about it, Rob. We took heavy fire just as we returned to n-space from the gateway. Destroyed the ship's own weapons before they could utilise their shield. Now look, we can exchange briefings later. I need to give you back command and your power. Then you'll need to keep station with the Eeeedle until we reach orbit. I must go back to the Deimos, ready to launch at the same time. We will have a small party of Zeder on board. A diplomatic mission. The Eeeedle will return to the gateway with the intent to go home and get repairs before returning."

"What about off planet activity in the meantime? Surely they have the ability to stand down the Guardians from this hostile status?"

"They hope so but have not had contact with them for hundreds of their years. They do have some doubts it seems. Again, that is for the future."

With that Pawl turned to the command seat and started giving the Phoebe's computer new instructions. A few minutes later the life support came back on as did the engines.

"All yours, Rob. Keep at around three quarters power. The Eeeedle will modify its own pace to match you. See you on the ground." And with that Pawl was gone.

"That was short and sort of sweet." Petra said as she popped her helmet open. "Are we going to remain suited or can we take them off, Rob."

"I think it would be best to keep them on for the minute but with helmets open. I don't much like the idea that we might take a ricochet if the Zeder ship should come under attack again. From what we saw if they were to hit us direct it won't matter if we have suits on or not."

"That's not the most comforting of thoughts." Hans muttered.

In the end the last two days of the journey went without incident and in due course the Phoebe and Deimos both landed safely on Eden. Even as they were disembarking, Commander Meeax signalled the departure of the Eeeedle.

Helga and Anton were back in Yablon, at the front of the crowd, waiting to welcome back the two teams and the small party of Zeder, who accompanied Pawl and his team.

20.   A Second First Contact

On the Einstein, a day after the rescue, Scott sought entry to the bridge. To John's surprise his, usually taciturn, engineer was quite excited.

"What's up, Scott?"

"We believe we have identified the aliens' propulsion type and you aren't going to believe it. I know I needed to double check everything several times, myself."

"Scott, you know my engineering skills are limited. Tell me."

"They have a warp drive that seems to operate only at the rear. I mean it does not seem to have a front torus."

"Are you sure?"

"Yes. Look the damage caused by the other ship's net was bad but it didn't, fortunately, cause a rupture of the power source. If it had there would have been no distress call and no ship left. We only identified it when the sensors were set up to monitor the various heat signatures and found an energy source similar to our own."

"Of course," John realised that he had overlooked the importance of that part of the call. "Their message stated that their star drive was no longer functional. Sorry I assumed that you had heard a recording. It might have helped your investigation. Having said that I wonder if there is any evidence that there was a forward torus - one that they might have jettisoned. Whatever. You'd better get Alan Piper involved. If a warp drive could work using a single torus it would mean that we might have to revise our understanding of the whole process."

"To be honest, John, I doubt that hearing a recording would have helped but we are now fairly sure we know how they could be signalling on a level that we could intercept, even if it doesn't explain how it could trigger our sensors in the way it did. They certainly had power available, just no engines to use it."

"Best to keep an eye on the ship then. We've no reason to expect trouble but let us be ready to greet our guests if they should wake."

"Aye, Captain."

***   ***   ***_

Three hours later.

"Engineering to Bridge. Captain, something is happening on board the Anthezedo. It looks as if they are waking up." Scott's voice showed excited concern.

"On my way, Scott." John acknowledged his chief engineer. "Comms, make sure Dr Carden and his team are on their way as well. Lieutenant Cheung, you have the com." Leaving the command seat John headed for the docking bays as fast as possible.

A short while later he reached the main entrance to bay four, to find Scott and Will Carden waiting. "What's happening?

Scott outlined the events of the past hour or so. "When we decided that we could not manage to access the ship without damaging it we left the bay but before we did, we set up motion sensors programmed to respond to any changes in the life signatures, increased heat or movement. About an hour ago they were triggered by an increase in the heat signatures. Then twenty minutes ago the motion sensor recorded movement. For some reason they appear to be coming out of stasis."

"Right, do we have adequate coverage so we can see any access opening, wherever it is?" John was thinking rapidly as to how to greet any aliens who might exit the ship. He was a conscious that they might be armed and nervous given the events back in the system. "Comms, do we have a translation of our first contact message in the language of the distress call?" he asked.

Teri responded. Why am I not surprised, he thought? "Just finished it, Captain. One thing, sir, this language was number seven on the list, as it were. Almost as if it was an afterthought by the Guardian."

"Okay, Teri. Please ask Comms to broadcast the message on the same wavelength, that their distress call used, to the ship. Just as a matter of course, if that is the seventh language, are we in a position to use a translation programme yet?"

"It might be a bit basic, sir. But then again that's likely to be true of all the languages at first. Should I bring a tablet down?"

"Yes, Teri, thank you. Right, Scott, Doctor. Now we watch and wait."

Over the next hour the sensors recorded increased movement within the ship, although a significant proportion of the beings on board did appear to be remaining in stasis. Teri, duly arrived, and with some excitement was able to tell John that one of her colleagues had found a "title" in each package of language data that appeared to have no purpose except to identify the language.

"We think that it is there to tell us which species uses that language. I had already, without realising it, named the first language as for a species called Zeder. This one appears to be for a species called Bedev."

Almost as she finished speaking Scott gasped and pointed at one of the monitors. As they watched a side of the ship appeared to vanish and a number of individual beings stepped out, looking carefully around the docking bay. To John's initial dismay two appeared to be armed with some form of hand weapon then, after what seemed to be a short conversation between two of the others, the weapons disappeared.

"I think that now is the time to make an entrance." John made the decision. "Just you and me, Scott, initially. We need to be aware that our relative size may be seen as threatening, so no quick movements."

"Captain, I feel I should be with you. I can run the translation software better if I can hear them speaking." Teri grinned. "And I am a little smaller!"

"Okay, but I make the point again - no sudden moves." John led the way to a side entrance to the bay area, speaking on his communicator to Ellen, suggesting that she might be needed in the conference room shortly.

Careful as they were, their appearance clearly caused a degree of consternation among those by the ship. Then, two of the taller ones slowly moved forwards and John understood even more the physical differences. These were the tallest of the group but were still, he estimated, less than a metre tall.

When they reached, what he assumed they considered, a safe distance from the humans they stopped and one started to speak. It took a few moments before the translator held by Teri reacted.

"Who are you? What ship is this?"

"I am John Lees, Captain of this ship, the Einstein. This is Chief Engineer Scott Bailey and, with our translation software, Teri Larding."

Again, there was some initial consternation as the tablet responded in the language of the Bedev but they recovered quickly.

"We do not recognise your species. How did you find us?"

Not the most forthcoming of people, John thought. Just questions. "We are known as humans or Terrans. We intercepted your distress call and responded as we felt we should. To whom am I speaking?" After a further moment of delay, he continued. "I regret that this is the first time we have used your language. It may be that some words are incorrect."

There was again a little delay before the leader responded.

"I am captain of the Anthezedo. I am called Fagoc Cless. Our distress call should only have been heard by one of our fellow ships, how could you hear it?"

"Captain, your message triggered our ship sensors while we were in warp space. We do not understand how but we were able to translate it. We were approximately half a light year away."

"What is a light year?"

"It is the distance light travels in one orbit of our home planet around its sun. In warp space we can, as I believe your ship can, exceed this universal limit."

"You cannot exceed the universal limit. Our engines can accelerate us to nine tenths of that limit quickly but no other species can do this. And none can exceed the universal limit. You are not one of the Seven, as we were."

"Captain, we clearly have much to discuss, but first, do any of your crew need medical attention? It is possible that our medical people could assist you."

"We have injured crew but they remain in stasis. I would rather that they be treated by our own kind."

"Understood, perhaps you and your fellow officers would like to accompany us to a more suitable place to talk. Please bring refreshments with you if you wish. Until we understand each other better, it might be wise."

"Captain." Fagoc nodded and turned to one of his fellows and spoke rapidly. That one moved quickly back into their ship and vanished for a few moments before returning with two bags.

While the conversation had been going on John was aware that Teri had been talking quietly on her communicator. With a raised eyebrow he raised an unspoken question.

Teri grinned, she does seem to enjoy life to the full, he thought. "Sorry, Captain. I thought it would be a good idea to organise things to make it a bit more comfortable for our guests. The conference room should be ready by the time we get there."

Fagoc interrupted. "Captain, we are ready."

"Come this way." John replied. "Scott, leave two of your people on standby here to help if needed. Teri, with me."

The journey to the conference room took a good fifteen minutes and it was apparent that Fagoc and his three colleagues were impressed by the sheer size of the Einstein.

In due course, they reached their destination. On entering the room John was pleased to see that Ellen was already present and two junior crew were just leaving by the side door. At first wondering why they had been there, he then smiled recognising Teri's clever thinking. A temporary dais held four children's chairs from the ship's school room, where youngsters had been training on the journey from Earth. An ideal size for their guests who had already recognised the thoughtfulness of being provided with furniture that was more suited to them as Fagoc said.

Ellen had managed to don her old dress uniform and John felt he could introduce her accordingly.

"Captain Cless, may I introduce Admiral Bayman. The Admiral is the leader of humans in this part of the galaxy."

"A pleasure to meet you, Captain." Ellen's voice caused the captain to step backwards a little but he recovered his poise quickly enough.

"I am honoured to meet you, <Dengen>." He responded, although the term of, presumably, respect was beyond the translation software.

"Please be seated," Ellen answered indicating the relevant chairs before turning to John. "Captain Lees, this is your party, please carry on."

"As you wish, ma'am." John smiled again before sitting down opposite the Bedev captain. They had to be Bedev, he thought, the language is translating too easily.

"Fagoc, I would like to understand how you came to be in such difficulty and to learn more about your people and how we can help in taking you, perhaps, to a safe place. You need to understand that we are already on what might be a rescue mission. One of our craft fell into a wormhole which seems to have been generated by an artificial intelligence in the system that we have settled in. We do believe that we have identified the system at the other end of the wormhole. We are still six light years away from there or about nine days - our time. I am sorry I do not have any numbers that might compare our numbers with yours."

"John, if I may, I am concerned that you seem to have, possibly, become involved with the Zeder. If you would, please explain how this has happened."

John thought for a moment before glancing towards Ellen. She understanding his unspoken question, nodded.

"The story is a long one, Fagoc. Would you like a break for food and drink? Or we can work through a meal."

Fagoc nodded. "We should work on if that is acceptable to you."

Over the next two hours John told the story of the Einstein, its escape from the Solar System, the devastating attack that destroyed the Earth and the various adventures and losses that had occurred before they found Eden. It was clear that the description of the attack on the Earth stunned Fagoc and his colleagues who were, so far as he could tell, almost distraught. Despite that, they remained silent until John had explained the most recent events in the Eden system and expanded on how the Einstein had been in a position to provide assistance.

"Captain Lees, John, the wormhole that you speak of. It opened as an AI messenger transited and you lost a small craft into the hole?" Fagoc spoke slowly and carefully, choosing his words with obvious care.

"Yes."

"Firstly, your craft will be able to complete its journey through the gateway. The gateway is an artificial construct and will lead to another system, as you appear to have identified. Your people are safe. The species at the other end will be concerned that a craft not of their making has made that transit. We have no love for the Zeder, for reasons I will explain later, but they are not hostile to newcomers once they understand that they are not an immediate threat. It is likely that one of their defender class ships will be sent to investigate a system that would seem to have been ignored by them for hundreds of years. If that is the case, you may find that your craft has already been taken back to your new home."

"You mentioned that you have no love for the "Zeder", why is that? And how do you know that they will be at the other end of the wormhole?"

"The Zeder control the entire network of gateways, although it is likely that one or more of the Seven, as we call them, will also be in each system, the Zeder's control extends to allowing only their own ships to use the network. We will tell you our own history in a while, John, but I am sorry that we need to rest. Stasis was a necessary action in the circumstances but it drains the energy from our bodies and it takes time for us to recover from that. We should return to our ship. May we meet again in, I estimate, twice the time we have been here?"

It was clear that the Bedev were struggling with fatigue and John agreed, arranging for them to be escorted back to the docking bay and their ship. After they were gone, he turned to Ellen.

"If that's a first contact why am I concerned more about future ones?"

Ellen smiled. "Probably best if we get some food and rest."

"It's a good idea but I need to take over on the bridge. Tung-Mei will need a break first. See you in a while." John left them to talk over the events of that morning.

***   ***   ***

John was on his way when his communicator pinged with a summons. "Captain to the bridge." Switching from a walk to a run he cut the time reaching the nearest lift and arrived on the bridge only a little out of breath.

"Captain on the bridge." He was pleased to see that only Tung-Mei moved, forsaking the command chair for the first officer's station before reporting.

"Captain, we have cut power to around half warp one. Forward sensors have identified a system about a light year from us which has evidence of intelligent life. In fact, there appear to be a number of spaceships in formation on the outer edge of the system. Should we drop out of warp?"

"Tracking, is the system's sun the one that we are seeking?"

"No, sir. We have been able to confirm that that system is still about five light years away."

"Helm, how close will our bubble get?"

"Too close, sir. Not sure how we would affect an actual ship but on current heading there is a least a risk of an impact."

Judy continued. "I would recommend a slight deviation, perhaps five degrees starboard now. It will only lose us a few hours in time."

John considered his options and decided that they could not afford any further delay. "We've lost enough time already. We can consider stopping here on the way back to Eden. Helm, five degrees starboard and return to warp five, back to our previous course as and when you deem it safe. Tracking, make sure we have a complete scan of those ships as we pass, as much detail as you can manage."

Turning to Tung-Mei. "Anything else? If not, go get some rest, I'll need you back in four hours."

With nothing to add to the reason for the summons, Tung-Mei headed off bridge pleased that John was looking to avoid any further delay in finding the Deimos and her partner.

***   ***   ***

Back on Eden, it was time for introductions and Pawl started the process, triggering Hal's translation software.

"Sugnay, our Mayors, Helga Nielson and Anton Tyler. Helga, Anton, Deputy Commander Sugnay Adzly. The Deputy Commander has been seconded to Eden as diplomatic representative of the Zeder, whose ship brought us back home.

"Welcome, Deputy Commander." Helga took the lead for the moment. "Perhaps you would introduce your colleagues"

"A pleasure, Mayor Nielson. Firstly, my deputy, Leader Zaster Hafzen. My junior officers, Officer Senior Calri Adzly and Officer Senior Binhal Hullint. We are also accompanied by our medical officer, Alldo Zardn and Leader Hafzen's partner - Finfal Jafzen."

"You are all welcome. Please come with us for some refreshments. If you prefer to use your own supplies please do so. We will need to check if our food is edible for you." Anton took the chance get involved.

"Thank you, Mayor Tyler. We will approach that process with a degree of caution but according to my historical experts, who include Leader Hafzen, the food obtained from this world was acceptable some four hundred of your years ago. There is no reason that that should have changed in any great way in what is ecologically a short time."

The small crowd that had gathered to greet the returning ships started to disperse allowing the Mayors, Pawl and the Zeder deputation to walk the short distance to the town hall.

Jenny managed, finally, to get Rob to herself. Looking at him she struggled to hold her tears back.

"A perfectly safe trip! Straightforward! Drop the sensors and come home! Remind me to believe you next time you look to go off planet. Rob, do you realise what it has been like back here? Not just me but Petra's family and Stefan's partner."

"Jen, I'm sorry but we are home now, safe and sound. I tried to get us back quicker when the wormhole opened, we were just a little too far and then Pawl killed our systems to make us look like a rock, I mean I couldn't do anything else, love."

"I shall be having words with that guy just as soon as he gets out from the shelter of those - Zeder, did they say?"

"Jen, please, let's just go home for now. Where's Evie?"

"She's with the other babes, being looked after by the Chans. They're running a bit of a part-time creche." The tears finally came. "Rob, I've been so scared. What really happened out there?"

Rob moved to hug her. It was a while before she released him.

"I wish I could tell you more. All I know is that the arrival of the Zeder ship caused the Guardians to instigate a defence programme. The ship survived but was damaged. Pawl had been warned of the possibility as the stand down codes would have taken time to reach Guardian One. The Zeder also believed that any of our active ships would be targeted. Hence the "make-like-a-stone" order. We will never know now, of course."

"But what about Pawl and his team? They must know more, surely."

"Of course. There is to be an initial briefing later, once the Zeders are settled in to their temporary quarters. And, if the Chans can continue to babysit, we are both invited. Before that let's go home, Jen."

That evening a select group gathered in a room near to the engineering centre to receive a lengthy presentation from Pawl, supported by his crew.

The story took some time and left his audience initially dumbstruck. Then the questions came swiftly.

Eventually, Jenny managed to get recognised by Helga and asked her question.

"Pawl, do you know how far away that system is? You didn't say."

"It's about fifteen light years and based on what Einstein reported back to Eden it is the system seen through the gateway. We are guessing that they will arrive in another fifteen to twenty days. The Zeder did find it difficult to believe that she will be exceeding, what they call, the universal limit. Rob, still talking to me?"

There were a few nervous chuckles.

"Just about, Pawl, let's say I'm giving you the benefit of the doubt. For the moment. You spoke of two species. The Zeder and the Hokaj. You also suggested that you felt that there was a degree of tension between them. At the same time, you also referred to a third race of beings, the Bedev, who are apparently extinct."

"Yessss. And your question?"

"The Zeder said that the Bedev were extinct and had claimed to have a starship capable of exceeding the speed of light but had never proved it. If they did, how do they know that they are extinct?"

"Their history says that one of their ships saw the Bedev home world destroyed and the gateway leading to the Bedev system had to be destroyed to stop the invaders. I guess, what you are suggesting is - how do they know, if they can't reach the system through a gateway and don't have FTL capability themselves?"

"It does occur to me that it is an assumption. Having said that, if some of them had survived and had FTL capability, why haven't they appeared in another system of the Seven?"

"And that's the sixty-four-thousand-dollar question, as we used to say," laughed Pawl.

"What about the Hokaj datafile?" It was Stefan who posed that question.

"It's with Hal and the language team. All I can say at the moment is that they think that they have a match but, if it is the correct match, then the language has evolved somewhat over the last few hundred years or so and that will make translating it harder. They hope to have cracked it by tomorrow night but aren't promising. Please, everyone, don't talk about that file outside of this room. We do not, as yet, need the Zeder to overhear. And before you say they don't understand English we don't yet know how good their translation equipment is."

Helga drew the meeting to a close with a promise. "As soon as we have the results from Hal and the team we will reconvene."

***   ***   ***

The next morning, Helga and Pawl met with Sugnay and his team and arranged for them to be given a tour of the settlement. Pawl also asked after the Eeeedle.

"The ship left orbit during the dark. Fortunately, the Guardian has stood down and its attacks have ceased. Commander Meeax told me, before their departure, that she does not anticipate any difficulty in reaching the gateway and returning to Zent. They will return as soon as repairs are completed."

"Sugnay, our satellites will be monitoring their transit, we have programmed them to record any changes in the gateway. If you wish to watch you will be very welcome. It will, of course, not happen for a few days."

"That would be good, Pawl. I have never seen a warship enter a gateway. It is, I think, a rare occurrence."

21.   An Upgrade for the Human Race

Across the system, briefly on the other side of the star, Guardian One continued to analyse the events of the past few orbits of its back up Two.

The humans had a ship capable of exceeding the universal limit - that was clear. That information had triggered long buried coding embedded by its designers. Such ability raised the status of such a race of beings above that of any others who might use the gateway network but who did not have their own FTL capability.

The Guardian was not a sentient being. Its analysis took the equivalent of several human lifetimes to complete but it finally came to the only conclusion its programming allowed.

It sent two messages.

The first to the gateway mechanism instructing it to transmit details of the humans throughout the network. The message process, while not instantaneous, used a method, unknown to any of the Seven or the humans, and meant that every Guardian throughout the network received the data within a few orbits of the Guardian's planet, now known to humans as Heira. If anyone had been watching those gateways that were closed, they might have seen an exceptional sight - the gateways flickering open for a few nanoseconds, as the message passed through, before closing again.

The second message to its fellow AI on Eden used more routine signals and took almost as long as the first. It was however shorter. Guardian Two was reactivated and instructed to make itself available to the humans but to no-one else.

Those actions complete, the Guardian recognised that momentous events were about to occur. Somewhere in the network there was a system with sentient beings related to the designers. Once raised from dormancy, future actions would be for them to decide on but, as the instigator of the news, it felt both satisfaction and excitement - emotions that should have been alien to it and would now take many more orbits to analyse.

22. A Dangerous Mistake

Two days passed without incident and the Zeder deputation seemed to settle in, mixing well with the humans despite the language difficulties. Stefan and his team were working hard on producing a miniature version of the linguists' tablets which would use remote linkage to provide at least some basic speech. The equivalent equipment that Sugnay and his team already had, also managed basic words learned during the time that Pawl and his team had been on Zent.

On the third day, Helga called at the embassy, as it had rapidly been called, to invite Sugnay and the others to join her to watch satellite images of the Eeeedle's approach to the gateway.

Two hours later live pictures, only delayed by the distance, began appearing on the screen set up for monitoring purposes. The swirling colours of the gateway dominated until the dark shadow of the Zeder ship started to eclipse the view. As it made its final approach two smaller craft appeared, one either side of the Eeeedle.

The two shuttles, as Binhal identified them, arced away heading towards the two planets still in alignment with the gate. In a clearly timed action, as they closed, multiple objects appeared.

Everyone turned towards Sugnay, as he stuttered. "They've fired missiles! What does Meeax think she is doing? Attacking Guardian locations! The Guardian has stood down. There's no reason."

"Father, look, the planetary units have responded." Calri's cry brought their attention back to the screen.

The watchers caught their breath as light beams erupted from the planets. The missiles proved of no value exploding as waves of heat swept them aside and seconds later both shuttles vanished in explosions of energy.

"Oh deity!" Binhal erupted. "How could she? They don't have the defensive screens of the ship!"

Attention was locked on the screen as they watched spellbound. The beams switched their targeting to the Eeeedle but, as expected, its shields were able to reflect them without apparent damage. The beams winked out as if the local automatic systems recognised that the energy was being wasted and the Eeeedle began to enter the gateway. Then…

"The gate, its closing. I don't believe it! The ship hasn't finished entering." Rob was one of those in the group. To their horror the gate didn't close slowly but snapped shut as if it had never existed. All that was left was the rear half of the Eeeedle drifting as parts broke away.

Sugnay, whose complexion was dark purple at the best of times, seemed to darken even further. His words caused a certain amount of difficulty for the translation software before it came out with some colloquial English. "The bloody fool. She always was impulsive but to do that. How many died for her stupidity?"

Rob was the first to respond. "Forget that for the moment. If the ship was at battle stations the different sections would have been sealed off, yes?"

270

Binhal nodded. Still in shock, he was unable to speak.

"Then we need to send a rescue mission. Helga, Pawl, we need to get Phoebe and Deimos launched now."

Helga blanched. "And get destroyed as well? You can't be serious, Rob."

"I don't believe the Guardian will attack them. Its local units only responded to an attack. Start broadcasting a message in English saying unarmed craft manned by human pilots are carrying out an attempt to save possible survivors from ship destroyed in gate closure."

Pawl had been evaluating the situation, while Rob spoke, before asking. "Sugnay, how many of the crew would be in that part of the ship?"

"Perhaps thirty or forty, it depends exactly where the break happened. They would have air for perhaps ten lights, if they conserve it."

"Then we must launch as soon as we can. But everyone must be volunteers. We will need two flight crew and two medics for each of the ships. I also want two shuttles to be in orbit around Eden ready for when we return, we may need to transfer people as the ships could be overloaded."

Binhal and Calri looked at each other before Calri spoke. "Captain, we are both medically trained. We wish to join the ships. Our knowledge of Zeder anatomy should help, if we are faced with injuries."

Pawl nodded. "Agreed. Now I can see others who are ready to go. I will select the rest. Helga, get your people to organise supplies. We can't delay and need to launch in thirty minutes. Rob, will the ships be ready?"

"They are already. They didn't need any significant work on either, since they returned, and the normal maintenance was completed yesterday."

As he turned to head for the door he ran headfirst into Jenny. "Where the hell do you think you are going? Another safe mission! And on your own again!"

"No, Jenny, it's not as safe as last time but it doesn't mean I can just avoid it. There are people dying out there and Pawl will need his best pilots."

"Good, then that's settled."

"Sorry?"

"I am going with you. There are only half a dozen qualified pilots and of those only Pawl and Hidecki have more experience than me. Hidecki isn't fit enough and Sophia is seven months gone. So, its Pawl and Stefan in Deimos and us in Phoebe." Jenny's voice might have been emotional but there was no mistaking the steely tone underlying her words. "And, before you ask, Helga will organise babysitting if the Chans can't continue looking after Evie."

Rob stood for a moment wondering how he might convince Jenny that she was wrong before realising that it didn't matter. He knew her well enough to know that once her mind was set nothing would stop her. Bowing to the inevitable

272

he replied, "Okay, I don't like it but I guess you're right and there really isn't anyone else. Let's move."

Much as he expected, Pawl had no difficulty with getting medical volunteers. Jenny was right, as he knew, fully qualified pilots were at a premium and, for this mission, using trainees, willing though they were, was not sensible. Thirty minutes later the two ships lifted from the ground and started their trips into orbit before using the planets spin to give them additional acceleration on the path to where the remnants of the Eeeedle were drifting.

On the ground Anton was repeating the message aimed towards Sol2 desperately hoping for a response from the Guardian at Heira to confirm that the rescue craft would be safe. It was almost an hour after the launch that he suddenly received an incoming message, not from Heira but from Guardian Two on Eden.

This is Guardian Two. I have been reactivated by Guardian One and am instructed to assist humans. I may not communicate with other races at this time.

Your craft will not be attacked. Our programming is to preserve organic life where it does not threaten our designers or ourselves. We recognise that your action in launching a rescue mission without knowing about its safety is in the same spirit that our designers admire.

We regret the actions that were necessary to keep the system secure. We do not know why the Zeder ship attacked our units after we had stood down from our defence mode. Guardian One is taking action to avoid a recurrence of such an event here or elsewhere in the network.

As the Guardian had said the two ships raced to the wrecked craft at full speed without drawing any direct action from the Guardian network. Passive sensors did in fact monitor both craft and identified the existence of two Zeder on board but the pilots were all human and that was enough for the ships to be allowed free rein.

It would take nine days but eventually the Phoebe and Deimos returned, a little more slowly, with the few survivors they could find. Despite Sugnay's hope that thirty or forty might have been saved the reality was much harsher with just seventeen Zeder being brought to Eden and five of those were in a critical condition. None of the five would survive.

23. Embargo

Guardian One might have felt some, what it understood were, emotions about the discovery of the humans but the actions of the Zeder ship as it attempted to transit from the system generated a cold, almost but not quite, fury.

The attack on its defensive posts had caused an automatic response which, without doubt, had led to the deaths of intelligent beings. While the killing of any organic life was contrary to its core programming this was overruled when it was directly under attack. Defence responses were designed to be no more than adequate but the ship had been able to defeat the units' beam weapons which had left only the auto closing of the gateway so as to ensure the safety of the next system in the network. That the ship was halfway across the entrance was not relevant. Guardian One would have preferred that its units could have stopped the ship before it reached the gate but that had not been possible. Gate mechanisms would eject that part of the ship already inside when it reached the other end.

The Guardian did not know what action might be taken at the next system but its analysis suggested that a fleet of similar ships might be deployed, large enough to overwhelm the protective structures in its own system. A further message was needed.

Using its own messaging process again, it sent orders to all Guardians. As an interim measure all military ships were to be barred from using the gateways. All Guardians were to advise the local intelligences of that decision. It also advised that humans were now under the protection of the network and local Guardians were to act accordingly.

Any permanent decision was outside its level of authorisation. Such authority was reserved to the sentients hidden somewhere in the network. The second message ensured that they would be properly briefed and able to take appropriate action.

24. Learning about Others

It had taken much longer than expected but finally, the day after the rescue mission returned, Hal called Pawl. "We have a translation. I'm sorry it has taken so long and I'm still not sure it's completely correct."

"Not to worry, Hal. We've been a little busy ourselves as you know. If you're ready let's go through it together." He thought for a moment. "Half an hour, at the engineering section, okay?"

"I will be there."

In that moment of thought it had occurred to Pawl that it might be wise to choose a location away from those frequented by Sugnay and his team, who, while occupied with looking after their fellows as they recovered from the events at the gateway, were often found exploring the settlement.

Thirty minutes later, he and Hal sat down to study the translation of the Hokaj document. "This looks a pretty comprehensive translation, Hal. I suppose two questions before we start. Why so long and why do you doubt the veracity of the English version?"

"Pawl, you know that we were given a database of languages which includes one which is a close match to the Hokaj?" as he nodded, he continued. "The answer to both your questions is really the same. Based on what we found out about the Guardian and how long it is since it was last active, the language database must be over four hundred years old. I am sure you know that languages evolve over time and this was our problem. In effect we had two versions of the same language. A simple translation using the historic data left huge gaps in the English version. So, we had to try and work out parts of the document using a contextual approach. If there was an English word that seemed to fit the gap then how did that translate into the older form. We then used the Hokaj word or words and tried to analyse what those words might have become over the centuries."

"A bit like a jigsaw then."

Hal laughed. "Yes, and you only have part of the picture! Where we still have any doubt, the text is underlined. Unfortunately, that means a lot of underlines."

"We had better get on, how long is it? Oh!" Pawl gasped at seeing the length. "I thought it would be a report sized paper but it is more like a book."

"Yes, would you like the executive summary?"

"Executive summary? You've analysed it to that extent?!"

Hal grinned. "Not a chance! That's way beyond my expertise. The summary was attached as a second file. As a start you can get away with reading the first three or four pages. Then, I suspect, you will want to read the rest."

Pawl read the summary, with occasional questions for Hal where the wording did not gel. As he finished, he recognised that Hal was completely correct. He would be spending the next few evenings or days, where possible, reading the full paper. At the same time, he decided that the rest of the Deimos's team should have the same opportunity.

"Hal, I think we should keep this under our hats for the moment. Will you let Hidecki and Molly have copies. I will speak to them about keeping it quiet until we have all had a chance to complete a reading and then we can discuss what it tells us."

"Will do, Pawl."

"And Hal, well done to you and your colleagues. Good job."

Two days later the four got together to discuss the Hokaj view of the universe and it was, as Hidecki in a masterfully understatement said, "Not quite how the Zeder tell it, is it?"

"Look, there is nothing we can do for the moment," said Pawl, "other than each of us should prepare a list of comparative points ready for when the Einstein returns."

"How long before we can expect the Einstein to be back?" Molly asked.

"So much depends on how long it takes them to reach Zent, if we got our estimates right when we met Uzbol they won't get there for another ten days or so. While I imagine that they will be aiming to return without too much delay its difficult to see the turnaround happening in less than ten days. I doubt they will be back inside a month."

"I guess I'll have to be patient then." Molly sounded quite low.

Hal smiled. "It's okay, Molly. We can use the time. You can help me come up with a good argument for my joining the Einstein on its next trip."

Hidecki, who had had other things on his mind, had missed some of the developments back on Zent. "Why do you want to leave Eden, Hal? I thought you were happy working on translations and being involved with the engineering work."

Pawl laughed. "Hidecki, I don't think work pleasures have anything to do with Hal's change of track!"

Hidecki looked over at Molly who was reddening even as they talked. "Ah. Understood. Good luck both. You make a good-looking couple."

"Do you have anyone, Hidecki? I haven't heard you mention someone you are close to." Molly tried to cover up her embarrassment by changing the target.

"I do, Molly, it's just that I tend to be very private about personal things,"

"Oh god! Sorry, I didn't mean to pry, Hidecki." Molly's face was in danger of resembling an older Zeder.

"Oh, it's not a problem, Molly, and it's not really a secret but Marley and I have been an item, as they used to say, from before we left Earth."

"Marley?! And I was trying to get a date. He led me on for ages. I would never have guessed. I'll kill him when I see him!"

"Molly, I am sorry. He shouldn't have teased you like that but I would rather you didn't. Kill him, I mean."

Pawl intervened. "Looks like we are all tied up! It will just be good when the Einstein does return. One thing Molly, at least now you know that Marley didn't not like you. He just doesn't have a leaning your way."

Molly ruminated for a moment. "It has its upside, I guess. I might not have found Hal if I'd been going out with Marley. But, Hidecki, tell him he owes me big time!"

Hideki's laughter was infectious and, amidst the general merriment, he promised Molly appropriate recompense would be arranged.

***   ***   ***

Some twelve light years away, John and Ellen were getting ready for the follow up meeting with the Bedev astronauts.

"How are things with Judy?" Ellen asked.

"Oh, they're good. I just wish we could get a little more time together. Its daft really, we spend more time on the bridge on duty together then we can manage off-duty. To be honest, it can be very frustrating. I really am hoping that we will be able to take some leave once we get back to Eden and get some quality time away from the ship. What about you and Jing?"

Ellen smiled. "We are good too. And, just to make you jealous, we are getting more of that quality time on this voyage than we usually manage."

"Typical, perhaps I should resign and dump you back in the hot seat."

"Not sure Judy would be impressed!"

"Probably not. Ready for the onslaught?"

"Ready to learn, first hand, about another civilisation. Try keeping me away."

With that they left the ready room and headed for the conference room. En-route John stopped to check with his bridge team.

"We're likely to be tied up for the next couple of hours. I don't expect you will need me but you know what to do." Tung-Mei, in the command seat, and Judy, at the helm, acknowledged him with a simple "Sir." before returning to concentrate on the screens and sensor reports as the ship continued its race towards the target system, now less than five days away.

"No captain on the bridge callsign then?" grinned Ellen.

"It took a little work but I finally convinced the computer that the ready room is part of the bridge."

"Well done. I was never able to find a command that ensured it would differentiate between one and the other."

A few minutes later they, together with Teri and the Pipers, entered the conference room to find the Bedev captain and two of his crew already waiting.

"Admiral, Captain, in these circumstances, I feel we should remain formal for the time being." Fagoc spoke quietly and seriously. "We are going to talk about our history and we will try to indicate how we believe that that history may impact on your actions in the coming days."

"As you wish, Captain." Ellen took the lead. "Please proceed."

"Admiral, this is a long story and I apologise for that."

Over the next few hours Fagoc led his team in telling a story that covered a thousand years.

"Thanks to your linguist, Terrey, we have been able to talk in time periods equivalent to your years. We have a written history going back about thirty thousand years but we only began venturing into space less than a thousand years ago. From what we understand that makes us slow when compared with humans but for us it seemed to happen quickly."

At first the Bedev had, like humans, explored their solar system with automatic and robotic probes before they ventured with manned missions to their satellites. There were no other habitable planets in the system and, at some point, several probes were despatched towards the closest stars. Although the Bedev system was on the edge of the cluster there were still four other systems within five light years. One such system turned out to have two habitable planets.

The Bedevs' home planet had become heavily over populated and, like the Earth, was facing serious problems with climate change. About six hundred years in the past a decision was made to send a small fleet of slow ships carrying colonists in hibernation. The journey would take almost a hundred years or nearly three generations. Each ship had a crew of ten with two replacement crews in deep sleep alongside the sleeping colonists.

Pawl interrupted. "Can you clarify that? As I understand it your life expectancy is lower than humans at around forty years?"

Fagoc nodded. "We did only live about forty of your years but we matured very quickly after birth. We reached adulthood in," he hesitated and one of his colleagues whispered in his ear, "our third year."

"And you have not experienced any increase in life expectancy over time?" Will Carden, had joined the meeting.

"In fact, we have. Since we colonised our second and third homes, we can now expect to live almost sixty years. Our medical people think that that is because of less pollution and a lower gravity. Both new homes are a little smaller than our planet of origin."

"Please continue, Captain." Ellen was intrigued by the history but would have admitted to being keen to learn about more modern times.

"Thank you."

The slow ships had gradually fallen out of contact with their fellow Bedev as they crossed the interstellar gap but a little over a hundred and ten years after departure a radio signal was received on the home world confirming that four of the five ships had reached their destination safely. Sadly, at some point, systems had failed on the fifth ship and it had been lost.

It was around that time that a gateway had opened in their system and ships of the Zeder arrived. The Bedev of that time must have seen that arrival as both amazing and helpful. Zeder technology was used to reduce the impacts of climate change and the offer of access to the gateway network using Zeder crewed ships allowed large numbers of Bedev to be relocated around the cluster thus providing a safety valve to the population growth.

In time it became apparent that the benefits of the gateways were limited by the Zeder insisting that only their own ships could be used. Bedev scientists were tasked with trying to find out how the Zeder could produce gateways, a task they failed at.

"We couldn't match their technology and, if I am honest, we began to wonder if they might have found the network by some chance."

"That it might have been built by another race of beings?" Pawl asked.

"Yes, that was reinforced by the refusal of the Zeder to open a gateway to the system where our colonies were. That decision seemed to support our doubts but even so the network covers almost a thousand-star systems, most of which have no indigenous space faring civilisations or any advanced intelligence of any sort. The Zeder have rules, which we agree with, that no contact is allowed until a civilisation has ventured into space."

Over the next hundred years, despite reservations over the Zeder domination of the gateways, the Bedev were able to take part in the colonisation of many new systems, sometimes with other races in the Seven as the group became known by their citizens, but mostly with Zeder teams. At the same time scientists on the home world continued to research ways of crossing interstellar space without gateways.

"We made a chance discovery four hundred years ago on one of the outer planets of our system. It was a source of immense energy that led our science teams to believe that, if they could find a way of controlling that energy, they might be able to design spaceships that could dodge the universal limit. In the event they could not manage that but did find ways to allow their ships to reach velocities close to the limit using exceptional acceleration."

By this point Megan was enthralled and, seeing that, Ellen interceded. "Captain, this is Doctor Newcombe. It was she who found the means to power our ship and her husband, Doctor Piper designed the means of retaining the energy."

Fagoc looked on with what was clearly admiration. "Doctors, you have achieved what our people failed despite their best efforts over almost a hundred years. You have my respect."

The story continued. Not satisfied with looking for FTL craft the Bedev also worked on other ships, using the same basic design as the Zeder and arming them with beam weapons as well as missiles. The argument was that if the Zeder felt it necessary to be armed then the Bedev could only be an equal partner if their interplanetary craft could stand alongside their allies.

It was to prove a wise decision, if ultimately unsuccessful. Fifty years later an Aash colony was attacked by a fleet of aliens. Zeder ships accompanied by a small number of Bedev flooded into the system in a vain attempt to save the Aash. The resultant battle with the aliens lasted several tens of days. In the end the surviving Zeder ships and a sole Bedev craft were forced to retreat through the gateway deserting the system. As they transited into the next system, a sole alien ship managed to follow.

"The Zeder closed the gate at both ends, if there were any ships still in transit they would have been crushed. The reserve Zeder ships attacked and rapidly disabled the alien. When they boarded the derelict, they discovered that its crew were all dead, apparently at their own hands, if they had had any. To the horror of the Zeder the aliens were shaped like insects not dissimilar to a form found on the Zeder home world. That is why the Zeder named them Pindat."

"Insectoid? The underlying fear of mammals will always be that. We have ingrained fears of some reptiles but it is giant insects that is the stuff of nightmares." Ellen shivered.

"It is not only mammals that fear insects. Intelligent cold-blooded animals have similar fears especially the Aash. They lost their colony and I suspect that they will have been arming their systems ever since that day."

"You speak as if you have not been in contact with them since." Alan interrupted quizzically.

Fagoc continued his story explaining that although systems close to the lost colony had been armed just in case, nothing had happened for some tens of years. Then the Bedev home system had been attacked by a fleet of Pindat ships travelling at almost half the universal limit. The Seven had deployed ships in support of the Bedev fleet in defence of the system. But the Zeder ships, the most powerful, had been ordered to only defend the gateway.

Even so some of the ships appeared to ignore their defensive role and moved forward together with their allies. Aash and Voin had forced the Zeder to permit them to transit large numbers of their own ships.

Fagoc's voice faltered a little. "We will never forget their sacrifice. They fought for our world as if it were their own."

His human audience was stony faced as they tried to control their own emotions. Megan, in particular, had sensed what was coming.

"We battled for many days but it was always a lost cause. The Pindat had sent thousands of ships and they outnumbered us many times over. Our people launched hundreds of ships in an attempt to allow a few to escape but almost all of were hunted down and destroyed. A few attempted to transit the gateway but were denied access by the Zeder commander who argued that it was more important that the defender class ships go first. The final result was inevitable. Despite losing most of their ships the Pindat drove their attack home and our world

288

was destroyed. Only our sole star drive ship was able to escape."

"Have your colonies been successful?" Ellen asked.

"From one view they have been but not as we would have preferred. Since the original fast ship reached that system, the colonies have been on a war footing. It will take many more lifetimes before we are ready but, eventually, we must launch a fleet against the Pindat. They cannot be allowed to destroy any more civilisations."

"You know where they came from?" John asked.

"Not yet. We have built four starships and these have been repeatedly sent on missions to try and track down the Pindat. You will understand that we have limited fuel. We have never found another energy source and the fleet when it launches will have to be made up of slow ships. Much faster than those that led the colonisation process, they can reach almost half the universal limit, but our star drive ships must be the search tool. We can reach as much as nine tenths of the universal limit. Slowly we are increasing the range and my ship has travelled the furthest from our new homes. We have been away now for one hundred and forty of your years and were starting to return when we were hit by an unidentified ship in the system where you found us."

"One hundred and forty years! Then you must be using deep sleep to allow such a journey." Will commented.

"Yes, we have five teams, four of which are in hibernation at any one time. Although all are now awake."

289

John and Ellen looked at each other for a moment. Both nodded to each other.

"Captain, how far are you from your home?" Ellen asked.

"Almost ninety light years by your measures. It would have taken another hundred or more years for us to return. That does not take account of the time dilation at top speed. Now I do not know if we will ever be able to go home. Our one chance is that the Zeder might allow us to use the gateways to reach the nearest system in the network to our new homes."

"You seem to doubt that they will."

"The Zeder are not vindictive or unreasonable but our history tells us that they fear one of the Seven finding a way to travel interstellar distances without the need for the gateways. Their status depends on their control of the network. If they realised that our ship could do that, they might decide that it was too important for them to release it. That our species has survived will be embarrassing, though I suspect the modern Zeder will not be fully aware of the events with the Pindat so long ago."

"You speak softly about the Zeder. Yet they might have done more to help at that time."

"We do not have much love for them but their leaders must have feared the outcome if the Pindat had managed to penetrate the network We can understand that."

"I believe that we can help you. We are not one of the Seven but our ship is not unlike yours. It differs in two ways, size and speed." John paused.

"Size is apparent, Captain. You suggest that you can traverse interstellar space faster than our ship. May I ask how fast?"

John smiled. "At this moment we are travelling at what we call warp five. We are crossing space at about two hundred and fifty times the speed of light, what you call the universal limit. We will need to find our fellow humans and then return to our new home but, even so, I think we could get you back to your home in less than two years. I am not sure that we would be able to sustain warp five for that distance but warp three should get you home in perhaps a year and a half."

Fagoc's colleagues gasped at this news and he was clearly stunned. "I do not know what to say, Captain. That is incredible. Both your ship and your offer."

"Fagoc," Ellen decided the time for formalities was over, "your species and ours have much in common. No matter how the Zeder take our arrival. I believe we must try to help you. It seems to me that there are two reasons for us to co-operate for the benefit of all civilisations. The Pindat and the fleet of machines that destroyed our world."

25. Confusion and Anger

Unknown to those on the Einstein, two light years ahead Uzbol was in a state of desperation.

The day before, three Defender Class spaceships had transited from Xonnt and now the Eeeedle or rather half the Eeeedle had returned. Rescue ships had been despatched to the aid of the stricken ship but, as yet, he had not been able to learn exactly what had happened to it. Only a few confused statements from survivors.

The news from Xonnt was even more disturbing. Despite the system being on full alert, the human starship had escaped the squadron deployed to ensure that it did not penetrate the defensive cordon.

"How did that happen?" he blustered when the Commander of the trio of ships reached his office. "Are your people incompetent?"

Commander Qert held his breath. He had no time for the pencil pushers of the political so-called elite but he did, for once, have a little sympathy for the local colony commander who was faced with happenings so far from his normal routine that he could not have dreamt of them in his worst nightmares.

"Commander, you need to understand that if the starship can by some means exceed the universal limit it would have passed us long before our sensors could register its very existence. As it happens something did pass our system edge, if you consider a thousand million gerts away, as at the edge. It generated a distortion in spacetime which briefly hid part of the cluster. That distortion was picked up by one telescope that happened, by chance, to be looking that way. Our local space force command centre deemed that sufficient to warrant reinforcing this system given that it is the apparent destination of the ship, based on what you learned from the humans and rightly sent to Xonnt."

"But what about the EEEEDLE?" Uzbol screamed. "It took a diplomatic party, as instructed, to the human colony and look at it now!"

"That, commander, seems to be something to do with a malfunction of the gateway. Our closest ship has sent pictures of the vessel which indicate that it was, quite literally, sliced in half. I have never heard of such a malfunction but in the war with the Pindat something similar happened when a local commander panicked and closed a gate before the last ship had transited."

"Are you suggesting that we did that?" Uzbol was getting more and more outraged.

"Commander, calm down. Of course, we are not but a malfunction is almost as unlikely as an error by the gatekeepers."

The rest of Uzbol's team had been keeping a low profile, wary of attracting the ire of their boss, but now one entered the room. If a Zeder could have looked ashen faced then she did.

"Commander," she started and then quivered.

"What are you doing?" Uzbol yelled. "I said I was not to be disturbed!"

Qert, sensing that only something of great import would have driven the interruption, interrupted. "What news do you have?"

"Sirs, it is a message from the system Guardian."

"What!" Both commanders cried out.

Uzbol was clearly now sweating. "That has never happened anywhere in the network since I was born, why now?"

Qert gritted his teeth. "What is the message, youngster?"

"Sir, you had better read it or, if you wish, hear it. It was recorded when we first received it." She looked miserable.

Qert was about to tell her to play the recording when his communicator chimed with an urgent message from his ship. "One moment."

Moving to one side he listened intently. "I see. It has been received here as well. I will listen to the full message and contact you with instructions then." Turning to the others he continued, his tone underlining the seriousness of the situation even without knowing the content of the message. "It seems this message has been received by every ship and each of the gateway command points in the system."

He indicated to the young woman to start the message and the two commanders sat back in stunned amazement at what followed.

"This is the system Guardian. As of now your access to the network will be limited. Due to the actions of a military ship in the adjoining system no such craft will be permitted to transit the network gates until further notice. We regret the death of any intelligent lifeforms. This interim measure will be subject to confirmation by the Guardians Ryx. This decision has been transmitted to all system Guardians throughout the network. Message ends."

Qert looked at Uzbol with undisguised fear, a fear he could not suppress. The space force had maintained the Zeder control for almost a thousand years, supported by their control of the gateways. Now they seemed to have lost that control.

"What in hell did Meeax do? Do we know if she survived what happened to her ship?"

Uzbol's previous belligerence had vanished.

"She was found in a state of diminished brain activity. It would seem that she may have taken poison. Her bridge crew are being questioned, on board one of the rescue couriers."

"And?"

"As far as we can understand the local Guardian had, after initially attacking the Eeeedle, received our codes and had stood down from offensive status. Despite that, it seems Meeax ordered two shuttles to attack the gateway defence units with missiles in a vain attempt to destroy them. The units responded. The missiles were destroyed followed by the shuttles. Then the gate closed with the ship only partly inside the entrance."

"I do not understand, just what was Meeax thinking? If the Guardian had not stood down and continued its offensive action her actions, however useless, would have been reasonable but she deliberately attacked Guardian bases!"

"But how!" Uzbol stuttered again. "How can a Guardian attack us or block our ships? Why did we give them such power?"

Qert's stopped his instinctive response. As the senior officer in that part of the network he knew that Uzbol's reaction came from ignorance and not stupidity. Carefully, he explained.

"Commander, I am going to disclose information to you but only because the current situation requires it. Should you repeat it outside of this office you will no longer have any need to be concerned about these events. Do you understand me?"

Uzbol looked up, a mixture of fear and curiosity showing on his face. "Yes, sir." He replied, his first acknowledgement of Qert's seniority.

"What I am about to tell you is normally known only to officers of my rank or above within the space force and it is only ever disclosed outside that group in the case of extreme circumstances. I believe that what we face here fits that criteria."

Uzbol held his breath before saying. "I understand."

You might think so but I wonder, thought Qert, remembering when he had learnt what he was about to tell the other.

"You asked why we would have given the Guardians such power. Quite simply, we did not. Despite what the vast majority of our people and all of our allies believe, we did not build the network. Its technology is, and always has been, beyond our knowledge or capability.

Several hundred years ago an early spacecraft stumbled upon a Guardian in our home world system and gained the codes to control the network. It seems that the AI was programmed to provide that data to the first space faring civilisation that found it or any of its counterparts, around the cluster. We still do not know how big the network is nor are we certain that we have found every gateway.

Since that time our race has been careful to work with the Guardians to enable us to maintain our dominance of the other civilisations. Only once, when the Pindat destroyed the Bedev's planet, have we acted against a local Guardian. In that case the network authorised the destruction of the local Guardian to avoid any chance of it falling into the hands of the enemy. And it was the network that destroyed the gateway link to that system. Not the Zeder ships in the next system as our history tells us."

"But if we did not build the network, who did? And what is the Guardian Ryx?"

"Nobody knows, the most the Guardians have ever said is that their designers, they call them "the designers", left them many thousands of years ago. As for the Ryx, there is rumour that one or more of the Guardians are sentient, it is possible that that term refers to it or them. Most Guardians are high level AIs but not sentient. The interim nature of action suggests that only the Ryx can confirm such actions. Our problems will only multiply should they do so."

"Our whole lives are built on a lie then. That we made the network a long time ago and then lost the knowledge that allowed it to be completed."

Qert gently, for him. "And that's why you would never have gained promotion from this backwater, Commander. If you had questioned such, when being educated, you would have been relocated to the core planets and a more important role within the bureaucracy."

"So, believing our tutors held us back, me and my fellow students."

"Yes. Challenging such inconsistencies in our history is generally seen as a sign of future competence by our home Government. I am sorry that you had to learn this way."

"What do we do now?" Uzbol's misery was obvious.

"We must ready ourselves for the arrival of the humans' starship. How they react will decide if we must look to capture or purchase their technology. I wish I really knew why Meeax acted the way she did. I must return to my ship and you must send an unarmed courier to Zeder. Only they can decide how we approach the Guardians."

"An unarmed courier, will they be safe?"

"If they are armed, they will not be allowed to transit the gate but no-one will know that they are not armed except for the local Zeder commanders. A short stop at each system to pass on my instructions."

With that Qert left for the spaceport radioing ahead to prepare his shuttle for immediate launch. Less than two hours later he was back on the bridge of his ship.

***   ***   ***

As the Einstein continued its journey, closing on the target system, Ellen and John were in his ready room discussing the Bedev and their history.

"What I'm still concerned about is why they have never contacted any of the Seven? It would have been hard in the early days after the war but it's been hundreds of years." Ellen voiced the question that focused on the main area that might affect them.

"I think that we can only ask that question direct." John replied. "They say that they do not hold a grudge against the Zeder and that the Zeder do not have a problem with other races that do not threaten them. Therefore, two more questions, yours and could or would the Zeder see us as a threat? If so, why?"

"We need to talk to Fagoc again. Let's go down to their ship. Meeting him there might help him relax and feel able to speak more freely about them."

John nodded and they rose to head down to the bay only for Tung-Mei to intercept them. "Captain, Captain Cless has asked to see you. He's just off the bridge."

Ellen looked a John with her eyebrows raised. "Speak of the devil."

John's response was as she expected. "Lieutenant, invite him to join us in my ready room."

"Sir."

Fagoc entered the room and, after an apology from John about not having a seat suitable for his size, sat down before speaking.

"Ellen, John. I must thank you again for your offer to take us home. I have another request. You are due to arrive in the Zent system, we think it is that one although our records are rather out of date. It is likely that you will be asked to entertain a deputation, from the local commander's office, on board your ship. Might I ask you not to tell them of our being on board? It would cause embarrassment and possibly affect the development of your relationship with them and the rest of the Seven."

Carefully wording her response, it was Ellen who answered him.

"Fagoc, we will naturally consider that request, however, we need to understand why. We also have some questions about your history, some aspects of which trouble us."

"Admiral?"

"We can understand that in the early days after the death of your home world you would not contact the Seven but it has been hundreds of years now and yet you still wish to avoid them. Why is that? Surely they would be glad that your race has survived."

Fagoc gave a sigh. "I am sure that the other races would feel that a heavy weight of guilt had been removed. That is a guilt they should not have but I suspect some would have wished to provide more help in the battle. The truth is that the Zeder might not be so happy.

In the period shortly before the Pindat came we had developed the star drive much as it is today but there was only limited fuel, as I told you. We went to the Zeder for help in finding other deposits of the same materials. They refused. Or rather they would have helped but only if we gave them the starships and the right to develop them as a part of the network.

We believe that they saw a ship capable of close to light speed as a threat to their dominance of the gateway network but if they controlled it then they would be able to reassert their unacknowledged control over the other races. Please do not interpret that as a bad thing. It was, or is, more like a benevolent parent laying down the rules for its children."

John then raised the concern he had.

"You talk about the Zeder's dominance of the gateway network and their acceptance of others who do not pose a threat but your people believe that your development of a star drive as a threat. Do you believe that they will see us as a similar threat?"

Fagoc hesitated for a moment. "I am sorry, I had not thought about this." He gave a few minutes to his thoughts before continuing. "I do not feel that they will recognise you as a threat at first. In particular when they understand how few of you there are, their space force would, no doubt, argue that they could prevent you from accessing the planet you have settled on. I suspect though that they might try to gain access to your technology with or without your permission."

John looked at Ellen. "I think we will need to be at full alert when we reach the system ahead. If their space force is armed, we will be exposed once we are in n-space."

Turning back to Fagoc he continued. "We will seal the docking bay your ship is in and look to ensure that no-one speaks of you in the presence of any Zeder, should they be invited aboard. Now I need to get back to the bridge, my duty session is already overdue and I need to brief my team. Until later, Fagoc."

"Captain."

His mind racing, John headed back to his command seat, taking over from Tung-Mei and allowing her to leave for some, much needed, rest.

26. Preparations for a Confrontation

"Permission to enter, sir."

"Granted, Commander."

The words, so similar to those of a human ship, meant that finally the ship commanders, and their deputies, from all five space-force major ships in the system, were now on board the Aaived, Qert's command ship.

A few moments later Qert entered his briefing room with his number one and his security officer. He wasted no time with pleasantries.

"You have all heard the message from the system Guardian." There were nods around the room. There was no humour, all understood the seriousness of the situation. "Questions?" he continued.

"I have two," one junior commander admitted, continuing. "how can the Guardians act in this way and the message implies that every Guardian has already been informed and instructed accordingly, how has the message reached the other gateway systems so quickly?"

Others nodded agreement as to the validity of those queries and Qert sighed. He was forced to explain the origins of the network to the group.

"Be aware of the sensitivity of this information, you would have learned it if and when you gained promotion. In these circumstances, it is appropriate at my discretion, that you should understand the nature of the situation we find ourselves in." Pausing to note the various reactions for future reference, he then addressed the second question.

"You are correct. The message states clearly that all Guardians have received the message. Unfortunately, I have no idea how that can be. It would be wise I think to assume it is a statement of fact. You now know that the race that developed the network was advanced in ways we can only dream of. A simultaneous message across such vast distances is beyond us but may have been a basic process for a race that could build the network."

"We must await the decision of the Ryx Guardian then?" Another voice interrupted.

"Or Guardians, yes. In the meantime, though, we must prepare for the arrival of an impossible ship."

"Sorry, sir. You said "impossible"?"

"I did. At least, by our understanding of the universe it is. If the humans are to be believed their home world is more than a hundred years away travelling at the universal limit."

"But it would not be impossible to travel that far, would it?" A third voice rose as the group struggled with what they were learning.

"It would not be impossible although extremely difficult to do so even at relativistic velocities. The humans claim to have covered that distance in about seven years." Again, he paused, allowing the shock to settle.

"That same ship left the system in which they have settled less than twenty-five lights ago and may well arrive here in the next light or two. And no, they have not been able to use the gateway network. That is around two hundred times the universal limit. Now you understand why I call this magic impossible."

"How can we prepare for such a vessel? And why here?"

"It is easier to answer the second question. A small craft of humans transited the gateway, it seems by accident, before it closed at the far end. The mother ship appears to have been able to identify this system and they decided to cross interstellar space in an effort to save their colleagues. That is largely surmise for the moment but it is possible for a ship in the right position to see the destination system's sun and, so far as the Eeeedle's scans of that system were concerned, no ship of the size indicated by the humans was near the planet.

Before you ask. The original human craft and its crew accompanied the Eeeedle back to its settlement. With hindsight it would have been better if one or more of that crew had been encouraged to remain to welcome their friends. We cannot change that now.

As for the first question. We need to obtain the humans' technology that allows them to cross interstellar space at velocities which are breaching some of the basic laws of physics."

"And if they refuse?"

"We must be prepared to capture the ship without damaging the drive or engine rooms." It did not surprise Qert that his last statement drew startled gasps from his audience. Despite having trained in the art of using force in space, none of the ships had ever seen battlefield action. The Zeder control of the gateways had ensured that only once had military action been necessary and that only to supress an uprising on a colony planet over a hundred years before.

Over the next few hours, the group discussed how they might ensure that the incoming ship would not be able to escape should its captain not concede possession to the Zeder delegation that would be ready to accept an invitation to visit the ship. In the end Qert was pleased to be able to summarise a plan he felt had an excellent chance of success.

"The Aaived will transport the local commander and his team to a meeting on board the human ship. Ibeed and Ugnet will take up station on the far side of the two gas giants. Yunh One and Yunh Two will start laying a wall of short-range missiles between Zent and the expected hold position of the human ship. Once that ship has arrived a second wall will be laid by Ibeed and Ugnet. That will need to cover a greater volume of space and the missiles will need to be programmed to spread out above and below the humans. It is not practical to do the same with the planet's protective shield but it seems unlikely, based on what our colleagues learned from the first humans, that given their experience with the loss of their home world they will launch an attack directly at Zent.

One last thing. Remember the missiles must be the smallest that we have. We are not looking to destroy the human ship, merely to disable it if they do not accept our right to take control of any ship found within our defence zone."

"Sir?" One of the most junior officers spoke.

Qert recognised the young woman as a promising officer and refrained from ignoring her interruption. "Yes, Hullint."

"Sir, my cousin met with the humans and was a part, I think, of the diplomatic team delivered by the Eeeedle. He told me that the human ship is large, possibly more than twenty times the size of the Aaived, can we really hope to defeat such a giant?"

"That is a reasonable question." Qert replied. "As far as we know the ship, though a giant, is not a fighting ship. It was built to carry humans away from the disaster befalling their planet, not to fight a war. It is unlikely that it could sustain a secure position against the volume of firepower that we can use, even if we restrain our attack to low level munitions. Now to work, everyone. We may not have much time to prepare."

***   ***   ***

John settled down in his quarters to wait for Judy to finish her stint at the helm. Twelve solid hours in discussions with his chief engineer, acting first officer and the Pipers had left him exhausted. Exhausted but finally satisfied that his ship would be ready for whatever the Zeder might throw at them. Certain that his best protection would be their wish to take the ship in one piece.

He still hoped that these preparations would prove a waste of time and that a good relationship would prove the way forward. Despite the concerns of the Bedev captain and others he found it difficult to believe that an advanced civilisation would look to steal technology rather than find a way to trade for it and work with others.

Judy came in and his concerns rapidly departed as she worked to take his mind off the plans for the next day. As they relaxed before sleep came Judy asked.

"Have you worked out how we can dodge any attack?"

"This was supposed to be part of tomorrow's briefing! Judy you will have to wait. I have better things to do without giving you an advance warning. Now come here."

The next morning John briefed his bridge team after having the ship slowed to warp one. He finished with a few words in summary.

"We will hold station on the warp boundary until we have made contact. Keep the warp drives idling so that we can replicate the process when we rescued the Bedev, if we need to."

As the Einstein accelerated back to warp five, John ran a check of all departments before accepting that all the preparations were complete. Seven hours later his helm team confirmed a drop to n-space engines as they crossed the local equivalent of the Oort cloud and entered the Zent system.

# 27.	A Time of Discovery, of Challenges and of Shocks

As the Einstein slowly moved in towards the inner system, they passed two gas giants. At that point two Zeder ships stealthily moved from the cover of the planetary rings, so like Saturn. Moving almost at a drift they began sewing the minefield of miniature missiles. Despite their care the Einstein's tracking team had spotted them and was carefully monitoring them.

"What are they doing?" Ellen asked as they watched the sensor images.

"Give us maximum magnification, Ensign." As the picture enlarged it gave the impression that they were speeding through space towards the alien ship closest. Then, quite suddenly, the results of the actions of the two ships became obvious. A network or web of small objects could be seen.

"Mines? Surely not." Ellen gasped.

"Not so simple as that," Alan Piper's voice broke in.

"Alan, where did you come from?"

"Scott and I have been analysing the first pictures of those things. In a sense they are mines but they aren't just passive explosive constructs. They seem to be short range missiles."

"Looks as if our preparations are justified." Said John.

"Captain, incoming hail."

"Translation as it comes please."

"Unidentified ship. You are in a prohibited zone. Halt. Identify yourselves."

"Not exactly a warm welcome is it." John grinned.

"Comms. Send this message. In English and Zeder." This is the Earth Starship Einstein. Captain John Lees. We are seeking the Earth ship Deimos"

Back on the Aaived, Qert turned to Uzbol. "Definitely not put off by our words and by some means or other they can translate our language."

"The first humans were able to do that as well. Better than we could at first. I still do not know how that was possible. How do we respond now?"

"First, we acknowledge their response. We confirm that their fellow ship was here. We then advise that we must inspect their ship for contraband."

"And if they refuse?"

"We request, I say request, that they accept a small delegation, including yourself on board to discuss how we can proceed. Remember they cannot know of the issue with the gateways."

"You told me that one of our ships was going to attempt a transit."

Qert nodded gloomily. "Yes. We sent a reserve space force craft to try and transit the gate to Xonnt. The gatekeepers opened the gate as it approached but that action was countermanded by the local system itself. It is clear that the message from the Guardian was real. The courier and two cargo ships have been able to transit, presumably because they are unarmed. We are not sure how the system is differentiating in their favour but, again, it supports the content of the Guardian's message."

"It must have been a shock to the gatekeepers."

"They had been warned of the possibility but you are right I imagine they are still questioning exactly what happened to override them."

As Qert expected the contraband message was rejected but, a little to his surprise, the request to send a deputation was accepted.

"Now, Commander," Qert spoke formally for the record. "You will be accompanied by four of my soldiers. If necessary, you can call on them to take the bridge by force. I would prefer that not be the case. I would rather have these humans as allies and prepared to allow us the use of the technology. Once we have that we can ensure that they do not cause us any more problems. Good fortune."

Uzbol, his two assistants and their escort boarded a shuttlecraft for the trip to the Einstein, exuding confidence that if they had been honest only the arms of the soldiers gave them.

On the Einstein, John was speaking to the head of his security team.

"I want the best unarmed combat guys in the docking bay ready for anything. I wouldn't be surprised if the Commander is accompanied by an armed escort which we are going to need to have disarmed. By force if necessary, but I do not want any fatalities. On either side. We know that they will be taller and bigger than humans but that is the only major difference. If you need to, use your tasers."

"Right, Captain."

"I sincerely hope that they will accept being disarmed until they return to their ship, but I don't want them loose on the ship with guns. Even if we can get them to stow their weaponry peacefully, the combat team must remain close by. We cannot assume that they do not have similar training."

"Sir." Sergeant Patel grinned. "No fatalities and make sure they can't or don't cause any trouble! This could be fun."

"Fun?" replied John.

"We have trained for years for just this sort of exercise. I have a dozen people all ready and raring to go."

"Be careful, Imri."

***   ***   ***

Two hours later.

"May I come aboard, Captain?" Uzbol's question did not match the normal protocol but John simply smiled and nodded.

"Welcome, Commander." Then, as the rest of the party followed, he continued. "Wait, Commander. I see that some of your party are armed. That is not permitted on this ship and I must ask them to surrender their arms while on board."

"Captain, I must object. My escort are necessary to protect anyone of my status and are always present."

"Then, I regret, you may not come aboard, sir."

One of the four soldiers, pulling his weapon from its holster, cried out, "Commander, drop."

Imri, stepped forward pushing John to one side, also yelled. "Drop that gun, officer." He did not appear to be armed and the Zeder simply turned towards him his gun coming up to centre on the smaller human. Before he could fire there was a blue flash from the bay roof. The artificial lightning hit the weapon causing the soldier to jerk backwards screaming in pain from the residual shock. His colleagues started to draw their weapons only for Uzbol to raise a hand. "Stop, this is not what is needed! Put down your guns, now."

The soldiers looked startled but, after a moment, returned their weapons to their holsters and Uzbol continued. "Help your colleague, take him and go back into the shuttle. Remain there."

"But, sir, we are to protect you." One soldier replied.

"I do not believe that that protection will be necessary and certainly not by attacking our host."

"Sir." The grudging response finished with the soldiers retreating into their craft.

Uzbol turned to John. "Captain, I must apologise. There have been issues recently which mean that my colleagues within our space force are extremely edgy. That does not excuse the reaction of that soldier who will be disciplined."

He was being honest in his words but his thoughts were that Qert must have instructed the section leader to force an entry, if needed. How could he control the demands of his military people, who were in a state of complete disarray? It was going, he thought further, to take the best of his diplomatic and political skills. Thank the deity that they were better than Qert gave him credit for.

John smiled. "I can remember times when such forthright actions by the military were both smiled and frowned on. Commander, please join us in our conference room."

The walk took almost twenty minutes, which emphasised to Uzbol and his two assistants the sheer size of the Einstein. The fact that there was gravity, only a little less than that of Zent, also gave them cause for amazement, they were on a spaceship after all.

Entering the conference room John introduced Ellen, as his Admiral, and the two parties sat down for what turned out to be a long discussion. It did not take long before Uzbol relaxed enough to provide a detailed outline of the events that had happened since the Eeeedle had transited to the human settlement and then returned.

"The crew of your Deimos returned safely to your settlement, that we know. What we don't fully understand is why our ship attacked the Guardian units that protected the gateway. We are now stopped from using the gateways to transit our space force ships. That means that our regional space force commander is now trapped in the Zent system and he isn't happy. He outranks me in the Zeder hierarchy when it comes to military matters and he sees your arrival as a part of his domain."

He continued to explain that the gateways allowed the Seven to work together and to feed those planets that needed support. But that they had been controlled, he had thought, by the space force whose reason for being was the protection of the network from a return of an alien civilisation called the Pindat. The Pindat had destroyed one home world before being repelled.

"Repelled? Not defeated then?" John asked.

"No. We did not have as strong a space force and they had thousands of ships. The only advantage we had were the gateways as they could not exceed the universal limit, as, it seems, you can and without the gateways that is a technology we now need to obtain." He paused. "Captain, that need is why the ships of our space force currently in this system have been laying minefields around your ship. I realise that that action does not reflect how you might expect of a would be ally but we are desperate. We hope we can convince you to concede this voluntarily but if not…"

"I see," Ellen's tone was as frosty as she felt and even the Zeder could understand her emotion. "you think," she continued, "that you can just take our ship with or without our agreement."

Uzbol nodded, gloomily as he sensed there was not going to be an easy agreement.

"Firstly, you should know that we are already aware of these minefields and that they are made of small missiles rather than passive objects. Secondly, we have no intention of giving up our ship, and, thirdly, Commander, you have overstayed your welcome. Our security team will escort you back to your shuttle. I suggest you get as far from our ship as you can as quickly as you can."

"Admiral, we will leave but I ask you to reconsider. If we do not hear from you within twenty darfs I do not believe I will be able to restrain the space force ships from an attack."

"Sergeant Patel, please escort our guests to their craft."

"Yes, Admiral. This way gentlemen."

With Uzbol on his way, Ellen turned to John. "What now?"

"We give the shuttle time to move out of the warp zone and then we engage warp for a couple of seconds. That should allow us to shift out of range of their mines or missiles and also give them an idea of the power we do have. I would rather dodge than use the exotic torpedoes, at least as a first move."

John had made his way on to the bridge just as the shuttle reached a safe distance, when the Einstein was hailed again.

"This is Senior Commander Qert of the Zeder space force. Your ship is surrounded. Signal your acceptance of an armed boarding party to take control or you will be destroyed."

"Nice fellow, isn't he?" announced John to no-one in particular. "His problem is that he really doesn't want to destroy us, as he would lose the technology, he most needs. Question might be, how much damage is he prepared to risk in trying to disable us? And are we really surrounded? Tracking?"

"Two minefields, sir. One between us and the inner system, one behind and below us. There are five large space ships that appear to be armed in one way or another. Can't be sure about that but they are positioned as if that is the case."

"How far away is the nearest?"

"A little over four thousand klicks."

"In that case. Helm, are the warp drives on standby?"

"Yes, sir."

"Ready drives for a two second activation at one fiftieth of warp one. Comms, send following in dual languages. "This is Captain Lees of the human starship Einstein. I regret that I am unable to comply with your demands. Please withdraw your ships to at least ten thousand kilometres. We will accept that as recognition of our status as a potential ally." Tracking, I want to know immediately there is any reaction."

317

Two minutes passed and then.

"Captain, two ships turning towards us."

"Damn. Maybe this will bring some sense to him. Helm, activate warp as previous instruction. Up ninety degrees. Maintain warp on standby."

On the Aaived bridge there were shouts of alarm as the Einstein simply vanished from view and more shouts as it reappeared more than half a million kilometres away above the system ecliptic only seconds later.

Qert was not amused nor deterred. "Activate closest missiles. Target that ship."

The minefield missiles began to target the Einstein's new position and within a few moments were tracking at high speed.

"Clearly not far enough." John muttered. "Prepare to activate warp drives."

"Captain, wait! Something is happening. The missiles are exploding!"

As the stunned bridges on both ships watched, multiple beams flashed from the gas giants hitting the missiles in an almost balletic motion until all were no more than wreckage floating in space.

Qert questioned his own eyes. The beams had originated from typical Guardian units, but why and how had they been activated? The answer came a moment later in the form of a message sent to all the ships including the Einstein.

"This is the system Guardian. The human ship and any other humans are now under the protection of the network. No attacks on them will be permitted. This message is being broadcast to all systems by their local Guardians. Further information will be sent in due course. Cease hostilities forthwith."

Qert howled in fury. "Attack!" he screamed. "Attack that damn ship!"

A second voice quietly cut across his angry outburst which his bridge crew were only slowly responding to. Unbeknown to him Uzbol had entered the bridge.

"Belay that order. Commander Qert, I hereby relieve you of command. Your actions place the entire flotilla at risk, if not all Zeders."

Qert looked as if he was ready to strangle the planetary head. "Security, remove this individual. Helm ahead full speed!" Then he realised slowly that his bridge team were no longer responding to his orders.

"Security, take the commander to his quarters and make sure he does not leave them." Uzbol's tone showed a deep anger and underlying capability that Qert had not expected. "Deputy Commander Xxsur, you have command. I strongly suggest you withdraw the ships into orbital station around Zent." The officer nodded and began sending orders to the other ships to clear the remains of the minefields before returning to Zent.

                    ***   ***   ***

On the Einstein, there was more astonishment on the bridge even than on the Aaived. John looked at Ellen with the unspoken question. "What have we done to warrant such protection?"

Tracking interrupted. "Captain, the Zeder ships are withdrawing. One ship seems to be clearing the minefield that was not destroyed."

Comms spoke up. "Incoming hail from the Zeder command ship."

"On speaker."

"This is Commander Uzbol on board the Squadron Lead Ship Aaived. Captain Lees, my apologies again. The flotilla commander acted without approval and has been removed from command. Our ships are returning to orbital station around Zent. I hope you will feel able, despite the circumstances, to visit our home. I can assure you that our visitors will be safe and well treated."

"Can we trust him, do you think?" Ellen's concern was easily understood and her quiet question to John unsurprising.

"You know, the Bedev did say that the Zeder are not a vindictive or nasty race, they just look for a dominance which, I believe, an accident in history enabled them to hold over the other races. The gateways are looking much less the invention of them but more a discovery of an ancient network. I'm guessing but I have to believe it was that way. Now they seem to have lost their control in some way and for some reason

                                320

and it looks as if we may be to blame. Though I really cannot understand why."

"But if they are blaming us, doesn't that make a trip planetside dangerous?"

"I didn't say they were blaming us. I doubt they understand, any more than we do, what is happening beyond the fact that their space force has been immobilised." John sounded more confident than he actually felt but his instincts were that to engage with the locals would be better than not to.

Ellen, having considered the matter further, finally spoke with her command tone of voice. "In that case I will lead a small team to meet with Commander Uzbol. You, John, need to try and contact the Guardian who sent that message and find out just why and what is going on. No arguments, this is why I am here and this is your ship."

John glumly conceded defeat as the truth of Ellen's words struck home.

"Who will you take?"

"Alan, for definite. I think it might be good to take Alejandro or one of his team anyway. We are going to be talking about some things where we may benefit from their astronomical experience."

"I will speak to Alejandro; you talk to the others. I will also send a message to Uzbol telling him that a deputation will be landing in, let's say three hours."

The conversation with the chief astronomer was fairly short. Alejandro decided it would be better to send Stephan Kolaski, a better fit with the team, he felt. John's message to the Zeder commander was acknowledged with an unexpected degree of warmth and a couple of hours later one of Einstein's shuttles launched for the short journey to Zent.

Ellen had agreed that they should be planetside for no more than two local days and accepted that one of the security team should accompany them along with the pilot, the latter two would remain on board the craft. A little reluctantly, John had decided that Judy was the correct person to pilot the shuttle. Without Pawl, Tung-Mei had to remain on board.

In his ready room amidst an emotional departure, John had emphasised his orders. "No risk taking, stay on board the shuttle and keep it secure, no visitors. Understood?"

"Yes, Sir." Judy muttered as she hugged him before lavishing a long, if unsteady, kiss.

Shortly after landing, there was a terse exchange between John and Ellen. He was adamant that the ship would not leave orbit before they were on board except to lift its position to an orbit further out than the Zeder ships. She told him that he should take the ship wherever was necessary, if contact with the Guardian required that movement. In the end they agreed to differ and to wait and see what happened next, both planetside and with seeking the Guardian.

*** *** ***

On this occasion, the human party were received with respect and a little razzmatazz before being flown by helicopter to the capital where they spent several hours in discussion with Uzbol and his assistants.

Ellen summarising the talks later would say. "To be truthful, we learned little new, except that the Commander confirmed that the gateways had not been built by the Zeder. It was something he himself had only learned in secrecy a short time before our arrival. I am not sure he was totally comfortable with disclosing this to the representative of another race but, as he put it, given the circumstances it was bound to get out sooner or later now that the Guardians had acted and, in any case, they might well tell us directly. The Bedev are, I feel, correct in how they saw the Zeder but it is difficult to see how they will react going forward. Uzbol's view is that they will ask us again to share our FTL technology so that they can reduce their reliance on the network. The past day or so has shaken their world view, and will be worse for the majority who have always believed that it was their race that had built the network. Such are the changes, he almost begged us to support his people in that way. At the same time, he admits he cannot speak for those in power on Zeder, the home world."

John's news was a little more startling.

"We initially tried sending a message to the Guardian. All that happened is that we were hailed by the Aaived asking if we needed assistance. Their Acting Commander seems very keen to get into our good books after their actions when under command of his predecessor. At the time I left it that we would get back to them. After that exchange, I decided to take us out of orbit and into a secondary orbit around Zent's larger moon and "bingo"."

"You made contact from there." Alan suddenly grinned, "Don't tell us the Guardian is on the moon itself?"

"No, but, a little like Eden, it does have a communication centre of some form which did respond, asking us to hold station. It appears that, again like Eden, the Guardian is in orbit around one of the gas giants, looking like a satellite!

"Did it give you any idea as to how long we should wait?"

"No. We did get one short message from the Guardian indicating that it was awaiting instructions from elsewhere in the network and it could not give a time."

"Then I guess we wait."

***   ***   ***

Down on Zent, the arrival of a courier vessel from Zeder brought both news and instructions.

Uzbol found himself promoted to regional commander. Qert was to be sent, under guard, to Zeder, to face a board of enquiry. The instructions seemed to support Uzbol's own views and the actions he had discussed with Ellen but went further. He was to arrange for a human deputation to be sent to Zeder for discussions about how the two races might work together. He sensed an underlying aim to get FTL capability was, yet again, the driver and would impact any relationship, unless the humans were willing to simply provide the technology to the Zeder and no others.

"Have they not listened to the Guardians?" he thought. "Do they believe that they can outwit the network?"

Two days later John was woken with a call. "Captain to the bridge, urgent."

Arriving a few moments later and still pulling his uniform top on John found Ellen, Teri and Tung-Mei standing in a group watching a screen. The scene appearing was that as would have been seen from a space ship orbiting a planet such as Jupiter or Uranus. "Do we know which of the giants we are being shown?"

Tung-Mei responded. "It looks as if it is the outermost gas giant. Not certain but the colouring of the bands seems correct. That assumes, of course, that we are seeing the correct colours and not ones that have been filtered by coloured lens."

Even as they talked a message started flashing on the screen. "Incoming hail, Captain." called his comms team.

"On speaker, English version if in duplicate."

The tone and accent of the message replicated that of the Guardians in the Eden system.

"Humans on the starship, Einstein. The network congratulates you on your discovery and development of a faster than light drive. Such ability was identified, by our designers, as an indication of an advanced race that would justify the complete support of the network.

I am advised that your presence in System Seventeen is requested. System Seventeen is approximately one hundred light years from this system. You are invited to utilise the network gateways. Do you have any questions?"

"How many transits will this involve and how long should we expect the journey to take?" John cut to the sharp end of the request.

"Eleven transits will be required. Total time including transit time between gateways will be approximately twenty Zent days."

"Can we transit back to the system we came from before starting that trip?"

"I am authorised to allow that. No other ships will be allowed to transit to that system at this time. Please note that that will add three or four days to your journey time not including time spent within the system. You are asked not to delay further."

"We understand. We will leave orbit immediately, how do we find the gateways?"

"Astronomical maps of each system you will transit are being downloaded to your onboard computer at this time. In each system all inter-system traffic will be held until you complete your gateway transit. This Guardian wishes you well."

"Comms, do we have that data?"

"No, sir."

"We have, Captain." Tracking announced. "It has been overlaid on our maps, I don't know how, sir."

"Right, not to worry about the how for the minute. Let's have routing for our gateway home. Helm, let's go. Quarter speed."

As they moved out of orbit, they received a hail from Uzbol. "Captain, you are leaving us? My colleagues on Zeder have requested that you allow us to transport you on a courier for a meeting."

"I am sorry, Commander, but we have also been asked to travel to System Seventeen by the Guardian. We will travel home first before returning to utilise the gateways to reach that system."

"I have never heard of that system." Uzbol paused and they could hear voices in the background. "I am told it is a deserted star with no planets. Why are you going there?"

"We have agreed to follow the guidance of the Guardian who expressed an invitation from the network. We will return after visiting our new home and then use the gateways to reach that destination by the fastest means. Commander, I promise that we will return here and brief you as to the outcome of our journey."

"How can you use the gateways? We, Zeder, control access. It is only military craft that are temporarily stopped by the Guardian."

"As we understood the local Guardian, it and its counterparts throughout the network will clear the way for our ship to complete transits as quickly as possible. I do not fully understand why we should receive such treatment but I do believe that it will be to the benefit of both our peoples to comply with the Guardians in this case."

"I understand Captain. Thank you for being open with me. I wish you a speedy and safe journey."

***   ***   ***

The Einstein completed the journey from Zent to the gateway's location. As they approached, they could see several smaller ships attached to wreckage of the Eeeedle working to salvage what could be saved. A message from the Guardian must have gone ahead of them as they and the other ships, stationed in a ring, apparently guarding the system from any incoming craft, started to move away, allowing the starship clear access.

With the size of the starship, it was possible that none of the Zeder ships had ever seen a gate opening to such an extent and the bridge comms team were able to report a large amount of radio traffic between them.

"Captain, incoming message from Guardian."

"Human ship. Transit time through the gateway will be approximately eleven of your hours. Guardian in destination system has been alerted to expect your ship."

"Acknowledge with thanks."

"Aye, Captain."

With that the Einstein transited the gate into a tunnel of light. Just over eleven hours later the unchanging surrounds gave way to the normality of normal space just before the ship exited and found itself, as expected, in the Eden system and close to home.

28. Together Again

Down on Eden there was sudden nervous excitement, as the satellite sensors, which had been focussed on the region that the gateway had previously opened in, reported that the gate was opening.

Helga and Anton called together a small group of scientists and then decided it was appropriate to invite Sugnay to join them. An hour later the excitement grew tangibly as a ship could be seen, about to transit the gate. It was Sugnay who realised that it was not a Zeder ship.

"We have no ships that would require such a large opening." He said. "How large is your starship?"

Anton replied first. "Twenty kilometres long not including its drive tori and around four kilometres top to bottom. Might it be that there is more than one ship in transit? After all I wouldn't expect the Einstein to be cleared to use the gateway, especially after the forward part of your ship reached Zent. Wouldn't they be wary of sending anything through?"

"We must wait. I am not sure what may be happening." Sugnay sounded as bemused as Anton could remember hearing him.

A few minutes later there was a gasp. "It's the Einstein! It really is!" Pawl almost yelled.

It would be almost three days before the Einstein moved into an orbital station but only an hour or so later the first shuttles left, to drop down to landings close to Yablon.

John and Ellen remained on board ship allowing the initial landings to transport those with relatives first chance to join the celebrations. Later that evening, leaving the absolute minimum of crew on the ship they too landed and joined the celebrations as the two crews were united with their friends.

One of the most emotional meetings was that between Molly and her parents and sister. The tears of happiness were rather mixed with both Megan and Judy berating the younger sister for not telling them she was heading out on the Deimos.

"I'm sorry, I didn't think we'd be away more than three or four days. Then everything went pear-shaped and I couldn't even send you a message."

"That's why you don't go without saying goodbye, especially when in space." Alan was quite gentle but his message brought Molly back to the edge of tears. "Now, let's have a drink and you can tell us all about your adventures!"

"Before we do, I need to get someone." Molly vanished into the crowd leaving her family looking at each other with unspoken questions. A few moments later, she reappeared dragging a young man behind her.

"Mom, Pop. This is Hal." Molly's look at her parents told all.

"Hello, Hal. You were on the Deimos too, weren't you?" Judy broke the initial silence.

"Yes, Lieutenant. I was." Hal's nervousness brought a genuine laugh from Alan.

"Hal, you've been looking out for Molly then."

"Yes, sir. I tried but I think she looked out for me more."

"Our daughters are both like their mother and I can well believe she did. No need to be nervous or shy around this family, Hal. Its Alan, Megan and Judy. Here anyway. Might be different on the Einstein but no formalities here, young man."

"I'm guessing that there is a little more to this friendship, Molly?" Megan grinned.

"Yes, Mom," suddenly it was Molly's turn to be nervous, "We want to move in together. Hal, he's the best even if he is a bit shy."

"You don't need our approval but you have it anyway, both of you. Now let's get that drink to celebrate."

Molly was beaming, hugging Hal so tightly he gasped. "I told you they'd be great. Now we can really get it together."

***   ***   ***

The following day, matters became more serious as Ellen called for a meeting with the mayors, Sugnay and Rob.

First explanations covered the events as the Eeeedle had approached the gateway on their way back to Zent. Sugnay was still suffering from an element of disbelief over the actions of his old commander and found himself faced with a decision. Should the Zeder contingent take advantage of the Einstein returning to Zent on its longer journey or remain, faced with the possibility that they might not be able to travel back themselves for some time.

The news of the events on the Einstein's trip did not help his emotional state. A member of the space force for most of his life he had had no reason not to believe the official history of his kindred. He realised that had he achieved the promotion he could reasonably have expected, then he would have been told the truth of the "designers". That there was also a contingent of Bedev on the Einstein who would be disembarking with their ship only added to his astonishment when told about the actions of the Guardians.

"We had promised to return the Bedev with their ship to their new home but the Guardians have vetoed any other race travelling with us to system Seventeen. Their block on that, they told us, is only for a short time until we have visited that system and spoken with the Guardian there." Ellen explained. "While here we plan to let our engineers lose on the Anthezedo. We'd like to repair it if at all possible but also to try and understand how their drive works. To be able to accelerate to nine tenths of light speed in a matter of a few days is amazing."

"I will have to discuss whether we look to travel back to Zent now or wait until the Guardians are more open to discussion." Sugnay nodded to the rest of the group. "Thank you for your understanding. Please excuse me."

The rest of the meeting was a collection of updates on progress on the planet which included, naturally, the fact that access to the Guardian on the mainland was now permanently available. This was not the fount of all knowledge they had hoped for as the Guardian had quite severe restrictions on what answers it could give. There had been quite a number of responses such as "Information not available at this time," which had led to a degree of frustration. Ultimately though the discussion inevitably turned to the reasons for the summons by the Guardians.

"We have been told that there have always been rumours that the network's designers left one or more Guardians that were fully sapient but none of the Zeder have ever heard of anyone actually finding one. The only Guardians there has been contact with have high levels of artificial intelligence but no more than that. I suspect that system Seventeen might include one of these elusive entities but why they consider it important to have a face to face is beyond me. We still have no real idea why we should be treated the way we are being." John's voice demonstrated his bemusement.

"Could it be because we developed an FTL drive, I wonder?" Rob, who had been very quiet, suddenly came to life. "From what the Deimos and you have learnt, John, no-one else has achieved that. The Bedev have a drive that allows them to get close to light speed but, while that is exceptional and beyond anything the other races have managed, it is still not in the class of the Alcubierre drives."

"Rob, where does your intuition come from?" Ellen laughed. "You are probably correct. One message from the Guardian back at Zent implied that any race that has developed FTL is special in the eyes of the designers."

Back in orbit, the shuttles were busily transporting the Bedev crew planetside where Sugnay and his team were alongside Anton and Helga to welcome them down. Without, at the time, knowing about the Bedev, the Zeder had decided that they should remain on Eden as their people's representatives. In the end, the meeting of the two races with ancient history separating them was amicable if combined with a degree of tension.

There had, of course, never been a question as to whether or not they should make the trip to Seventeen, and four days later the Einstein moved out of orbit en-route for the first gate.

It would have been sooner except that Jenny had convinced Ellen that there was a more serious event to complete before departure and so it was that the Admiral had the pleasure of conducting her first wedding service. Unbeknown to Rob, Jenny and her friends had been busy preparing a wedding dress and a suit for him. Other dress was informal but that did not stop many of the townsfolk dressing up for the occasion. The party went on deep into the night and it would be fair to say that not a few crew members were in a fragile state as the great ship left orbit the next morning.

29. Meeting a Designer

The trip to System Seventeen was uneventful. At each stage it was clear that the local Guardian had ensured that all other traffic was on hold and military vessels of the Zeder space force were noticeable by their absence having been withdrawn into planetary orbits in most systems.

The local Guardian messaged each time checking that John and his team were happy with progress. In some systems there were other messages, usually from the local Zeder commander, asking who they were and why the gates were closed to space force ships.

Then, they arrived in an unoccupied system. On this occasion the system had no planets and the star was a red dwarf.

"Have we arrived then?" Tung-Mei, taking a stint at the helm.

"According to the gateway map we should have. But where is the Guardian, they are usually around a gas giant. There are no planets as far as we can see. Captain, towards the star then?" Pawl was rather unsure.

"I don't think we have much choice, Commander. Other than the gate we have just come through there doesn't seem to be much else. This is a rare enough system. I doubt that there are more than a dozen red dwarfs in the whole cluster." John decided.

The Einstein moved on gradually closing with the star. Then, as they were halfway there, without warning, a second gate opened in front of them.

Pawl turned to the screen in surprise. "I understood that this system did not have any life and Sugnay did not understand why we had been summoned here. Well, maybe, we haven't been. This may just be a form of automatic routing."

"Well, it strikes me that this really will be a step into the unknown. Helm, stay on this course, quarter power. Tracking, keep an eye on the gate. We abort our approach if it shows any signs at all of closing."

"How long before we transit, sir?" Comms needed to know so that they could update the rest of the ship.

"Tracking?"

"At current power, roughly twelve hours, sir."

There were no apparent changes in the gateway, not even the flickering of the edges seen on all the other gateways that they had entered. Then as they made their final approach the ship was hailed.

"This is the gateway Guardian. Please proceed. I am instructed to warn you that it will take longer to complete this transit than any others you may have experienced."

"Now that is different. No controller but a Guardian responsible only for a hidden gateway and its going to take longer. I wonder how much longer?" John mused.

In the end it took them almost four days before the tell-tale signs of a gateway, as seen from the inside, began to appear. Slowly, very slowly, the Einstein gradually completed the transit to find itself on the edge of a star system that could not have been more different from the previous red dwarf.

"My lord!" cried Pawl. "Captain, that star looks like a white dwarf and there must be a dozen planets in orbit. How could they have survived the red giant stage? I've no idea where we are in the cluster. We never saw such a system when the surveys were running. Although given we never spotted any of the systems occupied by the Zeder and the others, maybe that's not surprising."

"Captain?" The lieutenant on tracking looked up. "I'm not sure we are still in the cluster. There are no other stars visible and, sir, I think you should take a look in the rear-view screens."

"Pardon? Commander, could that be right?" John was beginning to feel as if every step was a leap into the unknown. "Oh." As the rear-view screens were switched to the main screen a dull redness emanated across the bridge.

"The transit took nearly eight times the average time of the other gateways. Given that the distances varied from ten light years up to forty, with limited differences in transit time, we could be looking at as much as three hundred light years and, to be honest, that's no more than an educated guess. We are truly ignorant of the way the network operates."

"Captain, permission to enter the bridge." The voice of Stephan Kolaski interrupted.

"Granted, Stephan. What brings you here?" John was curious and already wondering why they had not thought to ask the astronomy team for their thoughts.

"Pawl, sorry, the Commander, asked us to take a look at the star and see if we could identify it."

"You know where we are?"

"I wish I could tell you. There is no record of any star with the same spectrum. We have run a computer search of all white dwarfs visible from Earth and this star doesn't exist."

"Doesn't exist?"

"There are a number of white dwarfs within the cluster, this is none of those. We've checked all the known ones that were in the Taurus constellation and again we found nothing. Then we saw the red glow and that gave us a real shock."

"Go on." John was totally focused on the view screens.

"The giant, if it is a red giant, has no spectra and we must be very close as it eclipses the entire night sky."

"So, we appear to have a red giant which doesn't exist or at least has no spectra, with an invisible companion which has a group of planets in close orbit in what looks be an impossible structure. Is it possible for any object to glow without a spectrum?"

"Well, yes, but it isn't or shouldn't be a star. It would have to have a totally uniform and unchanging structure."

"Captain," Pawl intervened. "the redness is all around us, not just behind us. Even the other side of the star and its planets."

There was a gasp from the helm. "Could we be inside a Dyson Sphere?" Judy looked up before apologising. "Sorry, Captain."

John turned to Stephan and Pawl. "Is that a possibility? I have heard of the term. An artificial structure, spherical in nature, that totally surrounds a star?"

"Until now, I would have called such an idea pure science fiction." replied Stephan. "There are numerous reasons why a Dyson Sphere should be impossible to build but then a stable gateway network shouldn't be possible either. What did someone once say? *"Any sufficiently advanced science would look like magic to a less developed civilisation."* It looks as if we may have come up against that magic." he smiled, a little grimly.

John came to a decision. "Helm, ahead quarter speed. I think we need to approach the planets. Anything in this system should be close to them."

Slowly the Einstein moved further in system. Sensors and crew all at full alert looking for anything that might lead them to the local Guardian.

As they approached the planets Tracking and Comms became deep in conversation. Finally, they called Pawl to their joint station. A little while later John returned to the bridge to take over from his deputy.

"Captain, most of the planets, if not all, appear to be artificial." Pawl announced. "They are spread around the star in what seems to be a single orbit. How that can be a stable set up, I have no idea. But something has been scanning us for the past half hour."

"Where are the scanner signals originating from?"

"We can't get a fix."

"Right. Helm, start a turn starboard. I want to reach an orbital position keeping station at twice the distance of the planets from the star. Let's see if that gets any reaction."

As they achieved John's desired position there was no immediate reaction except that the scans stopped. Hours passed. Then…

"Captain, we are monitoring some form of communications between three of the planets. Started a few minutes ago."

"Are they adjacent?"

"Yes, sir."

"Helm, port ninety degrees, then adjust course in direction of the middle one."

"Aye, sir."

***   ***   ***

As they completed this manoeuvre there was finally a response.

"Welcome to my home, starship Einstein. Please continue your routing and take up orbit about me. Please note that your star drive will not function while inside this system."

"This is Captain John Lees. Who are you?"

"I am Tryx, a designer of the network of gateways. With your agreement I will land your ship."

"This is a starship. It is not designed to land on a planetary body!" John's startled reply was echoed by Pawl's astonished cry.

"Captain, we are being pulled towards the planet!" Judy called out. "N-space engines having no effect."

"Cut power, helm. Tryx, what are you doing?"

"Captain, I have activated what you would call a tractor beam. This will enable you to land in me."

"Sorry, I don't understand. You said "In you"."

"That is correct, Captain. The planetoid you see ahead, is my principal physical person. Please be assured that when you are ready to depart the same beam will lift the Einstein into orbit again."

John and Pawl looked at each other in a stunned silence as the screen view of the planetoid showed what looked like a large entrance forming on the surface with the Einstein dropping out of its original orbit vertically.

In what seemed like no time at all the Einstein reached the planet's surface before dropping slowly into, what could only be described as, a huge hangar. A few minutes later the external sensors recorded an increase in pressure and Pawl turned from his station.

"Captain, outside atmosphere is breathable. Pressure is equivalent to sea level on Eden."

The voice of Tryx seemed to bypass the speaker. "Captain, if you and your team would like to disembark."

"Tryx, please allow us a little time." John decided to bring together his senior advisors and officers to discuss the situation before accepting the invitation.

It was a short meeting. As Ellen said, there seemed little choice if they were to learn more about their host. John handed over command to Pawl and accompanied by Ellen, Megan and Stephan took the unusual step of leaving the Einstein and stepping directly down on to a solid surface.

As they walked forward into the open space surrounding the Einstein, a figure appeared from the shadows. Although humanoid in size and shape, it was clearly a machine of delicate construction.

"Captain, if you would follow me. I am Tryx."

The four humans looked at each other in amazement, before following the humanoid through a doorway into a

343

smaller room with seating for a large crowd. "Please be seated, humans."

"Tryx, may I ask? What or who are you?" Ellen decided to cut to the quick.

"I am of the race of Ryx. In my current form I have existed for a little over one million of your years"

"In your current form?" Megan was struggling to understand that a being might be as old as Tryx had indicated.

"I was once a biological being, much as you are. When I was ten thousand years old, I extended my life by transferring my sentience to an artificial construct. You are, in effect, inside me. The figure that greeted you is also a construct produced to ease this conversation."

John's words focussed on trying to handle the existence of a being that was older than his species. "Tryx, your knowledge and experience dwarfs that of my people. Why would you ask for this face-to-face, as it were, meeting when I am sure that you could have conversed via the network. If indeed that was necessary."

The reply was immediate and clear. "Admiral, Captain, you should be aware that your species is unique at this time of the cosmic story and, as such, I wished to experience the physical reality of your presence. Your species has my respect and admiration."

Ellen responded. "Why us? Surely all species are unique."

"You are correct, in essence. All species are special but you are, to the best of my race's knowledge, only the third species in the entire life of this galaxy, to truly solve the problem of interstellar flight. Of being able to cross the void between the stars at velocities greater than light speed. Your recent history provides other reasons to admire you and, if you agree, I wish to aid your development and your future."

The human quartet were silent for some time. What might the implications of this ancient entity offering such support be?

To Come: The Hunt Will Begin.......

"I understand that there were another two starships that escaped your star system?"

"That is correct, Tryx, the Anticipation and the Europa. They fled in different directions," Ellen responded, "but you would know that if you have scanned all our records already."

"I realise that my ability to scan databases and records at such speed is, for the moment, beyond entities such as humans. However, it does not mean that I can claim to understand everything recorded without your assistance."

"How can I and my colleagues help?"

"With as complete answers as possible to such questions as I may raise from time to time. Firstly, do you wish to contact the other ships? If we can find them."

"I am not sure. I would prefer to discuss that with my colleagues." Ellen started. "How can you find them?"

"I am not the last of my race. Although there are but a few of us left in this galaxy, I can communicate with those who remain in this part of it. If you wish we will locate your fellow humans."

***   ***   ***

Also by the author

Fighting the Machines Saga

About the Author.

David Adams was born in England in 1952 and spent his working life in finance. First as a banker until, as he puts it, he saw the light and switched from poacher to gamekeeper spending most of his career in Corporate Treasury functions as Group Treasurer for a number of multinational companies. Now retired he spends what little free time he has playing golf, walking the family dog and, on occasion, looking after the grandchildren with his wife Marion and, of course, writing science fiction.

Printed in Great Britain
by Amazon

13262485R00203